Nectar Of The Gods

A novel by

L. S. Miller

ISBN: 0692230521
ISBN 13: 9780692230527

Library of Congress Control Number: 2014912810
lloyd s. miller, Llano, TX

Chapter One

Doc was sitting on the plywood deck of the townhouse units they were framing, his feet dangling over the side, none of the exterior walls in place as yet. It was Houston in April so the weather was always an unknown, today more typical of mid-summer than spring, a hundred degrees with the same humidity. He was tired and sore, too old for this shit he thought as he tried to make his back relax, unkink if he was lucky during their short break. He'd only been with the company a day, this his second and knew he'd adapt but God, the short term cost. The last thing he needed was to be harassed.

"A little old for this kind of work, ain't ya?" Doc turned and looked up at the speaker, an outline with a corona of afternoon sun shimmering around his head and shoulders.

"Yeah, I'd say so, especially the way my back feels about now."

"So why don't you do trim work? Nice light pieces a baseboard, your inside, outta this fuckin' sun," the younger man said as he hiked a thumb behind him.

"I'm more of a rough carpenter type," Doc said. "Not much on finesse. If I can't hit it with a big hammer, I pretty much can't work with it."

"Yeah, well, you're just barely holdin' up your end. If you work any slower, I ain't gonna want you on my crew."

"I didn't realize you were the boss, kid. I thought I was working for the Marone Brothers, George over there who hired me this morning."

"This is my crew, Pop, and if I say you gotta go, then you gonna go–one way or the other. You see what I mean, old man?"

Doc pulled himself up onto the deck and got to his feet, one hand massaging the muscles over his right kidney.

"You're the man, huh? The head honcho." Doc took a step to his left so he could bring the face into focus.

"That's right. I am the man. And you are the hired help. So get over there with the Mexicans and start liftin' those walls."

Doc looked over the shirtless young man standing before him. The boy had his thumbs hooked into his tool belt, feet spread wide. He was taller by two or three inches and wider through the shoulders and his arms were mapped with veins. Skin bronze, Mohawk hair, he didn't look like someone who would slip away from a fight but neither did Doc, braided steel cable to the kid's dock rope and he wondered if the kid had a death wish or something to prove, maybe to his uncle.

Doc ran through a short list of options and concluded he was too damn tired to try to re-educate the boy as much as he was tempted to, drive a shoulder into his chest, wrap an ankle behind and drop a knee on his stomach as the kid landed on his back.

"What's your name, son?"

"Bartolo. And don't ever call me son again."

"Are you always this friendly with the new guys or are you going out of your way because you like me so much?"

"I don't like you at all. You remind me of my father, look kinda like him from what I can remember. He was a worthless sack a shit too. Now get your ass moving or get the fuck out. You got it old man?"

"I got it now. That's why you're so fond of me, I remind you of your father. I bet I'd like *him.*"

"Yeah, maybe so," he said, dropping the redneck tough guy persona, "but you aren't likely to find out. I haven't seen him in four years and don't expect to anytime soon. Now get to work."

Doc turned and strode over to the pile of wall panels stacked in the center of the house deck, joining the four men who had watched his encounter with the younger man. Since Bartolo's stomping departure down the temporary stairs, they were no longer hiding their grins.

By four the panels had all been sorted and stood in their proper place, shot down onto the deck and into each other with pneumatic nailers. Three of the men were installing the top plates, walking easily along the walls like steel workers on a high rise, shouting measurements down to Doc who cut the material that was then delivered to the installers by the fourth.

Bartolo returned as the last pieces were being nailed on by one man and the others were wrapping up air hoses and extension cords and piling tools by the stairwell. Doc was reaching for the hose and nail gun of the last man up when Bartolo bellowed from behind him.

"What the fuck are you doing? Who told you to knock off?"

Doc turned, nailer in hand, one foot bracing the ladder for the man above.

"It's four-thirty," Doc said. "Eight to four thirty, a half hour for lunch. What am I missing, kid?"

"You're missing who's the boss. *I* say when we knock off, not you asshole!"

"It's too hot for this crap," a note of warning clear in Doc's voice. "It's four-thirty. Can we call it a day?"

"You can call it a career, Pops. You're fired. Get out. Give me that gun."

He reached for the pneumatic air nailer, Doc's hand wrapped around the grip, knuckles white, index finger depressing the trigger by instinct so when Bartolo grabbed the barrel and depressed the trigger safety, a sixteen-penny nail shot through his hand and impaled the front of his work boot, nailing his foot fast to the plywood deck as a second round glanced off his right shoulder.

He shrieked and clutched the wrist of his injured hand, staring at the bloody hole in his palm. He hadn't made the connection to his foot or shoulder but as he tried to retreat down the stairs and his leg wouldn't follow, his howls turned to sobs and he collapsed on the deck.

Doc handed the nail gun, butt first this time, to one of the laughing Mexicans and wrapped his arm around Junior's shoulder and sat him down on a sawhorse. He shooshed the other men away, telling them to find George and bring him a crow bar. Saying, "It's okay, we're going to get it loose," Doc cut a length of cloth off his shirt tail and wrapped it around the oozing hand.

As Doc was mulling over his alternatives, George pounded up the stairs followed by a dozen dark-haired men. "Get back, damn it! Give me some air for Christ sake." Leaning against a studded corner, George looked over his nephew's shoulder at the bloody rag and then the immobile foot.

"Holy mother of God. Looks like you toe-nailed him right good, Doc. Care to tell me how it happened?"

"It was an accident, George," Doc said. "But I think we should get him loose and to a hospital as quickly as we can. He's going into shock."

"Yeah," George said. "You hold him still and I'll pry the nail out. Did you boys bring a crow bar?"

When the iron rod passed through Bartolo's line of sight on its way to George's hand, the boy let out a hissing moan and fainted.

"Well, that's a break," George said. "Let's get him loose before he wakes up."

As the ambulance bearing the semi-conscious Bartolo pulled away, George and Doc exchanged a look.

"Tell me you didn't shoot him on purpose," George said.

"George, your nephew is an over developed bully. And I was pretty tired of his mouth. But I swear I didn't do it on purpose. At least I'm pretty sure I didn't. I'm sorry, George, it's hot as holy hell and he's riding my ass half the day. Then he fired me and when he demanded the nail gun, I thought I just handed it to him."

"He fired you did he?" George said with a chuckle. "He must have given himself a promotion. Last I looked, he was just a carpenter. And my sister's headstrong kid. He's worked for me off and on since he was big enough to swing a hammer. But it's too much like work most of the time. Sometimes he wants to be the boss and sometimes he wants to be a country music star. But the work sure put some muscle on him, didn't it? He was a skinny little pecker before I got a hold of him."

"Well, he's big enough to eat hay now. So what's my fate, George? Am I still in your employ?"

"How long you been doin' this kind a work, Doc?"

"Off and on for twenty years or so, but mostly just around the house, my own stuff. And it's been a while since I used the tools. I'm out of shape. But I remember how things are supposed to go together."

"You speak a little Spanish, don't you?" George asked.

"Yes, I do. Enough to get by on a construction site anyway."

"Well, seein' as you shot my self-appointed foreman, I'm a hand shy of a cattle drive. I'd like you to stick around till the boy's feelin' up to snuff. Then we'll see how it goes. All right with you?"

"Yes, sir. That's just fine."

Doc went from the job site to the Critical Care unit finding Bartolo bandaged but lounging on a couch in the foyer laughing with two young men and a pretty blond.

"What the hell do you want?" Bartolo said. "This is the son of a bitch that shot me."

"I thought I'd see how you were," Doc said. "See if there was anything you need."

"Feeling guilty, are you? Never shot nobody before? How's it feel, you like it?" Doc took two steps, his face reddening, the menace palpable as his expression changed from concern to something hard and dark.

"Yo! hold on, Doc," Bartolo said, hands up. "I'm sorry, man."

"You arrogant little snot," Doc said. "You don't know shit. Wake up, boy. The world doesn't revolve around you."

At quitting time the next day, George hailed him from the door of the job trailer.

"I have about ten minutes of paperwork," George said. "Then I'd be happy to buy you a beer if you're not otherwise occupied."

Doc hesitated, glancing back at his truck, then turned to George and smiled. "It would be a pleasure."

"Good. Come on in. The AC works and the water's cold."

Doc sat at a plywood table paging through a roll of dusty plans while George made several phone calls, jotting notes into a bound ledger as he spoke.

"All set. Let's hit it," George said. "The bar's just up the road. You can ride with me if you like."

"I think I'll follow, George, if it's all the same to you."

"Fine, fine, no problem. I'm a control freak myself, always like to keep the lines of retreat open, maximize my options, you know?"

Their destination was a replica of an old west saloon complete with swinging half doors, a plank bar with brass foot rail and piss trough, spittoons and a reclining nude etched on the mirror behind the terraced liquor bottles of the bar back. When George pushed through the swinging doors, the entire bar stool crowd produced a chorus of 'George' loud enough to make Doc flinch.

"My brother owns the place," George said over his shoulder as they headed for a pair of stools in the back, "and he started that 'George' crap. 'Cheers' reruns. 'Norm', you know? I only come in here a few times a year now, but the tradition lives on, don't ask me why."

George greeted ten men and women by name as they passed through the crowd at the bar and nodded hello or said 'Howdy' to fifteen more.

"You're a popular guy, George," Doc said as they sat down, mugs of dark beer already waiting in front of their seats.

"I guess," George said as he lifted his glass and toasted Doc. "Faster horses."

"Long life, George."

They drank then George announced, "Life is good, Doc. I'm so damn happy I could shit my pants with a smile."

Laughing, Doc said he had never heard that analogy before but somehow it made sense. He added, "I went to see the boy yesterday."

"Yeah, I heard. You shook him up pretty good according to his mom. What happened?"

"I reacted badly to something he said. It wasn't his fault. He couldn't have known what a raw nerve he was poking a stick at."

"Well, you're goin' to have to travel some to see the boy now. His momma took him back to her place in the Hill Country to recuperate. Keep him at the ranch, out of trouble, you know."

"Yeah. Maybe I could call him. I never even got to say I was sorry for shooting him before he pissed me off. What do you think?"

"I think a couple of days in the country would do *you* a world of good." When Doc gave him a look George continued. "I think Monday's a holiday and Saturday morning you should go with me to visit him and his mom. We'll fish a little, sit in the shade a lot, drink beer, eat barbecue, burp and fart, generally celebrate our good fortune. How's that sound?"

"George, I've been working for you for three days. For all you know, I could be Charlie Manson. How do you know you can trust me?"

"I don't for sure. But I trust my instincts and my instinct tells me you're a decent man down on his luck. And my dear mama taught us kids to help our fellow man. Besides, I like you. I like the way you work with the Mexicans, you don't look down at them, you work with them. And the fact that you went to visit Junior–that's what we all call him incidentally, don't ask me why– that shows character. And you didn't kill him in the first place, even if you did shoot him eventually," he said with a grin. "I saw how he was ridin' you. I would a stepped in if he'd a gone much further, but you didn't let him get to you, you kept your head, walked away. That's good self-control. I like that in a man."

"Well, I appreciate the job and I appreciate your kindness. Thank you. I think the country sounds good."

Chapter Two

Doc arrived at the jobsite at six Saturday morning, George already there.

"Mornin', Doc. I'll be right with you. You can put your gear in the pick-up if you like. There's coffee made in here and a couple biscuits." Doc tossed his sleeping bag and rucksack in the bed of George's six-wheel pickup, then mixed a coffee and selected a biscuit.

"What all's in that truck, George? Looks like you're going away for a month."

"I haven't been able to travel light since I got out of the army. I swore to myself, I can remember the date, lying in a rice paddy, soaked, shiverin', leeches on my back, my legs, that when I got back to the world I would always be prepared–prepared not to suffer I mean," he said laughing.

"You said *when* you got back, not *if* you got back. Were you sure you'd make it?"

"Yep. Emphatically positive. I never once doubted my life had more meaning than dying in that miserable hellhole. I just knew."

"That must have been a tremendous comfort to you, especially under those circumstances."

"It certainly sustained me. I wasn't afraid cause I just knew I wasn't going to die, not then, not there. Stupidity of youth probably. You'd think anybody with a brain cell left would see that it's all random, accident on accident. But I'm still here. Ain't my time yet."

They had traveled an hour west of the city and were well out into the cotton and cattle country, an occasional insect oil well pumping, when George asked Doc what he was going to do when the campground kicked him out.

"How do you know about the campground?"

"You mean that you're staying there or what its rules are?"

"Ah...you know I'm staying there because I put that address on my application. So . . . the rules."

"I haven't always been the fat, prosperous builder you see before you. I have had my *share* of misfortune," George said. "I have walked with the sinners and seen how they suffered," he said, grinning at his imitation of an evangelist. "My parents kicked me out about a month after I got back from Nam. I stayed in that campground for six weeks. There were so many hippies living there they couldn't keep track of anyone so they just let us stay as long as we wanted. In the spring of 1969, they purged the whole place, city and state police, horses, dogs. Peaceful for the most part, but everyone got kicked out. I went home and made peace with my parents. My brother took me into his company and the rest is history. In a way, Texas Parks and Wildlife is responsible for what I am. I was having so much fun in that park, if they hadn't thrown us out I might still be there."

"Sex, drugs, and rock and roll. The holy trinity of the sixties. I missed it," Doc said.

"What, too old or into other things? You look about my age, you should have grown up right in the middle of it all."

"Some of each. I'm fifty. The right age, the wrong place at the wrong time. And the wrong upbringing. My parents were....beyond conservative. I went to Valley Forge Military Academy for eight fun filled years. Came home twice a year for a total of two weeks. Then the Citadel. Yes sir, no sir. I did *not* question authority. I graduated in '64, a twenty-year-old second lieutenant so gung-ho I wanted to skip everything else and go straight to Vietnam. My parents would have been honored to have their only son killed in the line of duty."

"Ouch. So did you make it? To Nam?"

Doc was silent for so long that George was pretty sure he hadn't heard the question.

Finally, "Yeah, I made it."

"Have you ever been out this way, Doc?" George asked as they approached Austin and the land began to take on some texture after hours of table flat farmland.

"I spent a month at Fort Hood. Is that considered the Hill Country?"

"More or less, I guess, but Waco doesn't have the same pizzazz as the part we're going to. Not as hilly. Not nearly as pretty. My sister Maggie's place has a little frontage on the Llano River, lots of pink granite outcroppings, wildflowers that will knock your eyes out this time of year, live oaks, hickories, mesquite, cattle tanks full of big bass, deer, turkey, quail, doves, hawks, jack rabbits. It's really beautiful, especially now, in the spring. But even in winter it's always somewhat green, the live oaks, the cedars. It's magnificent country. I wish I could live there year round."

"Economically unviable?" Doc asked.

"Basically. We could probably move the company out there, but there just isn't enough work, enough large projects to keep us going. Especially not my brother. He is Mister Big Builder. Loves the whole persona, Cadillac's and cowboy hats. Yippie ki yi yo!"

"How's your sister get by?"

"Modest expectations. She leases most of her pasture to a neighbor for his cows. Big garden. Smokes and cans, all very back to nature. Nuevo hippie chick. You'll like her, she's unpretentious."

"Junior implied that his father wasn't around. That he couldn't remember him clearly. And that he thought there was a resemblance. That's why he took such an *interest* in me."

George smiled when he glanced over at Doc. "The boy remembers pretty good, I'd say. I noticed it right off, as soon as I opened the trailer door and seen you standing there Tuesday mornin'. Did a double take. You're a little taller and leaner, and you've got a lot more character in your face. And you're older than he was when we saw him last."

"Character meaning lines and wrinkles?" Doc asked.

"Pretty much. Daniel, my brother, called him Pancho Villa right from the start. Maggie would get so mad at us teasin' her, callin' her Missus Villa or Ma Villa."

"Worthless sack a shit."

"What?" George said.

"Worthless sack a shit. Junior's description of his father when he compared the two of us."

"Don't let Junior's opinion bother you. He took it pretty hard when ol' Pancho disappeared. He was about fifteen. I imagine he's been dead for a good long time by now, the way he made his livin'."

"What'd he do?" Doc asked.

"Dope. Ran it, grew it, smoked it, sold it, nobody's sure exactly but that's all we can figure, Daniel and me. That's how they bought the ranch we assume. Paid cash for eight hundred acres, five hundred an acre. Carried a shopping bag into the settlement. Pancho dumped it on the table then went down to a beer and set-up joint just outside a Llano and got half shit-faced while they counted it all. Four hundred thousand in hundreds. The story made the front page of the Llano Weekly News but Pancho wouldn't allow any pictures. It didn't matter. Pretty soon, everyone in town knew him but he went by a fake name."

"Didn't the sheriff get involved, ask him where he got all that cash, investigate?"

"Doc, out here a man's got a right to his privacy and as long as he ain't rubbin' nobody's face in the fact that he's breakin' the law, and he ain't hurting nobody, he's gonna be left pretty much alone. Besides, Texans love that fightin' the Comanche, Bonnie and Clyde, manly stuff. You know what I mean?"

"Remember the Alamo!"

"That's it. Pancho told me the sheriff stopped by a week or so after they moved in, set up camp really, they built the house later. He pulled ol' Pancho aside so Maggie couldn't hear, and gave him a little talkin' to. Establishin' the rules, you know? He said he didn't care what Pancho did for a livin', not actually callin' him a dope dealer, but that whatever it was, it better not find its way into Llano County or get in the hands of the local kids. Cause if it did, Pancho was gonna mysteriously disappear."

"Do you think that's what happened to him?"

"Nah. The sheriff was just makin' a point. He's an old Texas red neck but a pretty good guy. Pancho didn't bring anything home with him, except maybe the money. No, he was an importer, and a middleman as far as we can figure. He went away on a business trip and never came home. Probably killed in a rip off. That'd be my guess."

"Did he love your sister? I mean, could he have just moved on to greener pastures?"

"Sure, I guess. Hell, that happens all the time. You don't have to be a travelin' pot salesman to run into one a those affairs. But tell you the truth, I can't see it. Maggie ain't movie-star gorgeous but there's somethin' about her that, well she's my sister so this'll sound a little odd, but she's…special. Always was. Even as a kid, a teenager, the boys were just mesmerized. She was pretty enough, but it was an enzyme or somethin', a pheromone she gave off. Damn if I know. She was just serene. Quiet and dignified but playful too. Pancho loved her, would a done anything for her, except get a job, be a normal nine to fiver. There was no way he could a done that. Weren't in his make up. Daniel and I used to speculate about the might a been's for her, all the boys that wanted to be with her and about what she saw in Pancho, why she picked him."

"Because he was unique I imagine," Doc said. "Not like anybody who had ever come courting."

"Yeah, there was definitely some of that. He was the new kid all right. Showed up right near the end of her senior year in high school and by July they were gone. She left our folks a note but we didn't hear another word for like ten months. By then they were married, in Mexico I assume, and she was pregnant with Junior. She invited us all out to the ranch to get reacquainted."

"Did you go?"

"Hell yes! We packed up the entire Marone clan, Mom and Dad, Daniel, his wife, two kids, me and Gina, my wife, our gang of four, the little monsters–my kids are hell and a half. We even took the dogs."

"That's a pretty good response, the whole family going like that."

"This was Maggie, don't forget. Daddy's perfect angel, Daniel's and my protectorate. We all loved her more than about anything else. Still do. And she was still just a kid, eighteen going on thirty. Pregnant. We just couldn't believe Maggie was havin' a baby."

"How did you all feel about Pancho?"

"Old Pancho," George laughed. "Daniel was planning to beat the livin' hell out of him and Pop had a couple guns in the motor home, always did, and he must a been thinkin' about how good

Pancho would look with a load of turkey shot in his ass. It was Mom who put all that to rest. Before we got in our various vehicles, as we're millin' around in the folks' driveway, sortin' out who was ridin' with who, you know, all the kids wantin' to ride in Grandaddy's motor home, Mom shuts everybody up and gathers us into a big circle and she says, I know what you boys are thinkin'. She looks at Daniel and me but included Pop too, givin' us all her don't-cross-me-on-this look and I'll tell you, it's a good un, you don't mess with her when she gives you that look. She says Maggie has taken a husband and that makes him part a this family whether y'all like him or not, you treat that man good, like he's your kin, cause if I hear otherwise there'll be hell to pay. You understand me? Course we all knew exactly what she meant and none of us was gonna cross Ma, but it was a disappointment, especially for Daniel."

"So how did it go? It had to be an interesting weekend."

"Oh, you bet is was! We followed Maggie's directions through Llano, we're almost there ourselves. See the water tower up there to the right? Stickin' out above those live oaks? That's about where downtown starts." George chuckled. "Downtown is sort of an exaggeration. Anyway, we head on out a town followin' the river, countin' off the county roads as we go. Finally we come to the right one. These are gravel roads, mind you, and we've got a forty-foot motor home, towin' a boat no less. So we go about half a mile on this little gravel strip no wider than a driveway and all of a sudden we're at the bank of the river and the road just stops. We all pile out and we're lookin' at the river and lookin' at Maggie's directions and Daniel reads, 'Turn right on country road 117, cross the river and go two point three miles.' Cross the god damn river! he screams. On what? There's no bridge which a course we can all see plain as him.

"That's when Jake, my oldest boy, took off and ran right into the river and looked for all the world like he was runnin' *on* the water. He got about halfway across and turns back to us and yells,

'There's no bridge cause the road's right here under the water!' So we all go wadin' out there and sure enough just under the water there's a concrete roadbed. The river's so shallow it flows over the road. Until you get to the middle. There's about a hundred feet of road that's built up on flat concrete pads and here the water's a whole lot deeper and it's flowin' mostly *under* the road. Mom took one look at the deep part, looks back at that big old motor home, and says, 'No way in hell are we drivin' across that river!'

"It took us twenty minutes to convince her to walk across with Pop, the kids and our wives, and let Daniel and me risk just our lives by drivin' across. And then she made us maneuver around for another ten so I could get in front of the motor home and go first in the Suburban. I guess she could face the loss of one son, but not a son and that motor home. I tell you, it *was* a little scary. There was about six inches of excess road on either side of the Suburban and half a the outside tires on the pairs in the back end of the motor home hung clean over the sides." George stopped speaking and wiped his eyes with the back of his hand as he continued to chuckle, his belly bouncing up and down behind the steering wheel.

"Llano, Texas," Doc read off the roadside sign, "Population 2544. Nice size for a town. Big enough to have most everything you need, but not so big that it's got all those thing you'd rather not have around."

"Like crime."

"And smog."

"And traffic," George said. "There's three stop lights in town. We turn left at the second one. Across the bridge up there's the other light and the grocery stores–two of 'em, so you get a choice. On out a town is a bar and a liquor store. To the left at that third light is the barbecue district. I ain't kiddin' you. This here's barbecue country and Llano's the capitol. There's four or five places on about a half mile a Route 29. It's so smoky some mornings you have to put your lights on. Quit lookin' at me like that, I'm serious. We'll come into town tomorrow and have breakfast. Nothing like barbecued goat and ranch beans for Sunday breakfast."

"Goat, huh?" Doc said.

"Or brisket or sirloin or sausage, pork chops big as your hand and twice as thick, chicken even, if you're chicken. Slopped all over with sauce. Sop it up with white bread, big slice of onion. Oh man, we might have to stop now, I'm makin' myself so hungry."

George made the proper left turn, overcoming the lure of the barbecue district, then quickly turned into a parking spot in front of a hardware store.

"I'm gonna call Maggie, see if she needs anything from town. Gotta use a pay phone, the cells don't work too good out here."

Doc was browsing the fishing tackle ten minutes later when he heard several male voices simultaneously shout 'George'. George spotted Doc and, pulling him forward, made individual introductions to all of the men gathered by the cash register. "Doc and I are headed out to Maggie's for the weekend."

As they climbed back into the F-350, Doc asked George if there was anyone he *didn't* know. Anywhere.

"A town like this, it's pretty easy to make acquaintances. You have to earn people's *distrust* out here. Not like the city. Besides, they all know Maggie–and Pancho, the local hippie celebrity eccentrics.

"Whe it was pretty clear that Pancho wasn't coming back, all of Maggie's neighbors helped her out in some fashion. She wouldn't a made it emotionally without them. That's the comradery I'm talkin' about. Hell, city kid, hippie lookin', Maggie couldn't of been much more different from these folks when she moved here. And a course the rumors about Pancho and dope dealin'. But none of that meant squat when she needed help. I love these people."

"They seem to be pretty fond of you too, George. You have a gift."

"Not me. Maggie's got the gift–of empathy with her fellow man. You'll see. Care to hear more of the big weekend story?"

"Hell yes. You're like an audio book."

"It took us a while to get Mom back in the motor home. She just kept walkin' up the road with her arms crossed, wearin' a scowl that'd freeze your heart. Finally I went on ahead with the Suburban, Daniel readin' me the directions over the CB. After a while we crossed a cattle guard and the county road started curving back toward the river and I thought, if we have to cross that thing again Ma's liable to walk back to Houston. We came up over a pretty good sized hill and just at the top there was a wood slat gate painted about twenty colors and I knew without readin' the mailbox that this was Maggie's place.

"Jake jumped out and opened it up and Gina and I drove in. I told Jake to stay and close her up after Daniel came on. He'd finally got Ma in and was comin' up behind. We drove on down this rutted out driveway, almost a path, goin' about five miles an hour but that was okay cause the place was just beautiful, big live oaks hangin' over the road, the road snakin' along this ridge so you kept getting views of the river to the left and across the river those pink granite mountains shimmering in the sunlight, wild flowers under the trees, the grass full and thick. And the cactus flowers. Prickly pear clumps big as a Volkswagen with hundreds of yellow cactus roses bloomin'! It was just gorgeous everywhere.

"After about three quarters of a mile we wind downhill for a little then pull around a big granite knob to the right and into this football field sized flat clearing and sittin' right smack in the middle of about an acre of Indian paint brushes and the last of the season's blue bonnets is a huge tee pee. And sittin' cross legged out front on a blanket is Maggie–dressed in buckskins and tendin' a big iron pot hanging over a camp fire. If she'd of had black hair you would a sworn you'd gone back in time. Except just then Pancho comes rippin' down the ridge from the other side of the clearing in an old, open-top Land Rover and we all meet in the middle and start pilin' out and huggin' and Ma's cryin', Dad too–he couldn't help it. And my hellions start woopin' like Indians and runnin' around with the dogs howlin' and chasin' 'em. Then Daniel's kids get goin' and pretty soon you can't hear a damn thing and then we're all cryin', Daniel, me, Maggie, Gina, everybody but Pancho who's just sittin' on the top a the seat a that jeep thing laughin' his head off at the crazy Marones all over his pasture. It was a hell of a scene. I'd pay ten thousand bucks for a video of that moment. It sort of symbolizes the whole, nutty bunch of us."

"I think it sounds wonderful, George. I can only imagine what it's like. My parents were like museum pieces. Every once in a while I'd be allowed to admire them from a distance then go back to my real life. I was no different to them than a car or a painting. Just something you're fond of in an abstract way."

"How sad for you," George said. "Let's see what we can do to change that."

Doc was about to ask what he meant when George whooped and pointed out the windshield. "There's the river! And it looks like it's up some. Hold on cowboy, we're goin' in!"

Doc braced his left hand on the dash and grabbed the window post with his right as George accelerated down the gravel path toward the river. They hit the water hard, sending wet wings out to the sides and rear, barreling across the invisible road at a speed Doc thought was far from prudent. In a few seconds they were across the water and crashing up the bank on the other side, fish-tailing around corners, now sending up an immense dust tail to mark their passage.

"Did that sign say 'loose livestock'?" Doc had to nearly shout over the roar of the engine and the staccato drumming of the gravel spewing everywhere.

"Yeah, we're between fences, inside somebody's property."

"Shouldn't you slow down?"

George looked at Doc like, what's the connection, loose livestock and excessive speed? But suddenly it must have sunk in because he took his foot off the gas just before Doc yelled LOOK OUT! and the windshield seemed to fill instantly with a black shape the size of the truck. George ripped the wheel to the right slamming Doc against his door and then immediately whipped it back to the left. Doc was thrown across the seat into George's ample belly.

"Get the hell off me, Doc. I can't steer," George yelled.

"I can't help it!" Doc attempted to yell back but his face was mashed into George's armpit now. George swung the wheel right again and Doc fought his way back to his side of the cab as the gyrations lessoned and the truck straightened out finally, Doc thinking, seat belt, wear your fucking seat belt.

"Woo wee, that was close. We nearly had us a truck load of prime beef," George said, slapping his thigh with an open palm. "That'll get your pump goin'. You alright, Doc?"

"I just had four birthdays. Do that again and I'll be able to collect social security. Jesus H. Christ. That had to be a bull. It was too damn big to be a cow."

"Yes sir, I believe you're right. Good thing too. A cow might a jumped into us but the bull, he don't move for nothin'. Damn lucky."

"Lucky? Lucky we didn't get killed or lucky we almost didn't get killed cause it was a bull and not a cow?"

"Damn if I know. What you just said didn't make no sense at all."

"That's because you scared me senseless for God's sake. Can we just slow down now and enjoy the view?"

"We don't have no choice. At the top of this hill's Maggie's gate." They turned off the road and crossed a cattle guard beside which stood the old gate. "She put in the cattle guard about three years ago, when Junior came to work for me more or less full time. Didn't have him to get out and open and close the thing no more."

They rode in silence except for an occasional exclamation about the scenery and bounced slowly along the rutted pathway.

"Why didn't they ever improve the road?" Doc asked after a half mile of bumping along.

"Pancho said it was his last line of defense. I assumed he meant by the time the law got down that road he could burn the evidence if need be."

"Unless they came in low in a slick and set down in his front yard. Not much warning then."

"They'd have to rappel out the doors. There's no safe landing zone near the house." Doc looked at him and George continued. "You're thinking about the tee pee clearing. That was twenty years ago, Doc. Things change. Even these old live oaks are growin' although it's hard to tell if you look at 'em all the time. You'll see in a minute."

They wound down the ridge and made the right into the clearing but there was no open acre of wildflowers now. Instead there was a habitat unlike anything Doc had ever seen and it took him a while to grasp what he was looking at. There was a structure, that was clear, but it appeared to be made of living flora growing in an abundant profusion out of natural rock.

"What do you think, Doc? Different ain't it?"

"Different doesn't even come close. Who created this wonder, Maggie or Pancho?"

"Oh, it was a little a both. Maggie did most of the finish work but Pancho was an original thinker, I'll give him that. He'd say wouldn't it be cool if we had something or other over there and then they'd start working on it. They always had half a dozen somethin' or others goin' on simultaneously.

"Now listen, Doc. There's somethin' I want to ask you before we go in. I want to find out what happened to Pancho. You can see the boy's still fucked up about it. That 'worthless sack a shit' comment was just that—shit. That boy loved his daddy more than anything. And Maggie's still fucked up too though she won't admit it. I'll pay you and I'll cover the expenses for whatever you can think of that might shed some light on the whole thing. What do you think, sound interesting?"

"George, what did I tell you before? You don't even know me. What makes you think this is something I can do?"

"My instincts. I trust them and they tell me you're the right man for the job. You don't have to decide right now, just think about it, okay? And don't tell Maggie. She has to think it's her idea. You understand?" Before Doc could respond, George said, "Speak of the Devil, here she comes," pointing toward the flowering mountain. Doc looked but didn't see her for several seconds, then caught movement and saw a figure winding through the gardens growing at ground level in front of the boulders that extended almost to the front bumper of the truck, the whole expanse canopied by an artillery net, dappling the gardens below in a shifting pattern of light and shade, the cloth scraps billowing from the net's open weave, all the poles and ropes supporting the structure entwined with flowering Trumpet Vine, Bougainvillea and Wisteria.

"She's lovely, George," Doc said.

"Easy, cowboy. I told you she had a presence, didn't I? Just relax. Be yourself." With that Maggie was beside the truck and George hopped out and swept her up in a hug and swung her around and around, nimble as an elf, both of them laughing, Maggie's hair arcing out in a golden fan as she spun through the air. George slowed gradually, bringing her down in a soft landing directly in front of Doc and without any sign of exertion said, "Maggie, I'd like you to meet Doc. He needs your help, I think."

"Doc, welcome to my home," she said. After several seconds of silence, Doc forced out a squeaky sound.

She laughed then, a song of mirth, and took Doc by the arm and led him through her gardens toward the rock castle, the feeling of enchantment very real as she placed him on a granite settee under an expanse of overhanging live oak, limbs draped with Spanish moss, the air scented with a barrage of fragrance and humming with the flight song of a thousand honey bees, butterflies hovering, mocking birds and scarlet cardinals flitting in the branches above.

George joined Doc on the slab of rock, propped his feet on a varnished round of red mesquite and announced with a sigh that he could easily drink a beer about now.

"You've forgotten where the kitchen is, my lazy brother? Don't be expecting the handmaiden from me, George Marone. One time only then it's self-service. You too, Doc," she said. "Don't be shy."

"She means it," George said when Maggie had glided off behind a ten-foot chunk of pink rock. "If you wait to be served around here, you could starve to death. It's all very laissez-faire. No schedules. That's why it's so relaxing."

"That and the fact that it may be the most beautiful place on earth," Doc said. "The amount of work this must have taken is astounding. You said Pancho was lazy. I don't see how you can draw that conclusion," Doc said, gesturing around them.

Maggie returned to the patio and placed a tray on a flat-topped rock. "You are quite correct," she said as she handed a mug of honey colored ale to Doc and then George. "Pancho, as my brother so derisively called my husband, was an unusual man, a free thinker, totally unselfconscious. This led to some, let's say, misconceptions about his character, even his intelligence. Especially by Daniel, our older brother."

"Misconceptions," George said. "Man is that an understatement. Daniel about hated that boy after you run off with him. I don't think he ever much more than tolerated ol' Pan–'Arturo' – ever again. Ma's the only thing that kept him in line."

"Quiet, George." Maggie said. "Arturo could work incredibly hard," she said to Doc. "Tirelessly, day after day. When he became obsessed with a project . . . Let me start again. Arturo would have a vision, not like an Indian mystic or an acid trip but something he wanted to build. Or do. As I said, he had a unique point of view. When we first settled here I thought some of his ideas were impossible to build. You know how you talk with a friend or a lover and you dream together, vocalize your fantasies? Let your minds take off with a bizarre concept and then follow it to an absurd conclusion? Usually we'd be laughing our heads off by the time we exhausted the possibilities. But Arturo didn't always let it go. He would play with an idea, shaping and refining it in his head–sometimes for days. When he was working up a project he might lay under a tree for a day, or sit up all night and look at the stars. Sometimes he wouldn't get out of bed at all. It was pretty weird till I recognized the pattern.

"When he came out of the planning stage, he could turn manic. But happy. Always in great spirits, always kind, even when he was deeply consumed by one of his loony concepts. I'll take you on a tour, show you some of his things."

"The house. I want to see the house," Doc said. "The gardens are impressive enough but the house is . . . well, different seems so understated."

"Yeah, different don't do justice to Pancho either," George added. "There wasn't one normal thing about that boy."

"George, shut your mouth. What did Momma tell you a hundred times?"

"If you can't say something nice about someone," George answered, "just shut the hell up."

"Want to look around, Doc?" Maggie asked. She got up from the stump and gathered the bottles and glasses and led him toward the large pink rock.

"I think I'll go on down to the big tank and aggravate a few bass," George said as he got to his feet and stretched. "I'll be back in an hour or so." Maggie and Doc walked together down the path to the bolder that Maggie had seemed to vanish behind. She led him around it and through a carved, wooden door, the frame of which was bolted to the living rock. Doc soon began to see that the house was constructed primarily of slabs of pink granite stacked and piled, blocks leaning at odd angles, sections cantilevered over boulders below. At first it seemed that the entire eccentric mass was open to the elements but what appeared to be an opening between two truck sized stones, looking out above the plane of the immense artillery net, was in fact filled and fitted with a huge piece of plate glass channeled into the rock surrounding it. Similarly treated openings graced each combination of rock around what Doc began to realize was the exterior ring of concentric circles of stone. Likewise, the sky above was clearly visible through a dozen irregular portals, all protected by cut and caulked sections of glass.

Floors had been created of poured concrete, died a rosy pink to match the stone walls, and overlaid with Native American style rugs. There were wooden roof beams in some rooms and stone ceilings in others. Wood cupboards and cubbies had been framed into irregular nooks and pockets between the stones, some holding books, others odd nick nacks. Matching dark mesquite or golden pecan furniture groups were placed about in various rooms. The walls were decorated with all manner of flowering plants and climbing vines and petroglyph-style paintings, some juvenile in subject and style and some complex and skillfully applied.

There was electricity in the house as some of the rooms were subtly accented by hidden fixtures, here casting a glow across the ceiling, there inviting inspection of a small curving grotto. Switches and outlets, where visible at all, were connected by copper tubing bent to follow the curving stones and tucked in at floor level. And there was a current of cool, moving air. Doc asked of its source which, Maggie explained, was a series of ducts that ran to and from a stone filled thermal pit below the garden, the air circulated by low velocity fans.

The kitchen was the most 'normal' space, a thirty-foot long expanse, log rafters bearing on boulders behind and stacked stone piers in front, the spaces between the columns framed with mesquite planks for both walls and cabinets, the countertop hammered copper sheets. There were windows in some of the column bays and a set of glass doors flanked by wide side-lights that opened onto a deck suspended over a tumbling wash of granite boulders that ran out from beneath the deck and plummeted down the side of the hill a hundred feet below. Wandering over and through the boulders and in places falling ten and twenty feet at a time was a shallow watercourse, gurgling over the rocks, at the bottom flowing into a pool. At the far end of the pool another waterfall took the overflow down to the cattle tank below, on the banks of which George stood, casting spinner bait toward the sun dappled surface.

"We usually eat out here when the weather's right," Maggie explained, both of them now standing on the deck looking down at George and out across the wooded pastures, the river a half mile beyond and the view good for another ten miles beyond that, the horizon a broken line of pink rock outcroppings, the sun headed down behind them.

"My God, Maggie, this is breathtaking. And incredible, the house, everything. Arturo was a genius."

"Yes he was," she said.

"Do you mind if I ask what happened? If you don't want to answer I understand," he added.

"No, it's fine, Doc. Arturo's been gone for a long time. Let's sit out here and tell each other stories."

"I can't think of anywhere I'd rather be." Doc pulled out a rough sawn chair and held it for her.

After a few moments he turned toward her and was about to ask if she knew why George had said he needed her help, what he had meant by it, but as he was working up the nerve, with her quietly studying his face, she smiled. "George thinks I have the power to heal, to mend the broken spirit. Every so often he brings someone up here for a weekend and he says that after they return, they're well again, that just being here makes people feel better. It's probably the quiet and the clean air more than anything."

"I don't know, Maggie. George is an empathetic man. People react to him very strongly, very positively. Why couldn't that be a family trait?"

"I don't know either. Why do you need help?" she asked.

"George was in Vietnam. He may have picked up something from me that made him think I was as well. A brothers-in-arms thing. And of course everyone who was in the Nam is fucked up from it. Isn't that what most people think?"

"What you did in Vietnam. That seems more to the point than if you were there."

She looked at him while he watched a hawk soaring a thousand feet out from their aerie. Finally he turned to her and said, "I haven't talked about it in a long time" and she said then it's about time you did and so he told her, told her about his parents and the military schools, about the years of guilt and self-hatred, about internalizing his parent's rejection, channeling it into determination, driving himself to excel, to win, to conquer everything he faced.

He told her about his years at the Citadel, about being the most gung ho, the fastest in his class on the obstacle course, the best shot on the firing range, the brightest student. But he was never the class president or even the treasurer because they were elected offices and he was not fun to be around. He never let down his guard, never took part in hazing the freshmen, never looked the other way. He always upheld the code–honor, duty, God, country.

He graduated second in his class, beaten only by the son of a South Korean general who was so driven, so unrelenting, that Doc's "C" in freshman composition was never made up, the Korean never cracking, never once hearing Doc's footsteps, never even glancing back at Doc's pursuit.

Doc had been hounded by Army and Marine recruiters from late sophomore year. Finally he was ordered to the commandant's office in the spring of his senior year where the Army Chief of Staff himself greeted him by name and told Doc that he was by God going to join the United States Army, the finest fighting force the world had ever known and that was the end of it. Understand? He did.

He went from basic to advanced infantry, never considering tanks or artillery, then to Ranger training and jump school and finally he had a month of leave to consider his options. He had been invited to try out for the Green Berets at Bragg and offered a posting to the little known Army School of Jungle Warfare in their counter insurgency program. He spent his leave at Fort Benning, staying with his old Gunnery Sergeant from Ranger training, running in the mornings, firing every weapon in the armory in the afternoons, removing his lieutenant's insignia so he could drink beer in the NCO club at night and listening with rapt attention to story after story about Vietnam, how to fight and how to win the war, who was on the right track and which politician was going to throw them all to the commie dogs. But the words of a grizzled top sergeant, just rotating through after his second tour, stuck in Doc's mind. "It ain't the friggin' boy scouts with their Frenchy hats gonna win this war, it's the outfits you never see and never heard of." Doc went to guerilla school.

What he learned there severely tested his code of honor. It wasn't sniper training, crawling for two days through swamp and jungle, movement measured in inches, for the opportunity to cap an NVA political officer from seven hundred yards or the carefully planned insertions behind enemy lines, the target a civilian and his entire family. It was more the disregard for the lives of the soldiers themselves, the mission first at any cost through any method mentality.

He gave Maggie only a brief and sketchy overview of his first time in country. She didn't need to know the details of the horror to understand its effects. But then he talked about a second tour, cut short by savage wounds, nearly fatal, and about his recovery in Japan and his recruitment by the CIA.

His disillusion with the armed forces was nearly complete but his CIA contact spun a tale of righteous men fighting for the survival of the nation itself, of a comradery, an esprit de corps, that had been missing from his tours of assassination and sabotage. Their mission was a counter revolution, arming the freedom loving peoples of Vietnam and training them to fight the Cong, drive them from their home land.

Doc knew this approach had been tried from the beginning and had met with limited success but according to this recruiter, never with these mountain tribesmen and never with this commitment of resources.

Doc was back in country, on the ground with the tribesmen, for almost a year. He was constantly under supplied, he and his men barely surviving, and he eventually tired of the promises and lies, finally threatening his superiors with exposure if he did not get the material' they were so desperately in need of. He was sent by his section chief to a drop zone and ambushed, losing all of his men and nearly his life, his sniper training all that saved him, inching his way back to his encampment first through the corpses of his men and then through and around hundreds of NVA regulars.

Doc crawled into his own tent, found the section chief sleeping in Doc's bunk and a new guy in the other cot. He calmly slit the chief's throat–just deep enough to cause a massive, bloody smile. The chief bolted upright, saw Doc staring back at him filthy and blood covered, grabbed his chest and died on the spot from a coronary rupture.

Doc was cashiered out of The Company, stripped of his identity both military and civilian and cast back into society without a name, a past or a future. At the time, he felt damn lucky to be alive.

"Doc, that's horrible! How can they erase your identity?"

"That was the deal. Basically, I would disappear in exchange for immunity from the attack on the chief. They had me cold. The new guy saw it all and there were two other ops guys in the next tent which I didn't know till they were sitting on my chest, then tying me to a tree. I was pretty well gone by then. A head-case they said. It was true."

"But your identity. That's so . . . part of you. It's like they killed your whole family somehow."

"That's part of why it was so effective in my case. My parents are dead now but when this happened, they were informed by the Army that I was KIA, in the line of duty, honorably serving my country. If I would have shown up at their front door, they would have called the police. An honorably dead son was far better to them than I had ever been while alive."

"What did you do? How did you survive? Work as a carpenter?"

"No. That's chapter two. But we were going to *swap* stories, not listen to me till midnight. It's your turn. Tell me how you built the house. Assisted by aliens like the Egyptians?"

Maggie got up and stretched, closed her eyes and, fingers tented over her breasts, pressed her palms together, threw back her head and howled like a wolf. Doc laughed and joined her in stretching. George waved from the pond's edge below, hearing the she wolf, and they waved back at him.

"That was the dinner call. We can talk while I work out a menu. George will be here before too long and I expect Junior any time now."

As they walked back into the kitchen Doc said, "Oh shit! I forgot to even ask how he was. I'm so sorry. Does he still think I shot him on purpose and more importantly, do you?"

"No. Neither of us. He's really a sweet kid but he sometimes has a chip on his shoulder. Not to mention a gun nail," she said with a grin. "I think he'd like to be a little more 'average' but it just isn't in his genes."

"That can be hard for a boy, being different."

"For a girl, too. But I at least had my brothers to commiserate with. And they looked after me. Junior just has me. And George."

"Does he ask about Arturo? Does he know what happened?"

"None of us do, Doc. Not for sure. George and Daniel assume it was a drug deal gone bad but they always assumed the worst about him. That scenario isn't too good for Junior. It doesn't much help the quest for normal, Dad being a dead dope dealer."

"Is that part true, the dope?"

Maggie put down her paring knife, wiped her hands on a towel and turned to look at him. "Doc, I honestly don't know. He would leave for several weeks at a time and come back with bags of money. What would you think? He never answered me when I'd ask. He never fought with me about it, and I wasn't much of a scene maker, I don't fight, not unless I'm completely backed into a corner. I asked him a dozen times and he gave me a dozen beatific smiles and told me in a dozen ways that there was nothing to worry about, we were in no danger and nothing bad was going to happen." She turned back to the cutting board then added, "What else could it have been? What else can you do to earn bags of money in a few weeks? Kill people?"

Chapter Three

George returned as Maggie was lighting the grill, a rock and metal sculpture constructed on a massive chunk of stone, part of the sidewall of the kitchen.

Flopping down in a chair as Maggie fed wood chips in to a small fire, George asked, "So how's it going? Where's Doc?"

"Junior is showing him something in the house."

"Well?"

"Well what, brother?"

George laughed, hopped up and announced, "I'll get us a beer, then you start talking, girl." When he returned the fire was well involved and she was placing several larger pieces of wood into the pit.

"He's a troubled man, George. He's seen and done some terrible things," Maggie began, taking the bottle from him. "I think he's probably forced himself to adapt, to cope with his nightmares, but he's not well and far from happy. What did you think, to bring him here?"

"Much the same. A pilgrim, destination unknown. Nam is all over him. If you told me he was a shoe salesman from Des

Moines during the war, I would have lost all faith in my instincts. Prognosis?"

"I don't know. A good heart, but he needs to rest. And to forget. Mostly, I imagine, he needs to forgive himself, to move on. He's still haunted."

"How'd Junior react, seeing him here?"

"I think he knows you well enough to suspect you'd bring him along. When I told him you two were coming, he didn't seem surprised. Doc went right to him, asking how he was, apologizing. They talked for a bit, I was inside, I don't know about what, and then they went off together so it seems to be going well, yes?"

"Junior's growing up," George said. "A year ago he would have sulked in his room the whole time Doc was around. Course a year ago he wouldn't have braced somebody that looks like Doc. He's lucky Doc didn't throw him off the building. Wisdom don't always follow age, at least not right away. Still, I'm proud of the boy. Aren't you? I mean seeing the growth, maturing."

"Yes, George, and thank you for helping him."

"I wasn't fishin' for a compliment, Mags, I'm really proud of him, you know?"

"Yes I do." She smiled and wrapped an arm around his thick neck and kissed him on the head. "Thank you. I love you, George."

"I love you too, Maggie," he grinned. "When's dinner. I'm starvin'."

"Go get the boys, I'll start the steaks."

They ate on the deck, the sun approaching the tops of the hills across the river, the rib eyes delicious, smoky and pink, Maggie's pole beans simmered then sautéed with jalapenos in a big iron skillet over the coals, garden salad lightly tossed with olive oil and vinegar.

George finished first, wiping his mouth on a linen napkin then burping contentedly. "Hey, where's the dog. I haven't seen him around at all."

"Out chasin' jack rabbits probably," Junior said, gnawing on the end of his steak bone.

"You chewin' that bone's what reminded me. Mind if I try to whistle him up?"

"Be my guest," Maggie said, waving her hand out toward the end of the deck and the ranch land beyond. "I suspect he's down in the garden sleeping in the shade like he always is. That dog wouldn't chase a jack rabbit unless it was running off with his dinner."

George walked over to the edge of the deck, licked his lips and placed his thumb and index finger on the corners of his mouth, and let out such a blast that all of them winced.

"Jesus Christ, George," Doc said. "A *dead* dog would wake up and come running after that."

A few seconds later a faint jingling announced the dog's approach up the path that inclined from the garden level in the front to the deck level in the back.

"The old boy looks pretty spry, don't he," George said. The odd looking beast achieved the deck and trotted over to George, tail in motion, tongue lolling.

"What, ah, breed is that, Junior?" Doc asked.

"That is a Mexican bear hound. Pure bred, championship bloodline, right, Mom? That dog is worth a fortune in stud fees alone!" Junior said.

Doc looked the dog over again. "Bear hound, huh? I can see the bear part. That must have been on his father's side. But I think the hound part of the family tree might have had a little horse mixed in. That thing's big enough to ride. And where does one find a bear hound of such impeccable lineage?" Doc asked.

"Why, in Mexico of course," Maggie said. "Arturo brought him back on one of his trips. He was the size of my hand. We bottle-fed him for weeks. I would croon over him while I fed him, teasing him about how small and delicate he was and Arturo would say, just wait Maggie, I think he might turn out to be pretty good sized, and he'd laugh. I though he was nuts, but that was true about many things he said. Now look at the damn thing. Arturo must have known."

Junior tossed his steak bone to the dog who snapped it out of the air and crunched it down in two bites, then he picked up his plate and stalked into the kitchen.

"What's wrong with him?" George asked Maggie.

"Arturo. Talking about him," she said.

"Everyone assumes he's dead," Doc said. "But just maybe . . . A boy is going to dwell on those maybes. And the might have beens."

"Yep," George said. "I believe that's a pretty good assessment of what's botherin' the boy. What would you suggest as therapy for him, Doc?"

"I don't know, George. Maybe the answer's in the history. Educate him about his dad, help him understand. Or maybe a journey of discovery, take him places his father had been. Get to know the man that way."

George looked at Maggie. He had a smile on his face and as Maggie stared back at her brother, the corners of her mouth began to rise and she swung her head around to look directly at Doc.

"That is a wonderful idea," she said.

After dinner they watched the sun set in an explosion of orange and purple that filled the entire horizon. Junior eventually rejoined them. When the sky had faded to a muted glow, the air quickly cooling, Maggie suggested they adjourn to the observatory and asked Junior to start a fire.

Doc had thought he had been shown the entire house, with the exception of Maggie's bedroom, but there were more surprises in store. Junior led them down a stone walled corridor then up a steep flight of stairs, a ship's ladder, each tread notched directly into the sloping face of a boulder, the handrail a peeled cedar pole four inches in diameter, the pulp wood a bright white with stripes of red running down its length where the adz or axe had cut deeper as it was shaped, the pole bolted every few feet to the rock wall with copper brackets. The stairs discharged onto an irregular wooden platform that snaked almost completely around a large flat rock, the space thus defined about twenty five feet in diameter.

As Doc stepped onto the platform, he looked up and realized they were outside, on top of the massive pile of boulders that formed the backbone of the house, the stars surrounding them, the horizon unbroken except for a twenty foot tall rubble obelisk at the far end of the flat rock, the wooden platform butting up to the wider base of the obelisk from both sides. It took him almost a full minute, turning three hundred and sixty degrees, watching Junior begin to build a fire at the base of what he now saw was a fireplace of native stone, seeing George drop into an overstuffed chair, seeing the similar couch and matching chair, the ottomans and plank coffee table, the rugs, the end tables of flat boulders, to realize that they were not outside at all but inside. Inside an immense clear bubble!

"How . . ." he began. "What's it . .. ? George! Help me, damn it. This isn't possible."

"It's laminated glass," George said. "If you look real close you can see the ribs holding the wedges together. During the day it's obvious but at night it can shake you up some. You'd swear you were sittin' outside wouldn't you? It's the most dramatic space I've ever seen. Especially at night. Look at those stars. Ain't nothin' like the Texas night sky, Doc."

George stopped and put his head back and whistled a verse of 'Deep in the Heart of Texas,' the sound clear and sweet, Junior joining in for the one line chorus, then both of them singing, 'Don't Fence Me In,' full voiced, Junior standing behind George's chair, their voices blending perfectly, tenor and alto.

"You two are really good," Doc said, clapping. "I'm impressed."

"As well you should be," Maggie said. "They've been working on their act for fifteen years. I think they're ready for Nashville but they're scared to quit their day jobs and give it a try."

She placed a tray with a bottle and four goblets on the coffee table and asked Doc to please serve as she sat down beside him. "It's a shiraz, made with local grapes. It's quite good."

He poured for each of them then held his glass up to the light of the fire and gently swirled the red-black liquid.

"It's beautiful," Doc said. "To our lovely hostess." He bowed toward her then turned to George and Junior. "And her talented family."

"Here, here," Maggie said. "And to our guest. Well met, Mr. Doc."

"Indeed," said George.

"Yippee ki yi yo, mother fuckers," Junior said as he saluted them.

"Ah, Mags you've done it again," George said. "This is better than last year."

"You made this?" Doc asked. "Really? Here?"

"Yes. Right here. The grapes come from Herman Crenwelgie over past Fredericksburg. He put in the shiraz vines about thirty years ago. But the shiraz didn't work for his tastes and he switched to cabernet. His little plot of shiraz was an afterthought till he met Arturo. Their deal was pretty simple. Arturo directed the handling of the grapes, when to fertilize, how he wanted the vines trimmed, everything. Herman's men did all the work and Arturo bought the whole crop. Arturo taught me the rudiments of viticulture, bought me the equipment, some books. He built the cellars when he put in the thermal pit. He told me he thought I would have a knack for it, to experiment, follow my nose was his expression. So I did. He was right, I just love it. We have a half acre of Pinot Grigio and some Boudreaux grapes down by the river."

"And our own bees," Junior said, "plus peaches and pecans, the Texas two step. And pears for the special Elixir."

George laughed at Doc's quizzical look. "The elixir is pear brandy. There's a little still around here somewhere, hidden from the revenuers. Right, Junior?"

"Hidden from all humanity. And callin' the Elixir pear brandy is like callin' Nolan Ryan's fastball a pretty fair pitch. The Elixir is the Nectar of the Gods."

"Well, you got a point there," George said. "It is some potent stuff. Seriously, Doc, it has a real unusual kick to it, not a kick in the ass, more like a mental boost. Very strange."

"Arturo's old family recipe," Maggie said. "He built that first contraption, a still, as soon as we were set up in the tee pee. And he planted the pear trees from seeds he had in a little pouch. He said the Elixir wouldn't be at its best until we made it from the fruit of the 'family tree.' Yeah, weird," she said looking at Doc's expression, "but I've got to tell you, he was right. The difference was night and day."

"We'll give it a whirl tomorrow," George said. "You don't want to drink it at night unless you like weird dreams."

"Yeah," Junior said. "I think Pop crossed those pear trees with peyote cactus."

They all sat quietly for a time sipping the wine and gazing at the speckled panorama of the night sky, the air so clear that satellites flying through the stars were easily visible.

Finally Maggie said, "Have you ever been to Mexico, Doc?"

"Several times. After I was, ah, mustered out of the . . . well, you know, I spent a month kicking around California but the hippie scene was just too . . . I don't know, intense? The anti-war movement was gaining momentum and the war was still way too fresh in my mind, the deaths of my men, even the Agency debacle. I was still a soldier. So I took off to Mexico, got out. Ran away, call it what you like, I needed some quiet."

"Where did you go, any place in particular?"

"A week here, a week there. Moving South. I ended up in Yucatan. Spent six months laying on the beach, fishing, exploring the Mayan ruins, living off my meager savings. Maybe the Indian vibes helped, I don't know, but the place just felt right."

"It sounds wonderful. Do you ever think about going back?" she asked, glancing over at George.

"Pretty slick, Mags," George said. "Why don't you just ask him? Get it out in the open."

"Ask me what, Maggie?" Doc said.

"Because I haven't worked it through yet, George. I'm still considering the pros and cons."

"Would you two like to include me in this conversation," Doc said. "I feel like a steer at a stock show."

"I'm sure it doesn't concern *me*," Junior said, "but I have no idea what you guys are talking about either."

"Actually, it concerns you a great deal, boy," George said, taking his feet off the ottoman and sitting up. "It's all about you in fact. Right, Maggie?"

"I haven't decided yet, George."

"Ah hell, Mags. It's perfect. You knew it same as me, the second you heard it you knew. Now you're just scared to put it in play. You're afraid he won't come back either, is that it?"

"Yes, Goddamn it! That's exactly what it is. Now shut the fuck up, George!" Maggie said. "I'm sorry. I apologize, to all of you. Doc, what you said this afternoon, about Junior and Arturo? It obviously had an effect on both of us." She nodded toward her brother. "And I guess I know you're right but I'm having difficulty with the possible consequences."

"Ma, what the hell are you talking about?"

"I'm with Junior here, Maggie," Doc said. "What *are* we talking about? What did I say?"

"You said, my friend, what my sister and I have been worryin' over for years. How to help Junior here come to terms with his father's, ah, legacy I guess is the right word. And I think you were right on with the solution. And I think you are the perfect man for the job. You agree don't you, Maggie."

"Yes I do. But I'm not ready to see them off just yet, okay George? Just give me a little time." George got up from his chair, circled the table and put his arm around her.

"Sure, Maggie. There's no hurry. And nothings goin' to happen to the boy. I promise."

"Ma, what are you talking about?" Junior asked. "What's the matter? Come on, you're scaring me!"

"How about giving me a hand with my gear, Bub," Doc said. "I think they need some time to work this out before they let us know what's going on. What do you think?"

"Yeah, I guess," Junior said.

Chapter Four

Doc slept under the stars in the observatory, the couch enveloping him, the fire flickering. It was beautiful and serene and he awoke as the morning sun cleared the boulders behind the chimney.

As he entered the kitchen, Maggie was standin on the deck, hands on her hips, gazing down at the pond below. She was wearing cowboy boots, jeans and a Western shirt, hair cinched into a ponytail hanging out the back of a cowboy hat. She turned at his approach, a smile on her lips, face radiant and Doc felt such a bolt of desire that it was like a physical blow.

The smile left her face as she started toward him saying, "Are you okay, Doc?"

"I'm sorry. Yes, I'm fine. Good morning, Maggie. You look fabulous," he said "Thank you," she replied.

He made it to one of the sturdy cedar chairs and sat.

"We're going into town for breakfast. George said y'all discussed it yesterday. Are you sure you're okay? You're pale.".

"Yes. I'm fine," was all he meant to say but, "You are so beautiful" leapt out right after.

She put her hand on his chin, angled his face up and kissed him on the lips, lightly. "Thank you, Doc. I haven't heard that from a man in a long time." Then she took him by the arm, pulled him up and said, "Let's find those boys and go get us some barbeque! I am famished!"

'Those boys' were fishing and Maggie drove George's truck down to the pond's edge before she stuck her head out the window and yelled, "Come on fellers, we be gone to town!"

George and Junior tossed in their poles and climbed in the bed of the truck, slapping the fenders and whooping like drovers as Maggie fish tailed across the pasture and headed up the rutted driveway, bouncing Doc nearly to the cab's ceiling and almost tossing the boys right out of the bed. She slowed as they approached the county road then let out a rebel yell and took off in a dusty cloud.

Doc's frantic gesturing toward the road ahead and George's pounding on the back window finally got her to slow down but when the river came into view, Doc hid his face in his hands in mock horror as she hollered again, stomped the gas and barreled across, the columns of water shooting twenty feet in the air behind them.

When they piled out in front of Cooper's Bar B Q, George and Junior were half saturated and Maggie laughed so hard at their dusty dampness that her hat fell off at her feet and she picked it up and tried to beat some of the road dirt off her bedraggled payload.

They were all laughing when they got in line behind a dozen fellow diners, all of whom seemed to know either Maggie, Junior or George and in several cases, all three. Doc shook hand after hand, not remembering a single name.

When it was their turn to select from the 'menu', Doc's lack of barbeque education became evident. George looked at the befuddled expression on his face and said to the man tending the pit, a four by eight foot steel box three foot high with a counter-weighted lid, that ol' Doc was a Cooper's virgin and would Verdell be kind enough to explain the process.

"I surely would, George," Verdell exclaimed pleasantly, lifting the lid on the pit which let forth a billowing cloud of smoke and the scent of grilling meats. When the cloud lifted, Doc gazed down at a grate covered with fifty pounds or more of rings and slabs, haunches and ribs of a half dozen different animals.

"Now this here," Verdell explained, pointing with the tines of a three foot long wood handled fork, "is your basic brisket. And of course ya got yer ribs here, they's pork, and sausage, that's our own secret recipe so don't be askin' what's in it. Now that's a chicken as you can see and next to her, that big old slab there is sirloin and them's pork chops yonder. And then for yer barbeque connoisseurs like my good buddy George here, we like to keep a little cabrito on hand. That's goat, milk-fed baby goat. Dee-licios! Okay, now, what'll it be?" Doc was overwhelmed and turned to George.

"What you do here, Doc, is buy your dinner by the pound then go on inside, pick up your fixin's, pay for it all, then sit yourself down at these big old tables and honker down. How about if we get us an assort-o-pack and figure it out inside?"

Doc stood back to let the men get down to business, George pointing and Verdell cutting and piling until they had a red plastic tray heaped with some of everything and Verdell said, "Ya'll want sauce with that I expect" and the whole pile disappeared into a five gallon metal pail set down in the grate and re-emerged piece by piece on the end of Verdell's cavalry saber fork dripping a stream of red fluid that collected on the bottom of the tray, threatening to spill over by the time the last piece had been rescued from the sauce vat.

George led them through the swinging door, tray held high, and into the restaurant where they selected sides of cole slaw and potato salad and peach cobbler for dessert. George paid and led them to a table in the back.

"The beans and onions are over there Doc, they're all you can eat and so's the iced tea. The bread's here on the table and there's jalapenos and pickles in them big jars. Alright, dig in. You're on your own now, boys and girl," and without another word he ate nonstop for forty five minutes.

At last, slowing noticeably toward the end, he was done. His companions had wandered off at stages during his display but they were all back at the table toward the end, all staring silently as he ate the final few bites, faces blank, eyes following from plate to mouth, plate to mouth, mesmerized. George's prodigious burp, an epitaph, served to wake them from their stupor.

"George?" Maggie asked. "Are you sure you've had enough? Would you like a nice water buffalo for dessert?"

"No, nope, I'm pretty good," he sighed. "I'm thinking about curling up in the hammock for a little nap. What time is it, Mags?"

"It's 10:15, George. I'll take us home and you can sleep till lunch time. How's that?"

When they returned, Junior went inside and George climbed slowly out of the truck and headed straight for the hammock slung between two great, gnarly boughs of the big oak by the patio. Maggie asked Doc if he'd like to take a walk and he said he needed to do something to work off that meal and she took his arm and led him toward the river.

As they walked along, stepping over rocks and detouring around clumps of cactus and dead falls, Maggie pointed out and named the native plants and wild flowers that were blooming all around. A hundred feet from the river, close enough to see the sunlight flickering off the surface and hear the water, they sat down under the first of the fruit trees that grew along the bank.

“This is a lovely spot,” Doc said. “Your whole property is beautiful for that matter. It must give you great satisfaction to see it bloom and thrive.”

“It does,” she said, pulling a stalk of grass from its sheath and placing it in the corner of her mouth, her arms crossed hugging her knees. “But.... I don’t know,” she said. “There’s no one to share it with any more.”

“What is it you want me to do with Junior, Maggie? Are you ready to talk about it?”

“You know the rudiments of the situation,” she said. “You know Arturo disappeared, you’ve met Junior, you’ve seen him at his worst from what George told me about the ‘shooting,’ about how he was harassing you. And you’ve had a chance to see him here now, for a day. You can see he isn’t really a bad kid can’t you?”

“Yes I can. We talked some last night. And yesterday afternoon. He seems like a pretty normal kid to me. He’s so big though, I have to keep reminding myself that he’s only what, nineteen?”

“He gets that from George I think. George worked him like a horse when he had him during the summers, the last few summers. Plus he’s got George’s genes. More than mine anyway and Arturo wasn’t big like that. Muscular but not so bulky. Yeah, he is just a kid, it’s hard for me to remember that too sometimes.” She was silent for a time. Eventually she continued.

“It was hard for both of us after Arturo was gone. For a few weeks we didn’t expect him back of course. Then for a couple more weeks we were getting increasingly nervous, neither of us saying it. Junior was only fifteen but he was precocious. Mature might be more accurate. We raised him to be inquisitive and self-reliant. And he didn’t get to play with a lot of kids his age, he was home schooled so he was mainly around us, working with us, talking to us.

"I don't know if that was good for him particularly, in terms of his overall development or socialization, but he certainly had an interesting education. And he *is* smart. Arturo was too, scary smart, crazy ideas, like we were talking about yesterday, so Junior wasn't inhibited by two-dimensional thinking, that's for sure. And he has a lot of talent. You heard him sing and you saw his artwork in the house. The petroglyphs. They're all his. He's been painting them for years."

"Okay. I thought some were done by a child, Junior I assumed, but most of them are so elegant and complex, I don't know why, I just figured they were your work."

"Nope. All Junior. I will take credit for *those* genes though. Arturo had an artist's mind, the wild creativity, but as far as brush to canvas, that he gets from me."

"You're a painter as well?"

"I was. I haven't worked at it in a long time, since Arturo left, but I used to be pretty good, even made a little money at it. It was my pin money at first. Then I had to start investing it, there was too much to just let it lay around. We started a trust for Junior, for his education but he hasn't used it yet. We talk about college now and then and he says he'll go when he's ready but I think it's just lip service. And to be honest, I haven't really pushed him. It's probably selfish of me but he was allowed to make decisions for himself all his life, within reason, and I don't want him to go, not far away." She gave a wan smile and added, "Mother of the Year, huh?"

"Please, Maggie. I would have given anything to have had Junior's childhood."

"Maybe so. Anyway the money's there if he ever gets motivated to use it. I haven't checked one of those statements in a couple of years but it was two hundred or so last I looked."

"Thousand?" he asked.

"Yes. I told you I was pretty good. Didn't you believe me?"

"That's a hell of a lot of pin money, Maggie."

"The annuity reinvents the income back into the principle so it grows quickly. But some of my last stuff was bringing five figures. The checks were pretty big. I guess I miss it, painting. I'm not really sure. It's been so long and there are always so many other things to do. Now anyway.

"By the time Arturo'd been gone a couple months I knew he wasn't coming back. We pretended, especially Junior, but he knew too I think. Somehow it was just clear to both of us that we were alone now, that he was dead. Then we got the package. The poor UPS man carried it in the last four hundred yards. His truck got stuck under the limb of that oak that overhangs the driveway before you come down the big hill.

"Anyway, the thing had been all over the southwest by the look of all the stamps and postage on it. A big brown box." She held her hands a few feet apart vertically and then horizontally. "Full of money. And a perfect vase of Mayan pottery about this big." She indicated an object about the size of a small melon. "Full of ashes."

"That is too bizarre. You're serious aren't you? A pot of ashes in a box of money?"

"Oh, yes. The money was stacked all around, in bundles, with a space in the center for the pot and crumpled bills stuffed around to keep it from shifting. Very nicely packaged."

"A letter, anything? From Arturo?"

"A note. Typed on plain white paper. It said, 'He loved you very much. He is not coming back.' That was it."

He saw the tears coming. He put his arm around her shoulder and hugged her. She put her head back against his bicep, then wiped her eyes with her fingertips and smiled at him. "Four years. I could probably have him pronounced dead now, not that that would change a damn thing."

"It would be a release. Have a ceremony, a funeral? Bury the ashes? Is that horribly insensitive?" he said.

She laughed, shaking her head again. "Not at all. We could bury the hatchet, get it? Bury the hatchet, bury the ashes. Plant him, forgive him, forget him. Hey, it might help."

"I don't know that it could hurt unless you were trying to forget everything by repressing it, which it's pretty clear you're not or we wouldn't be having this conversation. But you and George weren't talking about a funeral last night, you were talking about a journey of some sort. Junior and I. What was that about? Specifically, if you please."

"Okay. You take Junior on a journey, a voyage of discovery, an attempt to trace his roots. Recreate Arturo's trips, find out what he did." After a pause she added, "Find out how he died."

"Okay."

"I know how vague that sounds but I don't know how else to say it. I'm not sure what it is the two of you need to do exactly. I just know that if you do it, it will help him. Junior will learn things about himself. And if he can come to terms with his father's life and death, then he can move on."

"Both of you, I suspect."

"Yeah, probably. We aggravate each other's sense of loss. Do you know what I mean? We see Arturo in each other and it's like picking a scab somehow. I can't forget him, Junior picks that up and it keeps him from forgetting, he gets mopey or lashes out like he did with you and that reminds me that he's still hurting. The cycle continues. I know we'll both get better eventually but it seems to me that without some sort of salve for the wound, the scars will be ugly."

"An appropriate metaphor. And I think the Road Trip concept has merit. But, ah . . . why me? That's what I guess I don't get. You don't know anything about me."

"Have you lied to me?" she asked. "Since you've been here, in our conversations, have you lied to me?"

"No. Why?"

"Because I know a lot about you. You're intelligent and passionate. You had a terrible childhood, your parents were harsh and unloving, your country screwed you. You've seen and done horrible things. But you're not crippled. That's what tells me the most really. You have every excuse to be a bitter, vicious man. But you're not. That means you have strength of character. The kind that you're either born with or that comes from a religious epiphany. I think you were born with yours. With a different accident of birth you could have been almost anything you wanted to be, Doc. An educator or maybe an actor, a scientist, whatever you put your energy into. Why are you grinning at me like that? Do you think I'm so far off base?"

"I'm not laughing because you're off base Maggie, I'm laughing because you were right on. With the educator part anyway. That's what I did for a lot of years. A PhD professor of military history, at a small college in Georgia."

"What happened, Doc? Why did you quit?"

"I didn't quit exactly. It was more a case of discovery. My past caught up with me. Or lack of a past to be technically accurate. Someone discovered that I had a few holes in my resume. That my personal history got off to a late start so to speak."

"Go on. Tell me the story. I knew you were more than an itinerant carpenter."

"Hey, I'm a Renaissance man. Soldier, scholar, worker of wood. 'If I were a carpenter, and you were a lady . . .'" he sang out of tune. Maggie was laughing as George came through the pasture to join them.

"I see you two are enjoying yourselves," George said as he lowered himself down beside Maggie.

"Have a nice nap, did we brother? Are you thinking about lunch now?"

"Not quite yet, lass, but I'll be sure to let you know when it's time for you to pursue your womanly duties."

"You'll be as skinny as a Hindu holy man before I'll wait on you're sorry ass, George Marone." Then she asked George if he often required a PhD from his carpenters. "I'm sorry," she said to Doc. "Is it okay to talk to him about this?"

Doc said sure, it was fine and George said what the hell are you talking about?

"Doc is a professor of Military History. What do you think of that?"

Doc said, "Was."

"Was, is, don't much matter," George said. "Once a man has done something, successfully I'm sure in your case Doc, then its part of him forever, right Mags?"

"That is correct," she answered. "I'm glad to see that something we've talked about has attached itself between your ears brother dear."

"Just cause I'm a fat old redneck don't make me stupid," George said.

"You are hardly stupid. Thick headed sometimes but never stupid. And your compassion makes up for most of your stubbornness. Like Mom."

"Let's not start slingin' around insults now, Mags. It's too pretty a day. So tell me more about this professor business, Doc. Is that where the 'Doc' comes from?"

"Yeah. One of the things that led to my, oh, downfall as an educator was my closeness to the students. And my informal approach. My colleagues were not all in favor of de-mystifying the profession. They thought it was a disgrace to allow one's students to address one as Doc."

George said, "So you got cashiered for being too chummy with the rug rats, huh?"

"Not exactly. I don't know if Maggie told you about my military background but I did get cashiered there. The only way I could get around my 'checkered past' was to create a new me, so I did. It really is pretty simple with a little knowledge and some patient maneuvering through the bureaucratic deadweight that's attached to almost everything governmental."

"Don't I know that. Try to get a building permit in Houston for anything bigger than a doghouse. So you got a new identity? Eventually?"

"Correct. And I got the PhD, a real one. From Texas Tech no less. A very good school for military history I should add. But I had to invent the rest. I couldn't use my B.S. from the Citadel and I didn't have a masters at all so I developed a transcript, forged documents, wrote letters of recommendation for myself from actual professors. Creative research. A little of my CIA training came in handy after all. My thesis was published as a text. It even got some play with the military, made me a few bucks. Very ironic. The military trained me to fight insurgency then threw me out, canceled my legitimate past, abandoned me, then bought my scathing indictment of their Vietnam policies as a text for the next generation."

"Where did you end up teaching?" Maggie asked.

"Georgia. The University of Georgia at Macon. Part of a legitimate university but isolated enough to be innocuous. And it would have been but I got cocky. After a few years you believe your own press, you know? I *became* Professor Robert Beaumont, PhD. And I published. That wasn't so smart considering my views on the military establishment. But what really screwed me up were the lectures. I was asked to speak at other colleges and my ego got the best of me. Instead of lying low, I went out on the lecture circuit and my best guess is somebody recognized me, probably from Nam. I'm officially KIA. My real name. Depending on their politics, it could have really hacked someone off, to see an Army officer, allegedly dead, making a living by biting the hand that raised him.

"The other possibility is the agency found me out. And someone got pissed off and decided I needed a little more punishment.

The local Georgia paper ran a piece on my dubious credentials. I know where they got their material, just not who clued that person in to me. The article alone was more than enough to get me kicked out of Macon. And I really was an arrogant prick, to the rest of the history department. I was so sure of my own rightness that I had no tolerance for them. I became the enemy. I can't imagine why the students loved me so much."

"So the professor's a goner. Now it's Doc the carpenter?" George said.

"No. Now it's Doc the tour guide slash private detective. Is that pretty accurate, Maggie?"

"If that means you'll do it, then the answer is yes."

"Maggie, you knew I'd do it before you even asked me."

"Thank you, Doc." She wrapped an arm around his neck and kissed him. "Thank you so much."

"That's enough, you two," George said. "It's time Miss Maggie started thinking about feeding her crew."

Chapter Five

When they got back, Maggie went off to work on dinner and George and Doc pulled chairs up to the cedar table on the deck and opened beers.

"Maggie makes the best home brew I've ever tasted," George said.

"She makes the beer too. I should have known after tasting that marvelous wine."

"Yep, the girl's got talent. Makes a brother proud havin' a sister that can make her own libations. Keeps me comin' back."

"I'm sure that's the only reason. You two being so cold to each other and all."

"Pretty obvious, ain't it. No love there at all," he said. "Hey, seriously. I'm glad you're willing to do this for her and the boy. We probably ought to talk some specifics though. Like funding. I'm paying for everything so don't let her even offer, okay?"

"Sure. I couldn't exactly get us there in style on my savings. I lost most of my assets to the college when I got the boot. Fraudulent pretext of creation or some such crap. They treated it like a Rico conviction, the burden of proof was on me. I can sue to get it back but it's not worth the bullshit. I'd rather let them keep it. Maybe they'll endow a scholarship in my name. The Imposter Award for Self-Education. What do you think?"

"Perfect. I'll make an anonymous donation, endow a chair in Revisionist Historical Perspectives."

"I like that. Let's make them take Junior as the first recipient. He could shake up the establishment I bet, keep up the tradition."

"Where are you sending me?" Junior asked as he plopped down beside them.

"Doc here needs someone to roust a bunch of pompous, windbag professor types. We thought of you, naturally."

"I'm flattered that you recognize my potential."

"When the votes were all counted," George said, "it was a land slide. Two for you, none for anybody else."

"Thank you, thank you. I'll prepare my acceptance speech."

"There's a different trip I want to talk to you about first, boy," George said. "Have you got a few minutes?"

"I'm at your service, Uncle. I've been waiting to hear what y'all have planned, bein' as I'm the topic of all this conversation it seems like."

"Ah, don't flatter yourself, we been talkin' about all kinds a stuff, eh Doc?"

"The problems of the world and how to solve them," Doc said. "But your name has come up a time or two. You want the short form or the long?"

"Short," Junior said.

"Your Mother and Uncle would like us to take a vacation, you and I." When Junior just stared at him, Doc continued. "To back track your father. See if we can find out what happened to him."

Junior looked at George. "You want to send me out into the world, with an old man you've known for what, a few days, to look for a dead drug dealer. That ought to work out real well. So tell me, Doc, what qualifies you for this mission? You a bounty hunter or somethin'?"

"No," Doc said. "I killed the men I hunted."

Without taking his eyes off Doc, Junior pushed his chair back and said, "I'm outta here."

"What's up with him," Maggie said as she joined Doc and George at the table.

"He got his self another little reality check from Doc here. Scared him some I think."

"Is that a good thing or a bad thing?" Maggie asked.

"In the long run," George answered, "the boy needs to find out that people ain't always what they seem. And to be more cautious."

"And less arrogant," Doc said.

"And more forgiving no doubt," Maggie said. "But I don't see how scaring him is going to help convince him to go along with this. Especially alone with Doc if Doc is what's scaring him. What am I missing?"

"Just give us a little time to work on him, Mags," George said. "It's a man thing. Now a woman thing would be to bring us a couple more beers, right Doc?"

"Oh, leave me so far out of this one, please." Doc got up and grabbed their empty bottles. "Would you like one, Maggie?"

"Yes, please. And bring the bottle of Elixir from under the dry sink. And three glasses." When he returned, brother and sister were staring at each other. Doc set a beer before each place and the Elixir and glasses before Maggie who pulled the cork with her teeth and poured a shot into each glass, then picked up her glass and held it up toward George.

"You two have a lot to talk about. I want a working plan, with details, by midnight. Tell me what you want for research and I'll get it." She swirled the coppery liquid in her glass once then tossed it down, picked up her beer and stalked away.

"Ouch," Doc said.

"Ain't she a pisser? God almighty, when she gets that temper up, you're best off just *shuttin'* up. That girl would bulldoze Attila the Hun if he got in her way. Part of the charm though. You ought to see her with my dad or Daniel. Both real manly men, macho, don't take no shit, you know? Except from Maggie. Her eyes flash and her neck starts to get red, you should see those two run away. No future in fightin' with her. Best just to grin at her and keep your mouth shut."

"I'm falling in love," Doc said.

"I know you are. But that woman is powerful medicine and I mean that not in jest at all. Just be careful. I don't want to see either of you get hurt. Now, try this here Elixir. It's mighty powerful in its own right."

Doc raised his glass and gave it the swirl and sniff tests, looking at it quizzically. "Pear brandy, huh? Great color, like molten pennies. And legs like a showgirl. What an odd, spiced apple smell."

"Shut up and drink it. That's when you'll really appreciate it."

They sipped. Then again and Doc said "Wow!" George agreed and they both finished their dose. Doc could feel the fire in his belly building, feel the numbing running down his legs and up across his chest and starting down his arms. His fingers and toes felt like they were electrically charged and the sweet burn rocketed into his skull and it was as if somehow a huge portion of his brain had suddenly snapped awake.

"Holy shit, George, what is that stuff?"

"Nectar of the Gods, Doc. Just what Junior said."

Chapter Six

When Maggie announced from the kitchen door that dinner was ready and could she get a little help, neither man heard her and it wasn't until she was standing in front of them, casting a shadow over the table now strewn with maps, a tablets, and a large atlas, that they finally noticed her.

"Time out, boys. I suggest we have some dinner then reconvene the meeting in the library. How does that sound?"

The library was a triangular space, two walls formed from the enormous slabs of rock and the third a combination of timber posts and beams and smaller pieces of stacked stone. Plank shelves covered the rear wall. A massive desk faced the timber wall and a fireplace large enough to walk in was built into the corner. Junior had a small fire burning at the back of the firebox and was preparing to feed several logs into the flames.

Maggie took Doc by the arm and led him to a chair in front of the desk and placed herself in the next one. George circled the desk and took the matching chair behind, pushing his pile of maps and tablets aside with an elbow to make room for a tray containing the Elixir and four glasses.

"Before we get goin' here," George said, "I'd like to propose a toast, to the success of our quest. But first we need the quest boy yonder to tell us if he's willin' to go. Come on over here, Junior. Let's hear what's on your mind."

Junior poked the newly placed logs a couple times with an iron pike then circled behind Doc and sat down on the other side of his mother.

"What did you tell him, Ma?" Junior asked.

"I didn't tell him anything. What we talked about this afternoon is just between us. And the decision is yours. All I wanted was the opportunity to explain my feelings and you gave me that. So it's up to you now."

Junior watched his mother while she spoke but then lowered his head and stared into his lap. Finally he looked up and met his uncle's gaze and gave him a scant smile.

"You obviously think she's right."

"Son, your mother is always right. Don't you know that yet?"

"Yeah, I guess," he said. "But hell, George, it ain't fair. *She* ain't fair. You can't even *argue* with her!"

George chuckled, his belly bouncing up and down. "Boy, you ain't tellin' me nothin' I don't already know. And I ain't laughin' at you, I'm laughin' at how long it took all your kin to accept what you're findin' out. Your father was the only person I ever knew that realized it right off. Everybody else had to test her, try to prove her wrong. Win an argument. It's a lost cause, Junior. You're lucky you found out at such an early age. Now how about that toast?" He poured them each a little Elixir and passed out the glasses.

"I think what you're fixin' to do," George said, "if it goes the way I hope it will, is going to make a big difference in your life, Junior. And in your mother's and therefore in mine and all your kin. Your mamma is the glue that holds this family together. Always was. She's the conscience. And that makes you the heir to that role, boy. That's an awesome responsibility and you gotta be trained for it cause we need you and your ma, all of us, including Doc and a lot a other folks that ain't blood relatives either. So I'm real glad you're doin' this and I'm real glad Doc's willing to go with you, to be your guide. Your mentor. Are you startin' to get that part, Junior?"

The boy nodded, glancing past his mother toward Doc who was looking at George with an expression of puzzlement and wonder.

"Good. I doubt if you could be in better hands. To us," George said, raising his glass high. "To all of us!"

They talked far into the night, first reviewing the notes and questions Doc and George had assembled during the afternoon, then trying to patch together a history of Arturo and his family and finally trying to tie the pieces into a conceivable whole. Maggie had led them to the library because it had been Arturo's private space, the only locking door in the house though seldom kept that way. Here were all the artifacts of their life together from the earliest letters to the box and pot. Maggie placed the latter on the desk with a thunk.

"Is the pot in there?" Doc asked.

"No. It's over on the mantel. See it there in the center? Why?"

"It just sounded heavy, the box, when you set it down."

She smiled at him. "Well let's take a look," she said as she opened the box and reached inside. "What have we here?" she said and began pulling out stacks of cash with both hands, heaping it on the desk.

"Jesus Christ, Maggie!" Doc said as he jumped out of his chair. "What are you doing, keeping all that money here?"

"Relax, Doc," George said. "It ain't gonna bite your butt. How much is left in there do you suppose, Maggie?"

"I don't know. Junior counted it when it arrived. It took you, what, three days?"

"Yeah, about that. There's everything but ones bundled in there. I finally just started riffling the bundles to make sure they were mostly all the same denomination and then sorted by amount and averaged the bundles. They don't all contain the same number of bills. I counted by the foot. There was four hundred thousand plus or minus."

Doc sank back into his chair. "Mother of God! This is very weird."

"To answer your question, George, I guess about a quarter million, wouldn't you say Junior?"

"Close enough. Maybe a little more."

"You're all very blasé about this. It just isn't that common, to have that much money lying around. In cash. Can't you invest it, put it in the bank or something?" Doc said. "It just isn't right somehow to have a big box of money sitting in your library."

"Relax, Doc. Christ, it's only money, eh Mags?" George was laughing now.

"Honestly, Doc? I'm afraid to. Not just for tax reasons. I'd pay the taxes gladly to get the damn thing out of here. I'm afraid of where the stuff has been. What it might be from. Does that make sense?"

"Like if it's the take from the Great Train Robbery or the Lindberg Kidnapping or some other heinous crime? Is that what you mean?"

"Yes. I don't want to know if Arturo was involved in something like that. Or I didn't until now. Maybe I should just deposit it and see what happens."

"There are a few problems with that, now that I think about it," Doc said. "If you plop a quarter million dollars down in front of some local bank teller, or even a hundred thousand, you'll have the sheriff out here before you get home and I'd bet the rest of the box that the FBI would be right behind him. If the money *is* dirty, or maybe even if it's perfectly innocuous, they'll get a search warrant and tear into this place. Then you're open to investigation by the IRS. I assume you pay some taxes but did you ever declare an income sufficient to have built all this?"

She shook her head.

"I can't see an up side to it, Maggie," Doc continued. "If you feel guilty about the money, and I don't think you should, at this point anyway, than give it to charity. That would be a lot better than having the government take it all and risking everything else. Even Junior's trust would be questioned. Don't forget, if they even think you acquired anything from illegal activities, they seize it and make you prove you didn't. You might get back the trust part of it, the lawyers would get most of it, but you might not get back anything at all."

"I'm not taking that chance," Maggie said. "I don't care how Arturo made this money, short of killing people. It's ours now and I'm not giving it to the fucking government!"

"Maggie! Such language!" George said laughing.

"Let's take a look at the stuff," Doc said. "The age and condition ought to tell us something. I wish we could test it for trace substances."

"Daniel can arrange that 'un," George said. "He's got lots of pals on the Houston PD and even the FBI. I think he gets a thrill out a hangin' with 'em. That's partly why he got that stupid carry permit, so he could be like his cop buddies."

"George, you're just being mean," Maggie said. "You love Daniel as much as I do." Then she snickered and added, "You're right though. He *is* playing cops and robbers with that pistol. A big kid."

"Okay. So take a few samples to him. I'd suggest hundreds," Doc said then added, "Maybe some of each would be better. We aren't really looking for cocaine. That's supposed to be on like seventy-five percent of all paper money anyway so what would it tell us? Yeah, take some of each. And make sure Daniel doesn't tell the cops where he got it."

"He can say he won it in a card game," George said, "and got suspicious when he noticed all the bills were the old style. Daniel's always playin' poker with some of his cronies."

Doc flipped through a few stacks, stopping now and then to scrutinize individual bills. "They look real to me, not that I'm an expert. Have you inspected much of it, George?"

"Yeah, a while back. Far as I can tell, if any of its funny money, it's in there by accident."

"I did a little investigating on the net. Bogus Bucks dot com," Junior said, "web sites like that. It's real all right. And by the dates of the newest bills, it doesn't seem to fit any unsolved crimes that are public knowledge, not of that amount of money."

"That's reassuring, Maggie, don't you think?" Doc asked.

"Yes it is. But we've known that for some time thanks to Junior's research. That's not exactly what I was worried about anyway. More the thought of a bloody drug massacre, where innocents were killed along with the dealers, Arturo blazing away with an assault rifle." They were all looking at her and when she saw their looks she laughed nervously and continued.

"Don't misunderstand me, please. I certainly don't think Arturo was capable of murder for money. That was just the most morbid of the fantasies that a lonely woman with too much time to ponder came up with, okay? Come on guys, stop looking at me like that, please. Let's have another little snort, George," she said. Doc set his glass on the desk, again amazed at the surge of energy the Elixir seemed to unleash.

"Let's check out the postage," Doc said. "Have you looked at that?"

"I did," Maggie said. "And later so did Junior. I can't see anything that jumps out at me."

"Me either," Junior said.

"Well, let me at least look." Doc had to stand to see the top of the box where the postage had been affixed. After a time he said, "It looks like someone was trying to obscure the actual origin, that's pretty obvious. But look at the amounts. The top one is for six or seven hundred more pesos then the last one and the one that overlaps the first group is for more yet. It's like the box got heavier as it went along. How is that possible?"

"Like takin' a collection," George said.

"Yes. Exactly," Doc said. "It went to several places, got re-mailed from each and each time the postage was a little more. Someone added something to the box at every stop."

"But why?" Maggie said. "If you received a box of money, anyone for that matter, what would you be most likely to do, add to it or take some for yourself? And not to be stereotypical but, aren't the post-marks from the south west and Mexico, rural places, villages and hamlets? You could easily assume that . . ."

"That the people were poor," Doc said, "and they would be (a) either incapable of making an addition or (b) more prone to take than to give? You're not stereotyping, Maggie, you're simply stating the obvious. Where would your average peasant get the money to make a contribution even if they were wont to make one?"

"Dope," George said. "Where else?"

"And U.S. currency. How does that fit?" Junior said.

"Where were the upper layers from, Junior?" Maggie asked.

"What upper layers?" Doc asked, turning to face Junior.

"I peeled off a few, trying to do what you're doing, but I didn't make the connection to the escalating amounts."

"Neither did I," George said. "How could we a missed that, Mags?"

"I don't know, George. We were a little preoccupied with the contents at that point."

"Yeah, I should think so," Doc said. "Do you still have the stamps, Junior?"

"Yes sir. They're right up there." The boy indicated the shelves and a metal box that shimmered in the flickering light. "Be careful, Doc. It's heavier than it looks," Junior said. He lobbed the box toward Doc who caught it with a grunt.

"What the hell . . . Is this gold?" Doc asked.

"Seems like it is, don't you think, Doc?" George said.

"Too heavy to be much of anything else, George. Where do you people get these things?" No one voiced the obvious.

Junior joined him and pointed over his shoulder to a small gargoyle-like face. "Push him on the forehead." The little rectangle opened slowly, as if raised by an oiled piston.

"I'll be Goddamn."

The box was only a few inches on each side and nestled in its cloth-lined interior were three different strips of postage, all actual stamp groupings, none simply a printout from some arcane postage meter, and all were U.S. in origin.

"These were the top layers?"

"Yes sir. And I think I got them in the right order. The top one was last on the box."

"Tell me that's not Elvis. Please. I don't know if my weirdness coefficient can take much more of this."

"It's sort a like the icin' on the cake, ain't it, Doc," George said. "You got this amazing story of drugs and money, mysterious disappearances, foreign countries and what's your best clue about it all? Elvis stamps! Enough to make a grown man cry I swear."

"This is all a little too much to handle on such short notice, if you know what I mean," Doc said. "Two days ago I was an ex-military, ex-academic carpenter minding my own business, trying to make a few bucks as a saw man on a framing crew and now I'm up to my armpits in a missing persons caper with a couple of country western singers and a beautiful artist slash hippie mystic.

No one is going to believe this. Not that there's anyone I could tell it to anyway."

Maggie patted the arm of the chair beside her. "Come here and sit down, Doc. I know it seems absurd, but some of the proof is all around you. If we were sitting in the study of a center hall colonial, four bedrooms, two and a half baths, would all of this make more or less sense? You've gotten yourself mixed up with a family of crazies, I admit it, that's what we are, but, hey, would you rather be bored out of your mind in an office somewhere?"

"What do you think, Junior?" Doc asked. "Is it better to be normal or eccentric?"

Junior's flat stare never wavered from the middle distance somewhere over all of their heads. Finally, with what seemed to Doc to be a great effort, he shifted his gaze down and tracked across to face Doc.

"How in the holy hell should *I* know!" He jumped to his feet and stomped from the room.

After a few seconds of silence, Doc said, "Excuse me" and followed the boy out.

"Well Mags, looks to me like them two is gonna get along just fine. Yes sir, just fine."

"I hope you're right, brother," she said.

Chapter Seven

Doc caught up with Junior at the door to his bedroom and he got a foot and a forearm in the opening before Junior could slam it closed.

"Hold on a second, Junior. Let me have a couple minutes, please."

Junior didn't respond but he didn't object either and Doc moved into the room and closed the door behind him. He was again overwhelmed by the scale and mass of Arturo's creation as he gazed around Junior's bedroom, boulders piled seemingly at random yet fitted all around with unlikely shaped desks and shelves and a sort of sub-cave for a raised and sheltered sleeping nook. The walls–rocks–were almost all covered with the same intricate petroglyph-like painting that graced much of the other rooms but here the work had a more intense quality and was wildly colorful.

"Do you ever work on canvas?" Doc asked. Junior shrugged, slouched low in a lumpy sack of a chair.

"Mind if I sit down? I'd like to talk to you."

"Curl up on the floor and go to sleep. I don't give a shit."

Doc crossed his ankles and lowered himself into a sitting position on a tanned hide, surprised that his back didn't object to the movement.

"I want to be your friend, kid. But I don't need to be. So let's use that as a starting point. Okay. Let me try again. Your Uncle, who I've known for less than a week . . ." Doc looked up at the forest of stars visible through the slab of glass that was notched into the granite ceiling. "I don't have a family. I never have. Your Uncle is an exceptional man. And I want to…I want to help him if I can. I like him. I want a friend like that. I'd like to have some roots. And you've got to start somewhere, when someone offers you a hand, and you need it, you accept. And you repay the kindness if you can. Am I making any sense at all?"

"You're a lonely old man and you don't want to die alone. How's that?" Junior asked.

Doc's face started to redden and he almost stood up but then after a pause he said, "Exactly! That's exactly what it is. I'm scared shitless! Thank you, Junior. I don't think I fully realized it till right now."

"Glad to be of service."

Doc looked at the boy. "And I'm falling in love with your mother. I can't help myself."

"Nobody else can. Why should you be any different? All my friends, their moms are these normal lookin', plain ladies, wear dresses with little birds or flowers on 'em, aprons, or baggy old jeans. They're nice, I don't mean anything bad. But, you know, they're *mom's* for God sake. They're not hippie love goddesses! It sucks, man. What are you laughin' at? I'm serious."

"I know you are and I'm not laughing at you. I was thinking of my mother and comparing them. My mother was a statue. I don't think anybody *ever* lusted after her including my father. It's amazing that I was even born. I can't picture her naked, submitting to anything so crass and uncivilized as copulation. It probably only happened once."

"Yeah, but at least your friends didn't hit on her."

"They couldn't. I didn't have any. And if I had, they certainly wouldn't have been allowed in my parent's mausoleum. Hell, they barely tolerated *me* there on the few occasions when I was allowed to come home."

"That sucks big time! They sent you to boarding school?"

"Military school. First to twelfth grade. Summers in some kind of camp, usually military oriented, never anywhere that 'fun' was tolerated. Yes. It sucked big time."

"Man, you're lucky you're not a serial killer or somethin'. FBI most wanted nut case. That was a seriously fucked up childhood."

"That's what your mother said, almost exactly. She said it spoke volumes about my inner strength. My ability to transcend the abuse and not turn it into hatred, lash out against society."

"Well, Ma's always right, about people anyway. About everything I guess. I just hate to admit it. It's bad enough to have a mother that's so good lookin' without her havin' to be so right all the goddamn time too. It ain't natural, she's like a saint or somethin'. You know what? I hope she falls for you too, maybe bein' in love would bring her down to earth. She ain't happy like she used to be. She needs to go skinny dippin' or get drunk or . . . or get laid, hell, I don't know. She needs somethin'."

"I don't, ah, want to pass judgment on the whole motherhood business, but, ah, I'm not sure it's socially acceptable for a son to be advocating sexual activity for his mom. Not that I disagree with your premise necessarily, it's just, um, a little odd, hearing it from you."

"I suspect you'd be more than happy to volunteer though."

"Junior, your mother is beautiful, more than beautiful, and I already confessed how I feel. And if I was blessed enough to have that feeling reciprocated, and if that eventually led to...well, you know, than I think I would be probably the happiest man–"

"Give it a rest, Doc. I get the idea. I ain't jealous, there's no oedipal thing goin' on. I think it'd be good for her, to fall in love I mean. And, ah, despite my first reaction to you, you don't seem like so big a shit heel as I thought. How's that, we makin' progress yet?"

Doc was still laughing a few moments later, Junior giggling along with him, when the door opened and Maggie padded into the room, apologizing for interrupting.

"It's okay, Ma. Doctor Doc has been analyzing my condition."

"And vhat condition is his condition in, Herr Doctor," she asked, stroking an imaginary goatee.

"He is in serious trouble, I'm afraid. The prognosis is extreme normalness which in the American Teenager can be a terrifying affliction."

"Shocking! Shocking I say! Vhat ever shall ve do?"

"We can only let nature take its course. But I think there is every reason to be cautiously optimistic. After all, the boy comes from good stock and he *is* motivated. I'm just not sure toward what."

"Amen to that, Doc. When you figure out where I'm going, let me in on it."

"Maybe I can help y'all with that 'un," George said as he entered.

"Be my guest, Uncle G. The floor is yours. And the hides and the chairs and even the bed, if you want it."

"I think I'll just stand here, thank you very much just the same. You boys is goin' on vacation, all expenses paid, take as long as you like, have a damn fine time, come back when you're done."

"Woop de do," Junior said. "And where are we goin' to on this adventure?"

"We were initially hoping you could back track the money box," Maggie continued for her brother, "but if that's not possible then I want you to go to some of the places that your father went." She cut off his protest with an upraised hand. "Places that he wrote to me about, postcards he sent, places he would talk about, and some places that we went to together maybe. George and I have been making a list. It should be fun. You'll love the southwest. New Mexico and Arizona, Old Mexico. Please, Junior, don't fight me on this, okay?"

"Okay, Ma." Then Junior brightened and with a quick wink to Doc he added, "Under one condition."

"What, sweetie?"

"You go too."

"Oh, no, Junior, I can't. It's not . . . I've got to watch the ranch, take care of . . ."

"I agree," Doc said. "If it's right for the son, it's just as right for the wife."

"No, no, I – "

"George. Tie breaker," Doc said. "Your opinion?"

George looked at all three of them. "They're right. You should go."

"Damn you, George!" she said then tossed her hair, stomped past her brother and slammed the massive door behind her.

"Wow. A little temper in the Marone clan?" Doc said.

"Yes, sir," George answered. "She definitely got the family temper gene. Woo, wee. She don't let it out too often but when she does, look out!"

"Why is she so upset?" Doc asked. "She doesn't want to go along?"

"Cause she knows we're right," George said. "But she don't want to face it. She don't want to face what might be out there. It's easier to stay here and not know. Mostly though it's just cause we ganged up on her. Blindsided her. Good 'un Junior. You got her right between the eyes."

"Don't blame the boy, George. He didn't say it out of maliciousness."

"Blame him? Hell, Doc, I'm congratulatin' him! You knew how hard it was to get one over on Maggie, you'd be back slappin' that boy too."

"How long before she calms down?"

"Depends, right Unc? Depends on who you are and what you did. She can stay mad at Uncle Daniel and Granddad for days. George not so long. With me it varies. She and Grandma never fight. You, you're probably okay now." After a pause and a quick glance at George he said, "Why don't you go see how she is, Doc?"

Doc found Maggie on the deck, slumped so far down in one of the big chairs that he wouldn't have discovered her at all if he hadn't heard her rearranging her position. Padding across the boards, he paused behind her, unsure how to proceed.

"Maggie," he whispered, "are you okay?"

"No I'm not okay, damn it. What took you so long?"

"I, ah, I didn't know where to look?" Doc said.

"Well, you found me. Now sit down. Why do I have to go? What did you say to him to make him want me along? This was supposed to be about him, not me. I'm fine. He's the one that hasn't adjusted. He's who needs the help. Not me. This is *your* fault!

"You think it's funny?" she said after a pause. "That's terrific. My self-indulgent tirade makes you laugh. I must be losing my powers. And don't worry, I may scream occasionally but I never hit. You can come out from cover now."

"Thank God. I didn't know if I was going to have to make a tactical retreat or jump off the deck. Are you really okay? Your reaction to my suggestion was, ah, unanticipated?"

"You just don't know me well enough, Doc. Although I'm sure my relatives gave you an unbiased picture of my mental health."

"They said you had an occasional temper tan . . . ah, occasionally your temper got the... You're just going to let me flounder here aren't you? That's not polite."

"Temper tantrums, huh? That sounds about like those two lunk heads. They consistently say the dumbest damn things, and once in a great while they say something that pisses me off to the extent that I am compelled to try to correct their wrong headedness. And *I* have temper tantrums. Okay, so maybe, possibly, I've been known to show a little"- she held her thumb and index finger a quarter inch apart and thrust her hand toward Doc's face - "just a little . . . enthusiasm in my response, to their stupidity, and *I* have a temper. Nonsense. I'm as calm and serene as a nun. You believe me of course, right?"

"Of course," he said. "You're a regular saint, Mother Superior. I mean Teresa."

"Thank you for that vote of confidence. Now that we have resolved all questions regarding my disposition, I am forced to admit that you three are correct–I should go along. It's not just for Junior, I'm fucked up too. So. There you have it."

"I'm okay, you're fucked up. I think I read that book," Doc said. "Happy ending, right? Boy meets girl, boy falls madly in love, girl feels sorry for boy, boy goes on impossible quest with girl and son."

"And dog," she added.

"Right. You need the dog to keep the book focused on reality. Anyway, they all live happily ever after."

"Especially the dog," she said. "But he was the least fucked up to start with so he had the shortest road to happiness. It's sort of not fair, the dog being so damn happy, always wagging his tail and slobbering all over everybody."

"Isn't that what we're all striving for? Some happy tail and a lot of bodily fluids?"

"Amen to that," she said.

Chapter Eight

The next morning they had a business-like breakfast in the library. George was going back to Houston, taking the money samples to Daniel for analysis and carrying their shopping list of equipment for the upcoming trip. Maggie was going to categorize her store of memorabilia from Arturo's travels and prepare the itinerary. Junior and Doc were going to prepare the items on hand and prep the travel vehicle.

The meeting was subdued and George pulled out in mid-morning, the others, dog included, standing in the shade of the ancient live oak, giving desultory waves. George wasn't expected to return till at least Saturday and all three were uneasy about the new dynamic. When the sound of the pickup finally faded, the dog wandered off a few feet and plopped down in a bed of buffalo grass.

"Well," Maggie said, "as comfortable as he looks and as much as I might like to curl up in a ball and go to sleep, we might as well get to it." She smiled at the others and returned to the house.

"What do you think, Bub," Doc asked. "You ready?"

"I guess. You want to check out the rest of the spread, I'll show you around the out buildings. Out caves is more like it. Come on dog, you gotta work too."

The three of them walked around the house, Doc again awed by the size and scale of the construction, trying to visualize the time and equipment, the planning and the manpower that must have been required to create such an awesome monument.

About a hundred yards beyond the curvature of the backside of the mountain, several smaller piles of boulders revealed themselves as structures. The largest was a garage, the overhead doors painted pink to match the surrounding rocks and distressed in a successful attempt to make them blend into the overall assembly. Inside was a vintage Jeep, military style, an old Ford four wheel drive stake body truck, and a thirty-six foot Winnebago motor home, twenty years or so old Doc guessed.

"I'd think we'd take the Winnie, wouldn't you, Doc? It's a custom job, four wheel drive."

"Yeah, just by sheer capacity if nothing else, although it looks like it's in the best shape as well."

"That was Dad's transportation of choice, that's for sure. He took all three sometimes but we always knew if he took the Winnie, he'd be gone awhile. He took his bike the last time. We thought he'd be back in a couple days. Go figure, huh?"

"Yeah. It's hard. Maybe we'll get a better handle on it, though," Doc said.

"Want to see the bikes? There's a couple cool ones." Junior led him past a bank of work benches and shelves covered top to bottom with every tool imaginable from vices and pliers to gas powered compressors and jackhammers, all seemingly well maintained, clean and in working order.

"Quite a shop. Arturo's?"

"Everybody's. We all dig tools. Arturo loved 'em. Grinders, nail guns, pneumatic everything. Christ, we got at least one of every tool ever made I think. Check this out." They reached a set of barn doors in the rear of the garage. Sliding them open, Junior caught an overhead cord and the interior was slowly illuminated as a series of fluorescent fixtures flickered on revealing a dozen motorcycles.

"He liked motorcycles, too," Junior said. "Those three at the end are my old dirt bikes. They got bigger as I grew up. Those two are Dad's. We used to have a motocross course down by the river but it's pretty overgrown I imagine. I haven't run it in, ah, well, a while. That 'uns Ma's. She ain't too big on bikes but she'd trail ride with us sometimes. She's pretty good and I think she likes it well enough, she was more just scared we'd kill ourselves. Dad was fuckin' crazy sometimes on the dirt bikes. Scared the shit out of me watchin' him. Man could he ride!

"And these are the street bikes. The obligatory Harley. And that's a – "

"Whoa, hold on. You make the Harley sound like a Schwinn. That's the most beautiful hog I've ever seen."

"Oh, yeah, it's nice, I didn't mean it was a piece of shit, but it's a Harley, you know? There's a million more just like it. I don't know why he bought it. He never rode it much. The others are more unusual, that's all. This is a Triumph 650 Trophy. Single carb. The Bonneville had twin carbs. This one's pretty rare. This is a 750 Norton Commando. The Commando has the chrome tank. Very distinctive. That's a 650 BMW touring bike. Ugly as hell if you ask me. That big monster is a suicide shift Indian. Very rare. And dangerous as hell to ride. This is a Kawasaki 500. Two cycle. Looks like mosquito control when you crank it open, clouds a smoke, but it's fast as a raped ape! Fastest production bike in the world when they first came out, like thirty years ago."

"Is there one missing?" There was an open slot between the Triumph and the Harley but a rack of parts behind the slot, much like all the others, indicated a former inhabitant.

"Yeah. That's the one he took off on last. That was his all time favorite, a real weird hybrid thing he built himself. It started as a Sportster, 900 series, but ended up as a kind of touring dirt bike, big custom gas tank, beefy suspension, all terrain tires, and built-in like saddle bags and a sissy bar thing that he'd strap a backpack to. He looked like a homeless biker on it. Pretty funny."

"Do they still work?"

"Oh, yeah. I crank 'em all up every couple weeks, let 'em run a little, you know."

"You feel like touring me around the ranch? I can ride enough not to be dangerous."

Junior eyed Doc for a moment. "Why not. What's your pleasure?"

"A dirt bike. Not too big."

"Good choice," Junior said as they walked back to the other end. "These two are both pretty mean, Dad's racers. How about my last one. It's a Kawasaki 350 Big Horn. Big enough to tote you around but unless you're stupid, it shouldn't get away from you."

"Sounds good. You going to take one of the racers?"

Junior didn't answer as he swung a leg over a lethal looking dirt bike, stripped clean of all lights, insignia, anything that might add weight or detract from function, function seemingly to go as fast as possible over anything in the way.

"It's a Huskavarna 500, stripped, bored and stroked, straight pipes, it gets it. I'll go slow. You know how to start that 'un?"

Junior explained the key location, the gas valve and the gear pattern and they wheeled their vehicles out into the daylight. Even expecting it, the roar of Junior's bike hit Doc like a fist and he would not have known his own had started on the second kick if not for the smoke and the vibrations. As Doc was revving his machine gingerly, toeing through the gears, Junior put down his kickstand, hopped off and ran back inside. He emerged a few seconds later and delivered an odd looking telephone operator's headset to Doc.

"Two way radio, voice activated. Clip this to your belt. Put this on your head. We can talk as we ride."

Junior roared off in a cloud of dust and fumes and Doc had to wait a full ten seconds before he could follow.

"Where the hell are you? You stall out?" Junior said over the radio.

"I can't see you for the dust. Just hold on, I'm coming."

Junior slowed sufficiently for Doc to catch up and then set a more leisurely pace as they toured the property, kicking out deer and jack rabbits, ducking under the branches of live oaks and mesquite, striking the old motocross course and following it across the river then back across upstream. The course wound through a series of sandy mounds that Junior explained had been a gravel pit for the County Highway Department years before but now made a great place to jump the bikes. At the top of the highest mound, after a spectacular vertical climb and a virtual flight of man and bike, Junior looked down at Doc idling at the bottom, eyeing the hill.

"Don't do it, Doc," Junior said. "That bike ain't got the guts for it even if you do."

Doc didn't respond but Junior heard the snarly growl of Doc's bike increase in volume and then watched as Doc spun one hundred and eighty degrees and sped away, whirled the motorcycle back around and raced toward the hill.

"Keep your rev's up!" Junior said into the radio. "Don't upshift, you'll lose power!"

Doc shot across the flats, hunched over the handlebars, weight on his legs and foot pegs as he hit the bottom of the slope. The bike roared up the steep incline, throwing a plume of sand thirty feet behind.

"Woowee!" Junior hollered. "Get it, Doc!"

And he nearly did but at about the three quarter point the rear wheel began to bog down as the sand deepened and in a few seconds his momentum was gone and the bike fishtailed in place, engine roaring, sand spewing.

"Give it up, Doc. She just don't have the snot for this hill. I'll meet you at the bottom."

Doc turned down hill and coasted to the bottom, Junior looking up at him now.

"You look like a summer hog, Doc, the waller all dried up and nothin' but dust to roll around in."

Doc shut down his bike, climbed off and shook himself, laughing at the dirt that flew off.

"I feel about like a hog. Is there a place in that river deep enough to rinse off in?"

"You got it. The old swimmin' hole, comin' right up. Follow me."

Junior stopped at the river and sat on the bank, pulled off his boots, shirt and jeans and jumped in. It took Doc a little longer but soon he too was washing off the accumulated trail grit, sitting in the neck-deep water. After splashing around for ten minutes, Doc stood up, stretched and turned to climb up the sandy bank.

"Holy shit, Doc! What the fuck happened to you?"

Standing on the bank now, Doc looked down at himself, at the road map of scars crisscrossing the ropey muscles of his torso and said simply, "Vietnam."

As they began to get dressed, Junior, still staring at Doc's pocked and tortured flesh, asked, "Can you talk about it?"

Doc had one leg crossed over the other, one boot on, one boot off, still bare-chested. He turned toward Junior but looked through him. Finally he said, "Sure." And they talked, sitting in the dirt, half dressed. Doc gave him much the same synopsis of his life as he had his mother but Junior was not about to accept a shortened version and was not at all too shy to ask specifically about every scratch and dent in Doc's poorly mended body work.

"All right, all right. Let's do this systematically," Doc said. "It's easier than chronologically, okay? Most of this stuff here and here," he said, indicating his chest and left arm, "is from shrapnel, a mortar round. We made a night drop, my team, five guys, into the North. We were after a political target, the Mayor of a big vil near the border. Very active chap this mayor, heavy propaganda speaker, traveled with an NVA regiment giving pep talks to the civilians in the South, all along the border. Apparently a hell of a public speaker, big rep among the villagers. Our special ops guys wanted him bad, wanted to send a message, you know, nobody's safe from our side, we'll get you even in the North. We were the third team they'd sent in. The first one couldn't find him–poor intel I imagine. The second team just never came back, not a word. Probably lost their radio in the drop, got ambushed somewhere.

"We got him. It took three days, nights actually, to crawl in on him. Dawn of the third night we hit the vil, killed everything. We took his head. Yeah, I know. It was that kind of war though and we were some gung ho motherfuckers. Maybe the most dangerous men that ever served in the US Army. Airborne, lurps, a couple Special Forces rejects. They actually had standards. My guys were just stone killers.

"Anyway, on the withdrawal, we had to go about five clicks through the same shitty jungle to get to our extraction point. We got shot up pretty good. The vil had a company strength guard contingent that we had bypassed and they were hot on our asses, pissed that we'd out gooked them I guess.

"Two of my team were dinged on the way out and one was gut shot. I had him over my right shoulder when we hit the little clearing, the slick just coming down. A beautiful sight. But the gooks knew where we were going, there weren't that many clearings in their area of operations. They had the mortars walking across, right to left, and we ran straight into the rounds.

"One of the dinged guys and one of the okay ones bought it and I was chewed up bad. The man I was carrying saved my life. He took most of the metal. See the right side's pretty clean. The chopper guys got us all in. We wouldn't leave our dead unless we were all dead. We got out of there about two seconds before the gooks came out of the tree line.

"A successful mission! Three dead, two wounded, one critical. Me. But we got the head. Those were acceptable losses, you see what I mean? We lost nine guys, the whole second team and half of mine, trying to stop this guy from giving speeches to a bunch of villagers who were either hardcore Cong to start with or didn't give a shit who controlled their hootches as long as they were left alone to try to grow a little rice. All the village men were already gone, drafted by one side or the other. It wasn't like they had to convert these people to get them to fight. Fear did all the convincing. An AK- 47 to the head of your kid can be pretty persuasive. Or an M-16 for that matter. It was such a waste, the whole war."

"Doc? Why'd you do it?"

"That's a hell of a good question. Why does anyone do what they do at the time, that's the easy answer. But the truth? More complicated. It's partially your upbringing, how you're indoctrinated by your parents, your culture. Mine was a culture of service, to your country, from birth. And of course the military doesn't want you to be exactly a free thinker. The first time in my life I had a chance to reflect on what I'd become, what I stood for, was my recovery from that mortar round. First on a hospital ship, then in a rehab ward in Japan. There were troopers all around me for months that had been shot to shit over there. Limbs missing, face blown away, blind, paralyzed. In the bush a man gets hit, you call in a dust off and you never see the guy again usually. There's no time to dwell on the consequences of the war. He was hit. He's dead, he's wounded, he's gone and you're still in the bush trying to keep from joining him. Even in the base camps when you're standing down, you're either too tired to think about it or you blank it out or you're planning the next op. It was cumulative for me, Junior. It took a long time to deprogram from all those years of training. And it happened slowly. If I had never been hit that hard, never had a chance to live with the consequences of what I was doing, who knows? I might have never seen the light. I might be a fucking two star training the next generation of killers. Pretty scary, huh?"

"I'd of been scared shitless the whole time. I can't imagine . . . how you'd do it."

"Everybody starts out that way. But it's like anything else, most people adjust. You see enough of your buds go down, you cap a few of them, dinks, you get numb. Life loses much of its importance, death is an everyday event, inevitable. *If* you're going to get it is a given, it's only a question of when. Once you reach that point, knowing you are going to die and not really caring, then you're a stone killer, a very dangerous adversary. The gooks had a lot more of them than we did but we had better support, better equipment and mobility. But it was their country and the only way we could have won that war would have been to kill every one of them. And then what would have been the point?"

"How'd you get all the scars on your back?"

"Aren't you tired of war stories yet? This should be depressing the hell out of you," Doc said.

"Yeah, it's scary. Sobering, you know? But it's like, living history or something. Like my old textbooks came to life and made it interesting for once. I'm curious, what can I say."

"I get it," Doc said. "I'm an anachronism, a talking book. Push the button and I tell you a story. That's okay though. Briefly. I got dinged twice in my first tour, both AK rounds, one a tracer by the way it burned. That one got me a three week R and R in beautiful Da Nang. The other got me a new field dressing every day for a week and I didn't have to walk point. The big slit scar on the right is a bayonet, just before the Agency and I parted company. It's so ugly cause a Montanyard medic sewed it up with cat gut while I was unconscious from a US rifle butt to the head as I was trying to beat the shit out of my section chief. I didn't know he was already dead. There's some buckshot holes back there too. That was 'friendly fire.' We were set up by the former section chief and his man in my squad wanted to make sure I went down first. That was just luck. My ruck must have shifted just as he hit me. I had a cut down piece of flack jacket in there that took a lot of the pellets. I was starting to distrust everybody by then, a raving paranoid. But obviously I had good reasons for thinking the Agency was, ah, not to be trusted, shall we say?"

"Holy Shit! You oughta write a book."

"I did. Several. That's what got me bounced out of the Ivory Tower. But that's a story for another day. You have to push a different button." Doc laughed and got to his feet. "Let's go see how your mom's doing. She probably did a hell of a lot more work today than we did."

"Yeah, but we had more fun."

"You two look like you've been *hard* at work," Maggie said as they came into the kitchen. "I ought to send you both to the showers and then to your rooms without supper. I heard you take off on the bikes but that was hours ago."

"You were gettin' worried, Ma? You could have called us on the radio."

"God, we haven't used those in so long I forgot."

"There's a base station in the library that uses the same frequency as the headsets," Junior said to Doc. "We went on a ranch tour, Ma and then took a dip in the river. Doc told me war stories. You should see his -"

"Can it, Junior. Your mother is not interested in my anatomy. What's left of it."

She gave Doc a stare and then told Junior to feed the dog. "He came back an hour ago with his tongue hanging down to his knee caps. And take a shower," she yelled at his retreating figure.

"You could stand a little soapy water as well," she said turning to Doc. "Did you have fun?"

"Yes we did. He's an interesting kid. Half adult, half adolescent. Full of curiosity. Reminds me of his mother." After a few beats, "Anything on your mind?"

"Lots. But I'm not sure how to . . . express it. I'm happy that you two are, bonding?"

"But the war stories scare you."

"Yes. No, not scare exactly. Well, partially I guess. I want to . . . protect him from that. I wish he didn't know about such things. But I'm realistic enough to know that I can't shelter him. War is reality. Vietnam is part of our history." She stopped, brow furrowed, gazing out the window.

"But you don't want it glorified, made to look like a grand adventure. Believe me, that was not my message. He asked about my wounds, saw them when we were swimming. He was shocked." Seeing her looking at him, he explained. "They *are* pretty bad. But he had the chutzpa to ask. I told him how I got them and he had the maturity to question why I went to war. And why I stayed. There was no glory in what I did. I made that clear."

"Thank you, Doc. I don't want him thinking war is something manly that all 'real men' need to experience."

"No. And I don't want him to be tutored by some beer guzzling, VFW bozo whose best memories in his life are the ten or eleven months he spent as a rear echelon poge then pretending for the rest of his life that he'd been a hard case grunt. Those guys are dangerous–to the youth of America anyway."

"Are there a lot of people like that? Pretenders?"

"War pretenders? My god, yes. Thousands of them. There's a professor, of history, at Columbia, I've read his books, who's made a career out of debunking other people's credentials. His subjects have to have some name recognition or position of relative importance for him to bother to attack them but, when he finds someone who arouses his suspicion, he goes all out on his research. Freedom of information requests, private investigators. He must also have some fair military contacts because a little of what he seems to have uncovered just isn't available to the public no matter how long you pursue regular channels. He's a son of a bitch."

"Why is that a bad thing, exposing imposters?"

"An imposter deserves what he gets. He's just a liar trying to embellish his own past. But this professor doesn't seem to discriminate. If he cannot verify the service record of any of his victims, they are automatically painted as liars or worse.

"I can see I'm not making myself clear," he said. "In every war in the modern era, there has been a certain amount of covert activity. Those involved in these activities, their service records rarely reflect what their actual duties were. In Vietnam there was an entire infrastructure of non-traditional commands, several layers, even multiple agencies. And for the most part, they recruited their operatives from the regular armed forces. And the operations that these agencies undertook were often not even remotely similar to mainstream military functions. Not things that Mr. and Mrs. America back home needed to know about. Or a congressional oversight committee. Do you see what I mean?"

"It was unethical. Or illegal."

"Or so horribly counter to most people's ideas about how America prosecutes a war that God help us if anyone ever finds out what we're doing. But Vietnam wasn't like any war that this country had ever fought. And the agencies that I'm talking about recognized that reality and experimented with some unorthodox solutions. Brutal, bloody, savage solutions. Ultimately it didn't make any difference and it was all a long time ago, but . . . no one wants these policies exposed and examined, not while a lot of the players are still alive anyway."

"So," Maggie said, "the bottom line is, this professor could never get all the information he sought on all his people . . ."

"And some of the people he's targeted can not or will not be able to verify that which they have alluded to in their . . . resumes, so to speak. Example. One of my insertion team members was a staff sergeant. He was never in a regular command the whole time he was in country. But his permanent record lists him as a clerk in a headquarters battalion in Saigon. No way could he ever prove otherwise. But that was the protection too. Why would anyone want to brag about their ability to live on bugs and swamp water for a month anyway? And you almost certainly wouldn't be telling your prospective employer back in the world about all your kills, the hostages you took, the prisoners you didn't take. Assassination and torture skills just aren't that in demand at Smith Barney."

"This guy targeted you."

"Oh, yeah. I was an enigma to him though. He looked deep enough to discover that Dr. Robert Beaumont didn't have much of a history prior to attending Texas Tech and that was enough to end that chapter for me. But I never made any claims to military service so he couldn't treat me like one of his poor wannabes. He went after me because of our political differences. He's an historical revisionist what-iffer. Like the novelist whose premise was, what if the Nazis got the bomb before we did? That's sort of how he studies Vietnam. Not what really happened and what we should learn from it but who fucked up what and what might have happened if they hadn't. Always why we should not have lost, but never with any morality involved. He's hopelessly stuck in the past. And not a very good historian. No. I'm not a fan."

"He read your books or heard you speak and didn't like your message? You alluded to that in the orchard. And he sought to debunk you?"

"Both personally and politically. He succeeded in getting me off campus which was probably his most pressing objective. I don't think he gives a shit about me but he didn't like me polluting the minds of the next generation. They might turn out to be free thinking individuals, not your prime candidate for ideological zealots which is what he would like all of us to be, as long as we support his ideology."

"Lots of people like that in Academia I suspect."

"Yep," Doc said with a shrug. "Lots and lots. But lots of others too and to eliminate any particular category would simply limit the cultural diversity so . . ."

"It takes all kinds," she said with a grin.

"Yes it do, Maggie Marone, but I've never met one like you."

"Oh, you silver tongued devil! You didn't tell me you were a poet."

"One of my myriad skills. You know I was the originator of the 'Roses are Red' sonnets? I should have copyrighted those in the beginning. I'd be rich by now, on royalties from Hallmark alone."

"Leave us not dwell upon the past, for tis the future that holds the allure. Pretty good, huh?" She laughed, took Doc by the elbow and led him out onto the deck.

"Take the path," she said pointing to the trail that led down to the draped garden and the big live oak, "and make your first left. It's only a little ways. That will bring you around under the deck where you will discover the most wonderful outdoor shower you have ever experienced. There's soaps and towels and even a robe that should fit you. There's a linen closet, you'll see it. Go. You're filthy."

Chapter Nine

Doc followed the path as directed and discovered a rock grotto hidden beneath the deck and beside the watercourse that flowed down to the pool and pond below. Overhanging shelf rock roofed in a small, darkened garden of moss and fern augmented by two cedar benches with storage compartments beneath, flanking a depression in the rock. Stepping down into the bowl, he turned away from the marvelous view window formed by a cleft in the surrounding rock and found himself staring at his own battered torso and then up into his face. Built into the rock and containing shower controls but no shower head, was a large piece of irregular mirror canted such that when standing above the bowl it reflected only the rock below.

Shaking his head yet again, he stripped off his trail gear and reached up to turn on the shower. The water seemed to flow directly out of the overhanging rock and, squint as he might, Doc could not determine how this illusion was created.

Fiddling with the controls, he found a flaw line in the glass and as his fingers played over the crack, a piece of the mirror seemed to spring out of the wall. Stepping quickly back to catch the broken section, Doc stopped short as he realized that the glass wasn't falling, it was opening on hidden hinges, a mirrored door behind which resided all manner of soaps and bath oils, fragrant and beguiling.

"I hope you feel as good as you smell," Maggie commented from a deck chair as Doc joined her, tucking the robe around himself as he sat down. "I see you found the shower. And the bath oils. Jasmine? How adorable."

"Somehow it seemed appropriate at the time," Doc said. "But even if I smell like a whore on Sunday, I do feel most improved. Should I even ask about the construction of that space or is it time to just accept the fact that I'm vacationing in Never Never Land?"

" 'Arturo World.' Forty dollar admission but all the gaping is free. At the end of the day we have chiropractors that snap your jaw closed for you. I can't tell you how he got the water to flow out of the rock. Lots of drilling I guess. Or Moses had a hand in it."

"I vote for Moses. It's easier to imagine. Where's the boy?"

"Down at the garage, I think. He said something about prepping the motor home. That was a couple hours ago. I was beginning to worry about you. Thought you drowned, or got lost. I was going to send the dog to look for you in another day or so."

"I fell asleep. I'm sorry, I should be helping Junior," he said.

"Sit down, Doc." She touched his arm. "I'm just pulling your chain a little. It's good for you. You need to lighten up, enjoy life. If I thought you weren't pulling your weight, I'd have turned off the hot water on you. The winterizing controls are up here, in the kitchen," she said. "And I'm glad to see Junior self-motivated. It means he's getting interested. That's good."

"Very good, I agree," he said settling back. "And for your edification, I have enjoyed life as much in the last few days, more so even, than in the previous fifty years. So there," he said. "I'm getting better."

She looked at him full faced and said, "Yes you are. I'm very pleased."

"So am I. I would not have believed it possible. And I *feel* so much better physically. Like twenty years ago. My back doesn't ache, I have more energy, it's amazing. Really. This is a magical place."

"It's the Elixir," she smiled at him.

"What? Pear brandy?"

"I'm only half kidding. Arturo always said the Elixir, made with the family pears, was the Fountain of Youth tonic. He always grinned when he said it so you always thought he was kidding but I'm not so sure any more it was all a joke. The Marones have been using it, as a tonic, for twenty plus years now. My dad is eighty-two. He still runs the law firm, with an iron hand I might add, twelve hours a day, still does trial work. Mom is seventy-eight, has her own foundation, they do mostly hospice work for terminal children. She speaks at luncheons three or four days a week, fund raisers, you know. Incredibly active and alert. Daniel is, well, Daniel. He runs every morning and lifts weights but he smokes cigars all day and drinks bourbon like its diet Dr. Pepper. Plus he's fifty-eight and he works like a field hand. Alpha dog all the way. His cholesterol is like 90, blood pressure 110 over 60, heart like a horse. He brags on all that stuff, that's how I know.

"And George. Looking at him you would swear he could not drag that belly across the street without stopping twice for air. But he can dance, literally, all night long, and never break a sweat or take a deep breath. We went to the dance hall in Luckenbach last year? He paid the band five hundred dollars to do two more sets after the place closed at one. The crowd loved him. Bought him about fifty beers, most of which he drank by the way," she said grinning. "But he danced for six hours, sang about twenty songs. It was amazing. The next morning he got up at seven and worked in my garden all day, chipper as a squirrel in a pecan orchard. And he's forty nine."

"And there's you," Doc said. "I won't make the faux pas of asking your age but you look about twenty five and you obviously have the energy of Hercules."

"I don't do stables. But thank you, I'm flattered, even if you are being that silver tongued devil again."

Sticking out his tongue he said, "Thee. My thoung ith as think as a those. I'm serious. You're beautiful."

"I didn't understand one word you said and put that thing away before I have to throw a bucket of ice water on you. Or me." And then she hopped up, blushing, and said she had to start dinner.

"Wait a minute. What about Junior? How long has he been allowed the occasional tonic?"

She sat back down and looked at him as she calculated. "Since he was about ten, I guess. Arturo said it was okay. In small amounts. About once a week. Almost like medicine. Now that I think about it, it was almost ritualized. With Saturday dinner, after, as dessert. We'd each have an aperitif, an ounce or so. Junior less of course. Even when Arturo was away, if he'd call he'd say, did you have your Saturday Elixir? Think of me when you do, I'll be thinking of you, that kind of thing, you know? It *was* a ritual but so ingrained in our lives that I never thought about him forcing the issue, creating the tradition. That's what he did though, didn't he. He created the tradition. And we still follow it. I wonder why?"

"Medicine, like you said. Be sure to take your vitamins. Or say your prayers before you go to bed. Make it a habit. Make it permanent. He believed in the stuff. And from what you explained, and how I feel, it's hard to argue the point. With you all it could just be good genes. And maybe you, and your Wonderland, have de-stressed me, but maybe it does have something to do with the Elixir. Have you ever had it analyzed?"

"No. Never thought about it. Do you think we should?"

"I don't see how it could hurt. Unless it turns out to have some narcotic or illegal component. That could be awkward. Junior joked that it was mixed with peyote."

"Or if it turns out to really *be* some magic potion," Maggie said. "That could get complicated. You don't suppose the Elixir is mixed up somehow in his disappearance do you?"

"I don't know, Maggie. If so, it might be a little more palatable for the boy."

"Yeah. Better than my dad the disappearing dope smuggler."

"Exactly."

Doc turned from the sink, dishtowel in hand, as Junior entered the kitchen. Seeing Doc in the white robe, Junior stuck his hands in his back pockets and walked over. Leaning in close he said, "If you had pointy ears, you'd look just like Mr. Spock. But I doubt Captain Kirk would approve of your smell. Miss Ohuroo maybe." He laughed as he bounced out of the way of the snapping dishtowel.

"You didn't take a shower yet, did you," Maggie said.

"Naw. No point. I was just gonna get dirty again anyway, not like some of the fine smellin' gentlemen around here I might add. Some of us got to work if we're gonna go adventurin'."

"I'm sorry, Junior. I was seduced by the bathing grotto and fell asleep."

"In scented oil no less," Junior said. "That happens to me all the damn time. No wonder I don't take more baths. I'd just sleep all day. That tub's big enough for two you know, Doc," he said with a wink.

"Junior!" his mother said. "You get your dirty body into a shower right now and take your dirty mind along and scrub it too." Doc turned back to the sink as Junior danced down the corridor toward his room.

"That boy. I should a whooped his ass more when he was small enough for me to do it."

"Too late now, Maggie. But I doubt you would have gotten better results anyway. He's a fine son and you did a fine job raising him."

"Thank you. Yes he is. But I do not need a nineteen year old to play matchmaker. My own son no less. And stop grinning like that. I can see your reflection in the window. You look like an adolescent at a peep show."

"I'll just keep my mouth shut and my dirty mind to myself. It's safer that way."

"Yes it is. And you might want to get dressed."

After dinner Maggie suggested they return to the library and review what they had accomplished. Doc apologized again for his lack of achievement but both Mother and Son assured him that it was okay and he promised to work more and play and sleep less tomorrow.

"We don't have a deadline. Relax," Maggie said.

"Yeah, Doc. Just chill a little. You like to fish? Tomorrow we could piss away the whole day layin' around the river tryin' to hook a catfish or two. George and I do it all the time, right Ma?"

"Your uncle comes here to relax mostly. And yes, he can in fact piss away the whole day in a host of creative ways. You are not going to though."

"Ah, you're no fun. That's what I been tellin' Doc. You need to have some fun once in a while. You oughta hang around Uncle George more often. Learn a few tricks of the trade."

She stared at him then said, "I do know how to have fun. I also know *when* to have fun. And when to work. What did you do this afternoon?"

"I got the motor home runnin'. Changed the oil, checked all the fluids, tightened the belts, filled the tires, gassed her up. She's about ready to go."

"Good. Anything else?"

"I, ah, cleaned out the, ah, compartments," he said. "Put the bumper rack on with a couple fives of diesel and one of water. Do you wanna take a bike or two?"

"What compartments, Junior," Doc asked.

Junior glanced at his mom who nodded slightly and then he turned to Doc. "The Winnebago has a few modifications. Additional storage areas."

"Such as?"

"Such as where one might . . . smuggle something," Junior said.

"Ah. An uncomfortable topic. Sorry."

"It's okay, Doc. They're pretty cool actually," Junior said. "There's an oversized gas tank, built in, but the tank's got a tank inside it. Impossible to tell from outside. The top deck has a false lid with a fair sized pit in there in a false ceiling. There's all kinds of nooks and hidy holes inside in the cabinet bottoms, under the floor. Plus the regular stuff in the sides of the body. We can take all kinds of crap along without gettin' jammed up. We can even put dirt bikes on the back bumper rack. That's what I was askin' Ma about, taking dirt bikes."

Maggie and Doc exchanged a look but Doc spoke first. "A couple little ones? Why not. Good alternate transport if required."

"Hell, Doc, we can put the Husky and the Bighorn on the back and hoist Ma's up on top. We can all ride."

"All right, Junior. Why not indeed," Maggie said. "Tomorrow can you and Doc clean up the inside and start laying away the provisions?"

"You bet. We could most probably be ready to leave as soon as George gets back. As long as you know where we're goin'."

"I'm getting there. I laid out everything we have from your father and I'm categorizing it chronologically and geographically. Tomorrow I'm going to plot it on a map and date it all and see what it looks like. Then we'll brainstorm an itinerary."

"Anything that's standing out at this point, Maggie?" Doc asked.

"A few things. There's little in the way of chit chat letters. That just wasn't Arturo. There *are* a lot of postcards and there seems to be a preponderance of, ah, religious overtones, I guess, in the postcards."

"Religious postcards? I didn't think even the Catholics had gotten that touristy."

"They aren't overtly religious," she laughed. "Not Christ with a long neck saying 'Greetings from Amarillo.' But there are a number of missions and a few monasteries and there's always something printed about the history of the structure, plus a brief handwritten description of the order that runs the facility, what they stand for or who they work with, orphans or an Indian tribe, you follow?"

"Sure," Doc said. "They're all over the southwest. Was Arturo a religious man? My impression, and it's just an impression, was that he was more of a pagan. Nature worshiper not motorcycle outlaw, Junior."

"I knew what you meant. My momma didn't raise no dumb boy," Junior grinned.

"God, I wish you would speak the English language the way I taught you to instead of trying to out redneck your uncle. They both do it just to aggravate me," she said to Doc.

"Nah we don't neither. We is just big dumb old country boys that don't know no better no how, Ma."

"White trash cracker hillbillies. My kinfolk from down the holler. And no, Doc, Arturo was not a church going man, not a good Catholic in the eyes of the pope but he was deeply spiritual and very much a pagan in the truest definition of the word, a nature lover like you said but he also believed in the pure Christian ethic of love for one's fellow man. It was an interesting combination."

"Part Christ, part Buddha, part Pan. I should say so. Why the missions do you suppose?"

"Possibly just curiosity. Arturo was always inquisitive. When he met someone who piqued his interest he would almost interrogate them with his questioning but he could do it in such a way that he never offended. People sensed his sincerity and they would tell him anything. I can see him walking into a church and seeking out the head man just to find out what they were about."

"He would have left a trail. People would remember someone like that."

"Absolutely," Maggie said. "The man was memorable."

"We should stop at all of those missions," Doc said.

Chapter Ten

The next morning Doc and Junior returned to the garage and Doc got the full tour of the motor home including the where's and how's of all the secret compartments. He noted with interest that each was lined with some form of cushioning and then lined again with tightly fitted, heavy gauge plastic and that when the compartments were closed they appeared to be virtually waterproof. Was this to deaden any incriminating smell or to protect a fragile cargo? The compartments probably would do both.

They worked for several hours wiping down all surfaces, vacuuming and deodorizing and by noon the vehicle looked ready for resale.

"Ma's real particular about where her things go so we have to leave her spaces alone but we can pack all the tools and camping gear and such. I got our list. If you want to read it off to me, I'll start pilin' it up. Most of it's right here in the garage."

"Rope, flashlights and batteries, socket set, jack, spare propane tank, bedrolls, no particular order I see."

"Nah. I just wrote down whatever you all said and threw in the stuff I thought of too. We'll pile first, pack later."

"Okay. Freon. For the AC units?"

"Yeah. It gets hot, they need a recharge, we got the stuff."

"Sounds good. It's like packing for a three-day hike in basic training only we didn't have these nice accommodations. More like shelter half, entrenching tool, canteen, gun."

"We'll get to the guns later. They're in a different place."

"You're serious."

"As a heart attack, man. Don't leave home without 'em."

"Okay. Ah, food. That's your mom's space?"

"Yeah. I just wrote it down so we wouldn't forget," he said with a grin.

"Shovel, pick, rock bar, axe, hatchet. Are we going to bury somebody?"

"Cut them up first. Wait till you get to 'chain saw'."

"Chain saw. All right. Radio, headsets, C.B. Is C.B. radio or are there two?"

"C.B. is car communication. Radio is motorcycle."

"Got it. Matches, waterproof in parenthesis, fire pit cooker, pots, pans, utensils, toilet paper. There's a must. Tank sanitizer. Chlorine tablets. Mexican water?"

"The sanitizer goes in the shit tank for the toilet. The chlorine goes in the potable water tank to keep it from gettin' algae. The heat again. And we try not to drink that water. Bottled water ought to be on the list."

"It is. Right after Elixir and before soda. Next is canteens. Tarp, cooler, ice. Motor oil, windshield fluid, radiator coolant, brake fluid. Christ, Junior, you've got this down."

"We used to camp some. But we always made a new list for each trip. Part of the fun was the planning. And we'd take different stuff dependin' on where we were goin' to."

"There's a list of 'to check' items. Generator, winch, AC units, awning, batteries."

"I got all that yesterday. There's more 'pack' stuff after that."

"Right. Next page. Clothes. We're each on our own there I assume. Bucket, broom, cleaning stuff. Rags. Pressure gauge. Tire sealant. Good idea. Tire patch kit. The bikes?" Junior nodded and Doc continued. "Spare plugs, all in parentheses. Small sledge. Duct tape and WD40. They're mandatory for sure. Bailing wire. You've got the holy trinity now. We can fix anything."

They continued through the list and when Doc looked at the hill of equipment Junior had accumulated he began to doubt the ability of the little motor home to pull out, let alone maintain momentum on an upgrade.

"What powers this thing Junior, a rocket?"

"You're wonderin' if it can carry the load, aren't you. Don't be. Like about everything around here, that thing isn't exactly stock. Pop drove it in one time with the bike he'd left on roped to the back. About a week later he drove it out the same way but with one of my little old bikes tied on this time. Had a helluva time gettin' it up the driveway. He came back in a couple hours on the bike. Then a month or so later he leaves on the Harley and a couple hours after that we hear this weird engine noise comin' and then there he is, sittin' behind the wheel of the 'new' motor home, only it wasn't a Mini Winni anymore, it was this here road monster. With the Harley sittin' on that platform.

"I told you it was four wheel drive. He had that done to it somehow. He also had it jacked up about a foot with an off road suspension. I guess all the little cubbies were put in then too. But the main thing was they took out the little eight-cylinder gas engine and put in a V6 Cummins diesel right out of a Kenworth long haul tractor and reworked that some while they were at it. It's got like three hundred and eighty horsepower and enough torque to about turn cartwheels. It'll pull anything you can put on it, in it or behind it. Don't worry about a thing that way, Doc. Hardest part is trying to keep it under ninety."

"All right," Junior said. "Let's run her up to the house and show the boss. Or maybe we should get the guns on board first. Hop in, we might as well drive over there."

Junior fired up the engine and eased the motor home out of the garage bay and turned away from the home mountain and across open pasture.

"This is top secret, Doc. George, me and Ma are the only people, other than Pop, that's ever been to the still. Where the guns are, mostly."

A quarter of a mile from the garage Junior stopped next to a single granite boulder that Doc judged to be fifty feet or more in diameter, dome shaped and unbroken by fissure or crack.

"Stay here a second, Doc, please. No offense but let me unlock it in private."

"Okay," Doc said. In a minute, he heard Junior's voice and climbed down and walked slowly around the immense block of stone until he came upon a perfectly round hole in the wall large enough for a man to bend slightly and walk through.

From the total darkness Junior said, "I got to start the damn generator and I think the battery cable's loose. Hold on. Okay, that should do it. Let me close that door, Doc."

Doc heard a whirring noise then the cough of an engine coming to life then light slowly illuminated the space as the engine picked up speed. As with the glass bubble on the mountaintop, Doc was reluctant to accept what his eyes told him he was looking at.

"It ain't a rock, Doc. It's concrete. A fake boulder. Pretty cool, huh?"

Pretty cool was to Doc the wildest of under statements as he appeared to be inside a perfectly hollowed out slab of rock, both by color and texture indiscernible from the surrounding natural boulders. The ceiling was as pink and pebbly as all the real stones but it was adorned with a hundred or more spotlights so that, with full illumination, there was not a shadow anywhere in the interior. And the interior contained a stainless steel contraption unlike anything he had ever seen, part brewpub, part space ship.

"The still, I assume."

"Correct. Most of it anyway. Hold on, there's more." Junior took two steps to the left of the shiny mass of tanks and tubes, and opened an invisible door in the floor of the chamber.

"Wait a minute," Doc said. "Take it easy on my brain cells, bub. Explain this to me before you smack me with some other weirdness. How's this behemoth function?"

"I'll give you the short answer cause the long one would take days. It *is* the still. The cooker part. There's a conveyer in the back of the rock. Fruit goes in there, up to the top vat, gets squeezed, pulp and crap comes down here and conveyed back out, the juice goes into that tank, gets cooked for a while, you put the miscellaneous stuff in through here." He indicated a small portal in one of the large tanks. "It cooks some more. The vapors go up through coils, see 'em? Then down into more vats below. Come on I'll show you."

"Don't you need water?"

"The whole thing is sitting on a well. Good one, too. Ten gallons a minute even when it's real dry. The water's filtered through those tanks yonder."

"What about the fumes? Doesn't it stink when you're cooking a batch? That's how the revenuers used to locate stills in the Appalachians isn't it. That and the fire."

"Fumes are filtered. You don't smell a thing. Smoke? There isn't any. Propane. There's a ten thousand-gallon tank buried under here. There's about four thousand left in it. Should last another three or four years, depending on the fruit crops."

"Unfucking believable. Okay, show me more. I think I can handle it now."

They climbed down a metal stair to a room as large as the one above, this one containing a hundred stainless steel barrels stacked like wine bottles in a massive rack that curved around the interior.

"All full?" Doc asked, trying to estimate the volume represented by the staggering display.

"About half, I'd say. An average crop of pears, from our orchard, we don't use any others now, makes about five or six barrels. Each barrel holds fifty gallons but you can't fill them full. Maybe forty-five each. I've made five crops since . . . you know, and of course there hasn't been any out go since he left. And there were two real good crops right around then, maybe ten barrels one year and nine the next. Plus there was some inventory before that so I'd say, yeah, about fifty barrels. We can count them if you like. They're all labeled."

"You said 'out go,'" Doc said as Junior's explanation sank in. "There hasn't been 'out go'. What did you mean?"

"Out go. What he took with him on his trips."

"He always took Elixir? Every time?"

"Yeah. Always at least a few bottles. Mostly gallons and gallons. Occasionally a whole truck load. He gave it to his friends. 'Promoting health and long life' was what he'd always say. I guess everybody likes the Elixir. Why?"

"Something your mother and I were thinking about."

"You gonna tell me, or is it another 'big secret'?"

"No, not at all. There was no intent to exclude you, quite the contrary. It was something we hadn't given enough thought to or didn't have any substantiation for, is more accurate."

Junior looked at him. "And?"

"And what if it wasn't dope at all? What if Elixir was the product, the cash cow that built all this." Doc waved his arm around the room.

"Elixir. Selling Elixir. How could. . . . We didn't make enough, especially in the beginning. We couldn't even with outside fruit, not with this still. Hell, this ain't Hiram Walker for Christ Sake."

"It's not the volume, Junior. It's the quality," Doc said. "Your mom says Arturo always espoused the virtues of the Elixir. Insisted that all of you have a little each week. I mean your whole family, grandparents, uncles, you even. What if he knew what no one else did, that the Elixir really is some medicinally significant tonic? Marketed correctly, it would be almost priceless. I should say marketed to the right people, it *would* be priceless. Do you see what I mean?"

"Hell yes, I see it. How much would Bill Gates pay to live an extra twenty years? A billion?"

"Probably. Or someone like him who had the wherewithal and who could be convinced that it wasn't some preposterous scam. It would explain an awful lot of loose ends."

"Yeah, it sure would. But somehow I can't see him trying to prolong the lives of a few rich folk. He didn't give a fuck about anybody's power structure. More likely he'd give the shit away if he thought it might help somebody. You had to know him."

"Hold on, Junior. We're talking pure supposition here. None of us knows anything about what your father really did. That's the point though. Let's find out."

"Hey, I'm with you guys. Have been. This just adds another weird-ass dimension to it, doesn't it?"

"Sure as shit does. The whole thing just gets weirder and weirder."

"You want a see the guns?"

"Why not? We might need a few."

Junior led him halfway around the curvature of the immense wine rack then stopped and turned toward Doc.

"Dig this, dude." He pushed in the spigot of one of the barrels, identical in every way to every one of its hundred neighbors, and a group of three barrels suddenly retreated, leaving an opening large enough for the two of them to enter the revealed room side by side.

"Check it out, Doc. Ex-military, you ought a love this."

Junior pulled another cord and again, slowly, the room within was illuminated. Racks, wall to ceiling, this time metal shelving with every second or third bay a vertically oriented gun case.

"What the fuck? Did you all rob an armory?"

"Dad liked tools, man. I told you that. He said guns were just tools, but designed for special jobs."

Doc reviewed the arsenal compiled before him.

"It isn't as bad as it looks, Doc. Pop bought everything this way. It wasn't enough to have one shovel if they were cheaper by the dozen. Same here. One M-16? Four hundred. Twelve? Three hundred apiece. Get the case. He was a wacker's wacker, man. Go ahead, look it over. Anything strikes your fancy, we'll take it along."

Doc started at the beginning. There was a set of metal shelves that contained an assortment of miscellaneous brewing equipment and large brown jars followed by a dozen twelve gauge shotguns, Remington 870 pumps upon closer inspection. Then shelves with cases of twelve gauge shells, from low brass number eight to pumpkin ball deer slugs.

"Did your dad hunt?" Doc asked, stopped in front of the shotgun shell library.

"Oh, yeah. We'd go out for dove and quail in the fall. There's usually lots of them around. And turkeys most years. It's been kinda dry the last few years so the turkey population is down." At Doc's look, Junior continued.

"When it's dry there isn't much grass. When there isn't much grass the turkey's nests aren't well concealed. The predators find them more easily. Raccoons eat eggs. Hell, raccoons would eat turkeys if they could catch 'em. But they can't so they chase them off the nests and eat the eggs. Now a coyote, he *can* catch a turkey now and again, especially if she's sittin' on a nest not payin' enough attention. And that varmint will eat the eggs too if that's all he can get. Plus there's foxes out there and skunks. Hawks. You see what I mean? If you can't hide the nest, you can't raise the hatchlings."

"Yes," Doc replied. "I see what you mean and there's an important allegory within that explanation but for the life of me I can't make the connection right this minute."

"That's okay, Doc. It'll come to you in your dreams."

"Knock that shit off Junior. You're scaring me."

"Ten four, good buddy. Now keep movin'. You got lots to see."

Doc kept moving. From pump shotgun to semi-automatic. Browning's this time. Then onto a mixed rack of sporting double barrels, most engraved with scenes of grouse and pheasant and none meant to be hauled around the country in the padded cubby hole of some vagabond's motor home.

"Now we're gettin' to the serious shit, Doc. Anything bring back memories?"

Doc moved to his right, past assorted bolt action deer rifles and a dozen M-16's, and then to a rack of weapons that did gave him a gut twist: the AK-47 Kalashnikov assault rifle. Doc knew every nuance of its assembly, all its strengths, how it sounded in all of it incarnations and what a huge bonus it was for those lucky enough to be armed with it. The image of green tracers lashing the jungle close over head suddenly flashed through Doc's mind.

"Full auto? Most illegal, you know that, right?" Then Doc shrugged and said, "One of these. Absolutely."

"How about some hand grenades? There's a bunch of different kinds here," Junior added. "I ain't sure which does what."

"Look at the pin color," Doc explained. "See what I'm saying? The green, red and purple ones are smoke grenades. You mark your LZ so the dust off chopper knows that it's you and not a bunch of dinks. The white is willie peter. White phosphorous. It will melt through solid steel. If napalm is hell's fire, this shit is the devil's own flatulence. Very bad. You definitely should not have these. The plain ones are frags. They'll only blow you to hell. In a hundred pieces."

"And a few Claymore's," Junior said as he uncovered another box on the last set of shelves.

"Of course. No home arsenal is complete without them. I'm surprised you don't have C-4."

"It's over here in a bomb box. Dad said to be careful around it."

"No! Really? But all this other ordinance is okay for a nineteen year old to play with?"

"Yo. Cool your jets there, Mr. Morals. I've known what this stuff was and how to work it since I was about ten. And I haven't blown up any of my little classmates yet, have I?"

"I thought you were home schooled," Doc said with a grin. "No little class mates to blow up." Then he said, "Sorry, Junior. Who the Holy Hell am I to pass judgment."

"It's okay, partner. Go ahead and pick out your particulars."

Chapter Eleven

Doc found Maggie in the library standing in front of the largest map of North America he had ever seen. She had nailed it to three of the vertical timbers that made up part of the doorway wall to the room and was now studying the groupings of colored push pins that she had inserted across the southwest and northern Mexico. Without turning she asked him what he thought.

"It's colorful. How is it keyed?"

"Red are missions and monasteries from postcards or letters. Yellow are other places he referenced in some form of correspondence. Green are places we went to together. They don't seem to have much relevance. They're mostly sort of normal tourist stops, the Grand Canyon, Petrified Forest, Vegas. You know, places everybody ought to see at least once. Blue are . . . I'm not sure. Things that just resonate to me somehow. I've been thinking about this for days, mentally plotting them. Here's the result," she said, standing back and making a hand gesture toward the map.

"It will be a protracted excursion," Doc said, "to cover them all."

"Yes. It would be. But I don't think we have to–cover them all I mean. Are you under a time constraint?" she asked, turning to face him and smiling.

"Not at all. We haven't even started and I already don't want it to end."

"Don't fret, Doc. I'm not going to cast you back into the cold, cruel world. Until you're ready to go anyway."

"What if I'm never ready?" She told him that he was a big, tough, intellectual commando, and that she was confident he could handle himself in any circumstance.

"You forgot handsome, silver tongued poet. My sensitive side might wither away in the harsh reality of the outside world. You wouldn't want that, would you?"

"Heavens no," she said. "We'll have to toughen up your poetic hide so it can protect itself. In my experience, work keeps a poet sharp and strong. What did you and your sidekick accomplish today? Catch any fish?"

"Ha. No. We did, however, clean and pack the motor home. We have enough stuff on board to create a new civilization, should this one collapse while we're away. And I saw the still. I didn't realize that Arturo made so much and that he always traveled with it, in quantity most times. Were you aware of that, that he transported a lot of the Elixir?"

"Yes and no I guess is accurate. If not exactly clear," she said. "I know they made quite a bit. The Elixir was a 'man' thing. Not that I was excluded, it was just something Arturo and Junior did together. Always. From the first seedlings. I'd help them harvest the fruit but then they would go off together and concoct their secret brew. Arturo made it a game at first. This is for the men to do! Like sorcerers, in their Merlin's cave. They had fun. I applauded their time together. But I don't know the details. I don't know how it's made. I didn't know how much he took with him. I don't know how much there is for that matter."

"I'd guess about two thousand gallons more or less," Doc said.

"Two thousand *gallons*! Not bottles, gallons?"

"Yes. More or less. The amount in barrels made me wonder and when Junior said there had not been any 'out go' since Arturo left, that's what piqued my curiosity about where he would take it. There was always 'out go.' Every trip. More than can be explained by a few good mannered gifts to people you might visit. I told Junior what we had discussed, the Elixir as product. We didn't really get into its possible medical benefits but we definitely should. He mentioned miscellaneous additives, besides the pears. I'd like to know what they are. I didn't ask because I assumed you would know."

"I don't. But we'll ask. After dinner. Are you hungry?"

"Famished of course. Fishing is hard work."

"So is poetry. Let's go get some grub."

Seemingly effortlessly she concocted a fabulous meal in a few minutes. They ate on the deck and policed the remains together then once more retired to the library to review the day's accomplishments.

"The Winni is road ready, Mom," Junior began. "All we need is your stuff and yes we left you all the usual spots to stick it in."

"Thank you. I am always gratified when the things I have tried to teach you have occasionally seemed to lodge themselves somewhere in your brain. Did you include some guns?"

"You bet! Two Browning autos plus that sixteen gauge Winchester pump you're so fond of. Lots of assorted shells. A nice .22-250 varmint rifle with a six to sixteen scope. Doc wanted an AK and we packed a half dozen extra clips. I threw in an M-16 just for the hell of it and there's a few odds and ends. We're all set there."

"Should I ask about the odds and ends?" she said to Doc.

"Probably not. Junior tells me that a motor home is considered a residence and therefore not subject to random search, like a car might be. So, ah, the way the, ah, unorthodox stuff is packed, should mean we are . . . sort of okay to take it? Christ, you know what I mean. We're taking military ordinance. Let's hope we don't get busted with it."

"Arturo never did," she explained. "We should be alright."

"And it's always better to be prepared. Right, Doc?"

"I guess. Certainly for a military exercise. I didn't know camping in Arizona could be so fraught with danger though."

"Junior," Maggie said. "You and your dad were the only people who knew what went in the Elixir. I would like to be included now."

"Why? Because of what it might be able to do for people?"

"Yes. Precisely. What's in it?"

"All right. Here's how it works," he said. "As I explained to Doc, you mash the fruit first to extract the juice. The pulp is discarded, automatically in our system. The primary cooker reduces the bulk juice to a syrupy consistency and then collects it in the secondary cooker. Filtered water is added at that stage along with the trace ingredients."

"Which are?"

"Which are I'm not completely sure. There are six big-assed jars down there and you put in a certain proportion of each one depending on the quantity of the batch."

"So you don't know either," Maggie said. "That's what you're telling me."

"Yes. I don't know what's in the jars, by chemical composition if you want total accuracy, just how much of each to add."

"How much," Doc asked, "is left in the jars? How many batches can you make?"

"Four or five. Depending on the amount of fruit. Four or five crops."

"So the propane and the additives will all run out at about the same time," Doc said. "Arturo had a long range plan but it was not self-sustaining."

"That's about the size of it, yeah," Junior said.

"On the off chance that this stuff is a miracle drug, we need to know what is in those jars," Doc said.

"Uncle Daniel's pals in the FBI?"

"Only if he can trust them completely," Doc said, "and if there is anything too hinky in any of it, no one can trust the FBI. If it becomes an enforcement issue, they won't be his friend. You see what I mean?"

"I do," Maggie said. "If it's illegal drugs, well maybe he found it in one of his trucks and big deal, one of the men dropped it by accident. If it's anthrax or powdered plutonium or something so esoteric that no citizen should have it, then they are going to investigate. Fully."

"Yes," Doc said. "And to protect you, Daniel would have to jeopardize himself. He may not even be *able* to protect you. If they need to dig deeply, they'll bulldoze him. They *will* get the answer."

"Hmm. Suggestions?"

"Maybe. Let me think about it a little. Why don't you tell Junior about your map."

She did so, explaining all the places and the significance of the colors. Junior's comments were much like Doc's. It would take a while.

"Yes it will," she said, "so don't give me any grief when I pack my stuff. I don't want to see you two starve in the wilds of America."

"Hey, you know me, Ma. Food is good. Lots of food is even better."

"No argument from me, Maggie," Doc said.

"Nor from me," said George. "That's for damn sure."

"George!" An exclamation from all three as the large man made his entrance and sat down in a desk chair.

"Hey, Unc. Didn't expect you for a couple days yet."

"I heard food and transported myself directly from Houston. Besides, I didn't want to miss all the fun. Not for something as mundane and ever present as work anyway. What have y'all been doin'? Fill me in."

Junior gave George an animated explanation of their endeavors including Doc's near climb of the big sandy hill and subsequent encounter with the bathing grotto ending with a description of Doc in the white robe.

"He smelled like a flowering shrub. You wouldn't hardly know it's the same dude."

"So, the motor home's ready but for the food which, if I'm going along, there better be a big old pant load of."

"George!" Maggie said. "Can you? What about work?"

"I told Daniel he'd have to get his ass out of the office for a change and get his hands dirty a little. He's okay with it, Mags. He loves the boy too, you know. And I may have to fly back and forth a little but I'm definitely joinin' up with this gung ho outfit. Wouldn't miss it."

"Cool beans, Unc. We will definitely kick some America ass! 'On the road again, I just can't wait to be on the road again.' So. When do we boogie on out a here?" They all looked at each other and then turned to Maggie.

"Two or three days?" she said.

"We could go tomorrow from my end, Ma."

"I'm good," Doc said. "Other than my truck and the stuff I left in Houston."

"I took the liberty of breaking camp for you, Doc," George said. "Everything's packed in your pickup which is parked in my garage at home. I also took the liberty of sorting through your stuff and bringing some things that I'd want if I was goin' on a big adventure with folks I didn't know too well so if I either brought too much, or left somethin' out, tough shit, buddy."

"Thank you, George. I'm sure you did fine. I guess, then, I'm ready to go right now."

"I may need . . . a little more time than you three anxious road warriors," Maggie said. "I need to make some arrangements. Let's say, tentatively, Saturday. How's that?"

"Fine, Mags. Whenever you're ready. Sides, that'll give me and the boys here a chance to rest up, do a little fishin. Relax a spell."

"Or two spells. Or three, knowing you my fine, fat brother. Well guess what, Mr. What's For dinner? You are going to help me pack. And can. And smoke. With your inclusion, we may need to pull a trailer just for the additional provisions."

Chapter Twelve

At breakfast the next morning, a meal that George insisted upon although the others had not been in the habit of eating in the mornings, they brought him up to date on their Elixir hypothesis.

"So," George concluded, "the big questions are, what's in the jars and how do we find out, eh, Doc? What were your ideas on that?"

"I had a friend, in the chemistry department at Macon, a certifiable lunatic. Doctor X the kids called him. Sort of an all-around conspiracy theorist, paranoid genius. If I couch my request correctly, he would test the stuff and keep the information confidential to a fault. I can call him, tell him I'm involved in something I can't discuss over the phone, imply a secret government connection. He'll salivate like Pavlov's dog. And he'll do it in a hurry. I should call from town though, a pay phone and a bag of quarters."

"No need, dude," Junior said. "We've got a scrambler. And a bootleg rerouter. On my computer. Nobody's gonna know shit about where the call came from."

"I should have known. And none of this security may be necessary but . . ."

"Why take chances," Maggie said.

"Exactly."

"Well, on my end," George picked up after a pause, "there is nothing of interest on or about the money as far as Daniel's local contacts can tell so that's a dead end. I did get the stuff on my shopping list, it's in my truck. You know where I had to go to get a spare solenoid for that Cummins engine, Junior? Waco!"

"Ah, poor Uncle George. All the way to Waco! A whole hour out of your way."

"Well anyway boy, let's you and me get that truck unloaded. We got some fish to catch this afternoon."

The two headed down the path to the flower garden and George's truck.

"I'll show you how to work Junior's spy gear," Maggie said to Doc. "If you'd like to make that call I mean. It's all in the library."

An hour later Doc finally reached the chemist, tracing him through a series of phone calls to his basement lab in the old science building on the campus of Doc's former employer. Doc had spent many hours in that lab while his friend puttered with various experiments, a continuous monologue of improbable theories spewing forth. Doc never knew what part of the man's diatribe was heartfelt belief and what part was tongue-in-cheek for surely there was a component of each and Doc didn't really care. Doctor X, for all his unorthodox opinions and contrived persona of eccentric scientist, had been a good and steady friend, even when the scandal broke around Doc and his tenure was revoked. The little chemist had been the last stop before Doc's exile began, his car packed and parked outside. Doctor X never asked if it was true, only that if Doc needed anything, then or in the future, to please call. Doc hoped his feelings hadn't changed.

"What?" in lieu of hello.

"Doctor X, I presume. A voice from your past. Can you place it?"

"Hmm. Let me see. A singular similarity to a certain professor of military history but with an undertone of western twang, perhaps newly acquired. Let me think. Nope. No idea. Kidding, kidding, Doc. How the hell are you, my friend! I thought our shadow government would have consumed you completely by now. Gave you up for dead last year. Talk to me, old son."

"I'm alive."

"And well?"

"Of late, yes. Very well. A month ago, only alive. But I need your help."

"Name it."

"It's, ah, delicate. But it's most definitely right up your alley. Interested?"

"Call back in five minutes."

When Doc called again he heard one ring then a series of muted beeps and a couple clicking sounds before Doctor X said, "Now we can talk. If your end is secure."

"It is. But tell me, Eugene, how are you? What has changed in your life? How's academia?"

"Fine. Nothing. The same. What do you want, gossip?"

"Yeah," Doc laughed. "Give me some old-fashioned, university, back-fence gossip. Maybe I'm a little homesick."

"For this place? No you're not. As you are well aware, nothing ever changes here. I've had exactly the same faces in every freshman seminar I have ever taught and that has been going on for eighteen years."

"I gather that the history department is substantially similar to the one that I knew and loved so deeply. Especially Doctor Depew."

"Old Shit Bag is as remarkably one dimensional as always, a self-aggrandizing blow hard absent any trace of personality or compassion."

"That sounds like my old boss. I wish I had a recording of our conversation when he terminated me. And an eight by ten of that plastic grimace he tries to pass off as a smile."

"I still have to look at it in person once a month at the faculty luncheon and it never fails to curdle my curds."

"I miss you, Eugene. I really do. Take a sabbatical, come and visit. You need to get some perspective. Time *moves* out here in the real world."

"That is a two-sided scimitar, my friend. And the only thing that makes this piney woods coffin palatable is my work. And the fact that they all think I'm insane so they leave me alone to pursue that work. Without too much oversight. They don't want to be around me," he said giggling.

"I knew you were a fraud! I just didn't know why you went to such great lengths to remain in character, around me especially."

"What makes you think I don't believe every word of every sentence I've ever spoken?"

"Bovine flatulence."

"Okay. Almost every word. Now tell me how I can help."

"I need some things analyzed, chemical composition, identification."

"What kinds of things?" When Doc didn't answer immediately Eugene continued. "If you knew what they were you wouldn't need me. Silly question."

"Yes and no. I think I know what they are not, but I don't have any idea what they are. I don't think they're poison, or radioactive, or even particularly obscure. But I need to know exactly what they are because I'm relatively certain that we'll need more of them. It's important, Eugene. Potentially paradigm shift important."

"This from an historian. When did you begin to dabble in the hard sciences, Doc? And who are 'we'?"

"They began to dabble with me. And I'd prefer to keep the we to me for now. Okay?"

"Certainly, my friend. But answer me this, please. There is a woman involved isn't there?"

A long pause ensued as Doc got up from the library chair and paced around the desk, stopping with his back to the door. "She's the sister of a friend."

"And?"

"And the most beautiful woman that ever walked the face of this earth."

"You're in love. Bravo, Doc!"

"Yes. I am in love. And she is much more than just beautiful. She's . . . indescribable. I don't have the vocabulary."

"I'm very happy for you, Doc. Now. Send me the samples Fed Ex . . ."

But everything else the chemist said was lost to Doc for, as his friend began to speak, an arm encircled Doc's chest from behind and a hand took the receiver from his hand and placed it on the desk and then he was turned in place and Maggie was in his arms and she gently pulled his head down to hers and kissed him.

"I think its mutual, Doc," she said. "But it scares the hell out of me."

"So take it slowly, right Maggie?"

"Please." She kissed him again. "Did you get what you needed?"

"I'll have to call him back I think. I got distracted toward the end."

"I should hope so," she said laughing. "Come see me when you're done. I'm in the kitchen."

Doc picked up the phone as she left, preparing to go through the security procedures to reconnect with Doctor X but, to his surprise, he could hear Eugene chuckling on the other end.

"Eugene? You're still there. I apologize. I thought I cut you off."

"Cut me off my hairy ass! You were getting a little! From Miss Maggie with the marvelous laugh."

"You have the hearing of the Devil himself, you little bastard."

"No secrets amongst old friends, Robert. I'm sorry. She does sound wonderful though. Christ, you deserve it, all you've been through."

"Thanks, Eugene. I'll cover your costs, of course, but I, ah, missed the actual mailing instructions, if you could repeat that part."

"No costs involved. Compliments of Shit Bag Depew. Now write this down."

Chapter Thirteen

George and Junior were casting lazily into the pond, a state of affairs not lost on Maggie and she directed Doc to join them for a while if he so chose but then to 'drag their worthless butts back up here so we can get some work done.'

"Doc," George said. "Perfect timing. Me and the boy were just discussin' personal defense techniques and I told him you were more than likely a hell of a lot more qualified to give him pointers than I was."

"Ah, that's sort of, ah, not as simple as it sounds, George," Doc said. "Explain what you mean."

"You know. Karate, Kung Fu, some things the boy could use to defend himself. If the need arose. In our journey. You see?"

"Yes. Self-defense capabilities are ah, admirable. Unfortunately, I don't really know any."

"But you're such a bad ass. No offense, Doc," Junior added.

"None taken, Junior," Doc said. "But that's exactly my point. We weren't taught self-defense. We were taught offense. Hand to hand combat isn't about subduing an opponent without permanent injury. It's about killing him as quickly and as quietly as possible. It's ugly, messy work. And irrevocable. There's no 'Gee, I'm sorry, did I hit you too hard?' You stick an eight inch serrated blade between the third and fourth rib, go for the heart. Smash a man's nose upward with the heel of your hand and drive bone splinters into his brain. A stick in your eye? Yeah. Sharpen it on a rock and shove it right to the back of his skull. Or into the jugular. You don't need to know this stuff and I don't need to remember it."

"Sorry, Doc," from both of them.

"I didn't get taught any of that stuff, Doc," George said. "I guess us regular grunts didn't have the need. Least wise I never did. Hell, I didn't see much combat anyway. Mostly we were guardin' the arty, 155's, usually way back from the front line stuff. We did do some night patrols, set up ambushes, listening posts, you sure as hell know what I mean. But we didn't get lit up too much. Too remote."

"You're lucky," Doc said.

"I'm sorry I brought up the topic, Doc," Junior said. "It was my idea, not George's."

"It's okay. I'll tell you what. There are a couple tricks I can show you. Come on over here. George, you spot."

An hour later the three of them, dirt brown from hair to boot, followed by the dirt brown dog, tramped across the deck toward the kitchen door.

"Don't even think about coming in here, boys," Maggie said through the kitchen window. "Not till you're all a hell of a lot cleaner than you are now."

"Ah, come on, Mags. We just wanna get a beer and rest up a little."

"From what? Playin' in the dirt like a gaggle of little boys? And I thought you were on a beer-free diet."

"That's when we're on the road, not now. And we weren't playin', we were learnin' self defense. From Doc. It's important Mags, for the boy's self esteem. Right, Doc?"

"Why do you drag me into this? Why do I let myself get *dragged* into this stuff," Doc said with a shrug.

"Because," she said, "they are two charming men who can make the most obviously inane proposal sound like a perfectly reasonable request from a normal, sane individual. I should have warned you."

"Yeah," George said. "We used to really get after her boyfriends when she was a kid. Most of 'em wouldn't come back a second time. They'd still pine for her but me and Daniel, we'd run 'em off. You ought to get me a beer just for protectin' you all those years."

"Alright. One. Then you get clean. Doc, can I talk to you a minute."

"Uh oh! You're in big trouble, Doc," Junior said as he swatted off some dirt on his way to the door.

"What is it, Maggie," Doc asked.

"Do you think the boy needs to know how to fight?" she said.

"If you mean because he's already big as a linebacker, no, probably not." She shook her head and he continued. "If you mean will it make him an aggressive bully, again no, not what we were practicing. They are truly defensive techniques to disarm or ward off an attacker. And I don't know much. Most of my training was more offensively oriented and I wouldn't teach that to anyone. So, I thought it was okay."

"Of course. I just wanted to understand. Are you going to join the ne'er do wells?" she asked.

"Can I help you?"

"Yes. But a cold one sounds pretty good. I'll come out."

The next morning George and Maggie began to stock the motor home with the last of the required items, Maggie's supplies and the food stores. Doc and Junior walked across the meadow to the still, Doc carrying a box of Ziplock bags.

Doc was shown the hidden locking mechanism for the still boulder, a small rock indistinguishable from the others nearby that, when turned appropriately, caused the round portal to open silently inward. They activated the generator and proceeded down to the gun room and the brown jars.

"Okay, Doc. Here's how she works. All the proportions are in units per barrel of syrup, before the water is added and the secondary cooking starts. They all go in together more or less and Pop always said we didn't have to be super precise. As long as we got enough, a little too much wouldn't hurt nothin'. So. This here's the first one," he said as he unscrewed the lid on a ten-liter brown glass pharmaceutical jar.

Doc ran his hand across the top several times, trying to draw any aroma up to his nose but none was detectable.

"Ain't none of 'em got any particular smell, Doc, if that's what you're checkin'."

"Just a technique I remember from chemistry class. You stick your nostrils over a bottle of the wrong stuff, take a big whiff and then find out its sulfuric acid or something."

"Yeah, I know. I probably had the same course. They don't smell much."

"I believe you, I'm just being safe."

Each of the jars had a glass measuring spoon inside with a handle long enough to reach the bottom. Doc removed a few grams from all of them and placed the samples individually in bags labeled simply jar one to jar six. Then he took a sliver of wood and put a pinch of the first sample on the shelf, dampened his index finger and put a few grains on the tip of his tongue.

"No taste either," he said. "I'm assuming that if it's in the Elixir, it's probably not poison."

"Damn, Doc. I don't know that I'd assume anything where pop comes into it. What's that crap they shoot into lady's faces to freeze their wrinkles, bostic or somethin'? It's made from some poison ain't it?"

"Botox," Doc said spitting on the floor, "and you make an excellent point. It's a derivative of the botulism enzyme I think." Never the less, he continued with the second and third samples, spitting after tasting each. The fourth one brought a frown.

"I'm not an expert and I was never much of a druggy, even in my professor days, but this tastes like cocaine to me."

"Let me give it a whirl. I confess to having tried a line or two," Junior added with a smirk. "Yeah, sure does. Mostly it's the numb tongue though. Could be anything like that I'd think."

The fifth and sixth jars were no more readily identifiable than the others although the fifth had a brownish hue and a distinctly bitter taste and the sixth looked like red dirt.

"Well, let's send them to the expert, see what we've just ingested," Doc said.

"Yeah, if we ain't dead by then. How long'd he say it'd take?"

"Just a day or so from receipt. I told him we would call Monday. I thought we would probably be in transit by then."

"I expect. You ready to go to town, ship this stuff out? I thought we'd run over to Fredericksburg. It ain't that far and it's a whole lot bigger than Llano. Full a tourists. We won't draw any attention there."

"Sounds good. Are we going to invite the rest of the gang?"

"You bet! Do a motor home shake down cruise."

They crossed the river in the motor home and Doc got a first hand impression of the consternation it must have caused Mrs.

Marone all those years ago. A sand and gravel county road brought them to Ranch Road 2323 which was smooth and paved and Junior ran the little bus quickly up to eighty five.

"Slow down, Junior," Maggie said. "We aren't in a hurry."

"I told you she weren't no fun didn't I, Doc," but he eased off and settled down to sixty five, then began a tour guide's spiel describing the flora and fauna that they were whizzing through, as well as anecdotes about the ranchers he knew. "That there's Mrs. Augustine's spread, Doc. You can see part of the roof stickin' through the oaks, yonder. She used to tutor me when Ma was out a town with Pop. Retired school teacher from up north."

"It's funny," Doc said. "I would have assumed that all these ranches were run by third or fourth generation descendents of homesteaders. Family affairs where nobody ever really leaves home. Not expatriate Yankees."

"There's all kinds, Doc," Junior said. "We ain't so easy to categorize. Look at Mr. Reuche, am I right, Ma?"

"Yes," she said. "Jim Reuche is about seventy-five I guess. Both he and his wife have college degrees. Both work all day, every day. Last summer Jim won his third or fourth consecutive Llano rodeo, you get a big gold buckle, for all around steer roping. At seventy-four. Hardy folks. Arturo loved the Reuches and the Augustines."

"Maggie," Doc asked. "You said Arturo was close to these folks. And that they're elderly and very active."

"I see where you're going," she said, "and yes, I think he gave Elixir to several people, the Augustines and Reuches included."

"Do you know how he, ah, instructed them in its use? Or if he did?"

"No, Doc. I do not but we can certainly ask."

"No time like right now, eh, Ma?" and without waiting for a response Junior braked the vehicle sharply. Within a few minutes they were crossing a cattle guard at the entrance to the Augustine ranch and Maggie again admonished Junior to go slowly.

Doc thought the ranch house was rustic-quaint until they rounded the corner of what turned out to be just one of the components of the home and entered a landscaped courtyard surrounded on three sides by a timber framed covered porch.

"Wow," he whispered to Maggie. "This is unexpected."

"Wait till you see the inside. This is probably the nicest home in Llano County."

By the time they got inside, Junior was already hugging a silver haired woman of indeterminate age, mid-sixties, Doc guessed. George was greeted by name in an exclamation of surprise and delight and received a hug of his own and a big kiss on the cheek.

"How wonderful to see you again, George. On a weekday even and not during hunting season. Are you playing hooky?"

"Yes ma'am, I surely am and don't you tell Daniel."

"I wouldn't dream of it," she said with a smile. Then she turned to Maggie, opened her arms wide and enveloped the younger woman in a tight embrace. "Maggie, my dear. I don't see you nearly enough. I miss you, sweetheart. I'm so glad you came to see me." After a pause, she turned to Doc and extended her hand. "I'm Meredith Augustine."

After a house tour for Doc, Mrs. Augustine led them out to an open deck with a view of the ranch spread out below and asked Maggie what brought them to her home.

"Meredith, Arturo would stop and see y'all sometimes wouldn't he? Before he . . . left?"

"Yes he would, Maggie. Why do you ask?"

Maggie explained their plan briefly.

"So, Doc," Meredith said. "Are you the tour guide or the voice of reason in this enterprise?"

"Meredith," Maggie said before Doc could answer. "Did Arturo ever give you any of his pear brandy?"

"The Elixir?" she said. "Yes he did. Every couple months he'd come by and visit with us. You remember what a terrific storyteller Fred was. They would sit out here for hours swapping yarns. Fred Lee just loved that boy. He kept asking about Arturo right till the end. The Alzheimer's was pretty bad by then, Doc, but he never forgot Arturo."

"Did he ever say anything about the Elixir, how to, ah, enjoy it?" Doc asked.

"You mean like instructions? Of course he did. You all act like the Elixir is some big secret. Arturo was very straightforward about it. 'The Elixir is a pear based tonic'," she quoted, "'with certain medicinal properties that should increase your energy levels and stimulate general good health.'

"He brought a bottle or two every time he came by. At least once a week, a good hearty shot were the 'instructions.' It's not something he had to force on us. It's delicious. And it works. Fred had cancer, as well as the Alzheimer," she said. "At the time, they gave him six months. I didn't tell him, he didn't need any help to enjoy life, make his last days count. He was always so full of life anyway. Your father had the same attitude, Junior. Every day was new and exciting, an adventure.

"Arturo came by the next afternoon, brought a bottle of Elixir. We sat right here on the deck and he explained it to me. He said Fred should have a little every day for a couple weeks, then not so often. Arturo knew something was wrong, I don't know how. He told me privately, in the kitchen, not to worry. He said 'the Elixir can't save his life but it can prolong it. And he will not suffer in the end.' I remember his exact words, I always will. And he was right. It did. He lived almost three more years. Died in his sleep, right here."

"Ms. Augustine, do you know if he gave Elixir to other folks in the area?" Doc asked.

"Sure. The Reuches for one. Emmy and I swap Elixir stories. She claims it cured her arthritis and Jim swears he could not ride a horse without it. His knees were giving out on him."

"Are they all elderly?" Doc asked.

"Yes, Doc. All the old folks in the neighborhood get crocked on pear brandy on a regular basis. It beats the hell out of afternoon tea! Seriously? Yes. Arturo seemed to have a special fondness for us old buzzards. I think he had a regular route, like the Schwann man only he didn't charge anyone as far as I know."

"You must have run out by now, Meredith," Maggie said. "Why didn't you call me?"

"Maggie, I imagine I still have a two or three year supply left. The last time Arturo stopped, he lugged in a big box with four gallon jugs in it. He helped me put them up on the shelves in my closet. And we filled some regular bottles so I could handle it easily. A fifth lasts about six months. I always assumed you two knew all of each other's secrets, you were both so in love. I'm sorry, that was a silly thing to say."

"No it wasn't, Meredith. We *were* in love and we didn't keep secrets. Except about the Elixir. That was Arturo's business. And Junior's. And I really wasn't aware of the scope. I'm still not. That's another reason for our trip."

"Whatever you discover, Maggie, I'm sure it will be positive. About Arturo. That man did not have a selfish bone in his body."

They had driven several miles in silence before Doc spun the passenger's seat around to face Maggie and George in the living quarters and said, "It occurs to me that the scope of our journey is beginning to clarify itself. We were going to attempt to . . . back track Arturo, see if we could discover how he, ah, disappeared. Ancillary questions involved source of funds and perhaps his family history, relatives, which you do have some leads on right, Maggie?"

"Yes. I think I know where his family was from, in Mexico, and the family name. There are still some de la Madre's in the area according to some information I got from the internet. We don't know how common the name may be although there were not a lot of them mentioned, not like Garcia or Rodriguez."

"Okay," Doc said. "So we can do some on site research there, see what develops. What fascinates me is the Elixir tie in. Is this stuff really a miracle drug? Does it have any medicinal properties? It certainly seems so. Is it the product that generated the revenue? Arturo certainly gave enough of it away so if he was selling it as well, to whom? And why mostly the elderly? Does it prolong life, ease suffering? And if that's all it does, why give it to you and George and especially Junior? It's much easier for me to accept the possibility that the Elixir can 'ease the pain' and as a corollary, prolong life than it is to believe in a fountain of youth. And why the missions and monasteries? That I think will be the simplest question to answer and hopefully lead to some answers on the other issues. Finding out who, if anyone, bought the stuff I suspect will be more difficult."

"Follow the money," George said.

"Meaning?" Doc asked.

"Doc. 'Follow the money,'" George said. "Motive. Crime of passion? Doubtful. Then who stood to gain and gain what? If it ain't passion, random crime, accident or natural causes, then there probably was money involved."

"And we know for a fact," Maggie said, "that there was money involved. Lots of it."

Chapter Fourteen

Fredericksburg, Doc thought, was a charming, western-style town, the old stone buildings housing shops and restaurants.

"Why are the streets so wide?" Doc asked.

"This is the width required," Junior answered without hesitation, "to make a U-turn with a team a twenty mules."

"Bullshit!"

"He ain't kiddin' you, Doc," George said. "They had to accommodate the supply wagons and the mules that pulled 'em back then."

"There's a UPS store over by the grocery store, Doc," Junior said. "I'll take the box in. It's all ready, ain't it?"

"Yes. Make sure they mark it 'fragile' though. I don't want the Elixir bottle to break. And don't put a return address on it."

"I ain't stupid, Doc. Want me to put on latex gloves? Probably nobody'd notice."

"No, it's too late for that," Doc laughed. "If the FBI is watching Doctor X closely enough to open his mail and check for prints, they're going to find that a twenty five years dead army officer sent that box. That will shake them up some I'd think."

After the box had been mailed and Maggie had filled a small shopping list at the grocery store, George insisted they stop for lunch. They ate an assortment of nachos, fajitas and knockwurst at an outdoor cantina then piled back in the motor home and headed back to the ranch.

"Take the back way, Junior," George said. "Through Cherry Springs and Castell. We'll show Doc some of the outstanding scenery. And stop at the Hill Top, I wanna get a six pack. The Hill Top's a gas station turned restaurant, Doc. Used to be a fun little place with a couple pool tables in a screened in room and a cooler full a dollar beers. Then some city boy bought it and's tryin' to turn it into a silk purse. I wanna see how he's doin'."

The parking lot of the Hill Top looked more like a Harley dealership then a fine dining establishment and Junior had to park on the shoulder of the road.

"Looks like the old crowd ain't got the word yet," George said as he looked out the side window at the motorcycles parked randomly across the lot. "Get me some Shiner Bock, boy," he continued, handing Junior a bill.

"George! He's not old enough to buy beer."

"Yeah, like anybody's gonna notice with that bunch in there. Besides he looks plenty old enough to me."

Junior grinned at his mother as he opened the driver's door. "Chill, Ma. It ain't like it's the first time or anything."

Junior had only been gone a few minutes when Doc looked up with a puzzled expression. "Something's happening. I'm going to check," he said.

Before George or Maggie could respond or Doc exit the vehicle, a man flew out the open door of the restaurant and landed in a heap in the gravel parking lot. All of them were in motion then and only Doc saw the next group of bodies come surging out, Junior in the middle of a nasty scrum, his blond head encircled by a meaty arm, two denim clad figures clutching his arms and another piggy-backed on top.

Once the group cleared the confines of the doorway, the man holding Junior's head drew back his arm and punched Junior in the face, then again and was cocked for a third blow. Doc's forearm, delivered with all the momentum of his sprint across the lot and the full rotation of his body and shoulder at the point of impact, caught the man holding Junior's head flush on the side of the jaw.

Junior, free of the choking constraint, snapped his head back, smashing it into the face of the man clinging to his shoulders. Simultaneously he swung his arms together and ran the two men holding them into each other.

Doc, standing over the man he had hit, saw a wave of reinforcements roiling out the door of the bar and then a flash of dark as George hurtled past him and slammed into the new group, his charge knocking them down like bowling pins and his momentum carrying him and three of them back into the restaurant.

Doc was striding toward the restaurant's door, Junior still grappling with one of his attackers, when the blast of a shot gun rent the air followed almost instantly by a second and third explosion. Doc turned to see Maggie marching across the parking lot, the Browning held at port arms in her left hand, the right calmly feeding shells into the breach beneath.

She walked through the restaurant door and before Doc or Junior could follow her in, George was thrust out. A second later Maggie emerged, walking backwards till she cleared the doorway. She turned and without looking at the men around her and said quietly, "Let's go, boys."

They got as far as the doors of the vehicle, only George making it completely in, when the first squad car slid across the highway and came to a stop behind the motor home. Two Gillespie County officers jumped out, hands on the butts of their service revolvers as they looked first across the parking lot full of motorcycles and the dozen bikers congregating near the restaurant entrance, then down at the four fallen men who had engaged Junior.

A wailing siren announced the arrival of a Department of Public Safety highway patrolman. He was as big as an offensive tackle Doc thought, his campaign hat shadowing his face but unable to conceal the scowl that further darkened his already chocolate complexion. Another Gillespie cruiser with two more sheriff's deputies on board arrived right behind the highway patrolman. The trooper strode directly to the motor home, ignoring the bikers and the county cops.

"What the hell went on here," he demanded in a deep bass voice, inches from Doc's face. "Don't you give me that hard case look, mister! I'll run your ass in so fast you'll think you was *born* in jail!"

Doc's fists were clenched at his sides, the muscles in his forearms bunching, when the window on the driver's side of the motor home slid open and George's face appeared in the opening directly opposite the crown of the trooper's felt hat.

"Now Clarence, there is no need to be so uptight. We was just having a good natured disagreement with them nice biker boys."

"George? What the fuck are you doing out here? And why are you interrupting my lunch hour?"

"Good to see you too, Clarence. How's Ellie doin'? And Jed and Justin?"

"Jesus Christ, George, what am I going to do with this mess? And the family's fine. Yours?"

"All good. Healthy as little savages which they are, a course. Gina's good too."

"And Maggie?" the trooper asked. "How is that fine woman. I haven't been out that way since I got transferred over here. A year or more."

"She's right behind you, Clarence. And that big bloody monster behind her is Junior. He's how we got introduced to our new friends."

"Maggie!" the trooper said. "How good to see you!" He swept her up in his left arm and gave her a kiss, then stuck his right hand out at the grinning Junior and said, "I don't know that I'd of recognized you, boy. You're twice as big as you was and bleeding like a head shot hog. You alright, son?"

"I'm fine, Clarence. Just a bloody nose."

"Good, good. Well, you all stick around here a minute. I'm going to do my duty to the state a Texas.

"Take your time, Clarence," George said. "We were just out for a Sunday drive."

"George?" Doc asked as the trooper stomped over to the bikers.

"Yeah, Doc," George said. "We know him. Pretty good in fact. And no I don't know everybody in Texas, it's just a happy coincidence."

Clarence announced without preamble that the bikers were going to get on their motorcycles and get out of his sight within thirty seconds. They all turned away and began to shuffle over to their respective machines except for the man who had punched Junior who said to the trooper, "They started it. This isn't fair."

Without a word, Clarence slammed the man against the side of the building and the concussion brought the Gillespie County sheriff's deputies running.

"Easy, Trooper Little," their sergeant said as he reached Clarence's side. "Let us help you here, sir. Please. We'll take care of these boys now," and when Clarence released the man, two of the other deputies grabbed his arms to keep him from falling to the ground. The sergeant walked Clarence off a ways and began a whispered conversation with the trooper. Doc could not hear anything the sergeant said but Clarence exclaimed, "You're shitting me!" in a loud voice followed shortly thereafter by, "Get the fuck outta here!" and then a torrent of rumbling laughter.

Within a few minutes the parking lot was empty except for the motor home and Clarence's patrol car. Clarence was still chuckling when he walked over to the motor home, all four of its occupants now standing outside watching his approach.

"Well boys, y'all just beat the crap out of the younger half of the Fredericksburg Lion's Club. They was on their yearly 'Outlaw Day' outing and this year they thought it would be a hoot to rent motorcycles and pretend to be Hell's Angels or some such. Last year they were the James Gang. You could a shot them for real then, Maggie. Yeah, I heard about the shotgun so don't be giving me that Miss Innocent look.

"That fat boy was Dr. Matlack, the proctologist. I hope none of us need a rectal exam in the near future. And the little skinny guy that Junior head butted? He owns Greenleaf's Flower Shop." After a couple minutes of raucous laughter, Clarence asked them how the fight had started.

"Junior, answer the man," George said. "We ain't had a chance to find out ourselves, Clarence."

"Hell, Unc, all I did was walk in the door and ask the waitress if I could get a six pack. Then this little shitheel elbows me in the side and says this here's a private party, boy, get the fuck out and grabs me by the arm like he's gonna throw me out. So I showed him Doc's hip and flip move and y'all seen the rest."

"Well," Clarence said. "You're all damn lucky Mr. Hard Case here," nodding toward Doc, "didn't break fatso's neck. We all are. I'd have been writing reports till the fourth a July and them Gillespie cowboys would have had to lock your asses up. All of you. It ain't nice to fuck up the local butt doctor. I think they're all too embarrassed at the moment, fifteen a them getting whooped by two old geezers, a kid, and a girl, to make an issue out of it but that could change once they get back to being a bunch of outstanding citizens, take off their fake outlaw suits and put their Dockers and loafers back on. They might get to rearranging the facts a little, start bitching to the Sheriff. Y'all ought to get Annie Oakley here and Doc Holiday back to Llano County and lay low for a spell."

"We're gonna do better'n that, Clarence," George said. "We're gonna skip town completely! Seriously. We're leavin' tomorrow."

"Good. Go around Gillespie County. I'm off tomorrow so I won't be available to get your asses out a trouble." Clarence shook hands with the men and gave Maggie another feet in the air hug and another kiss and made her promise to call him when they got back. And to keep her men folk out of trouble and to be careful with firearms and they all had another big laugh before the trooper drove away.

"Well," George said, "I'll get the six pack this time and then we can get out a here."

They got back to Maggie's mid-afternoon and spent the rest of the day loading the perishables in the motor home and preparing the homestead for their absence. After dinner Maggie unpinned the immense map from the library wall and gathered her store of notebooks and travel guides and packed everything into a leather knapsack.

"I think we're ready, boys," she said looking at the three of them.

"A toast to our success then, Mags," George said.

"Here, here, Unc. I'll do the honors." Junior poured the Elixir and each of them held their tumbler, looking expectantly toward George.

"Here's to the open road," he said. "May our vehicles run smoothly and the roads be smoother yet. Let the cops all be like Clarence so our troubles we forget."

"Bravo, Unc! To the big adventure," Junior added turning to Doc.

Doc took a second to gather his thoughts. "A safe trip of course. And a successful one. But we need our expectations to be realistic. I don't want you, Junior, or you either Maggie, to expect something miraculous and then be disappointed."

"You're a windy son of a bitch, Doc," George said. "I wasn't expectin' one a your lectures. This here trip's supposed to be fun."

"You're right, George. Here's to fun. May we all be happier upon its conclusion. Maggie, you're up."

"God bless all of us and our journey. Keep us safe and make us wiser from this experience. Thank you. All of you."

Chapter Fifteen

By six o'clock they were all up and by seven they were all in the idling motor home, Junior at the wheel, George on the other side, Maggie fussing with the last of the carry-ons. The dog had climbed in the side door and without so much as a sniff, walked to the rear bedroom, hopped up on the bed and went to sleep. Doc, sitting at the dinette, commented that it looked like he'd road tripped before.

"He'll sleep till he's forced out of that bed," Maggie said. "Then maybe he'll go outside and do his business. If he can make it all the way to the door without collapsing from exhaustion. Junior! Did you wash that mutt like I told you?" His answer was lost in the rising decibels as he goosed the throttle and eased the vehicle up the driveway.

They got all the way into Llano proper, ten miles almost, before George demanded that they stop for food, the only venue available at that hour being the 'U Tote 'Em' where he stocked up on chili flavored corn chips, salsa in a jar and Slim Jims to the horror of his sister who had packed all manner of home canned vegetables, mesquite smoked jerky and sausage, fresh fruits and other nutritious food stuffs which he had shown no interest in.

Their first travel decision had to be made in the parking lot, take Clarence's advice, however tongue in cheek it may have been, and go around Gillespie County or save an hour plus of travel time and go right through the center of Fredericksburg. They went around, after a unanimous vote.

The four missions just south of San Antonio, Maggie said, had all been referenced on one postcard, she'd been there with both Arturo and Junior and they probably fell into the category of places to see at least once. Like the Alamo. They went west and picked up I-10.

"Only four hundred and fifty six miles to El Paso," Junior hollered when they passed the first highway marker. "We'll be there in no time a'tall."

After six hours of smooth, high speed driving, George spelled Junior just west of Fort Stockton by holding the wheel with his right hand while Junior slipped out of the driver's seat and scooted under George's upraised left. The vehicle maneuver, obviously practiced, transpired at eighty miles an hour and Doc began to wonder if the motor home ever needed refueling.

"Does this thing ever need gas?" he asked George from the passenger's seat.

"Yeah, every thousand miles or so, depending on your speed. At fifty five it'd probably go from Austin to San Diego. The drivers wear out before the fuel supply."

"Maggie," George shouted over his shoulder, "where do we turn for the mission?"

"Follow the sign for Horizon City if there is one. I don't have a road name. Or look for Socorro Mission."

They exited the interstate on a two-lane blacktop access road that rapidly deteriorated into barely improved gravel. Five miles later they came to a dusty intersection, the four corners of which were occupied by a weedy vacant lot, a boarded up general store, a two pump gas station and a fifties style, steel shelled diner, the sides streaked from roof to driveway with foot wide stripes of rust

"No sign a no mission, Mags," George said. "How about we go on in and check out the 'Early Bird' dinner specials."

"Yeah," Junior said. "This place's probably got the best food for miles around!"

"Alright, let's go in. But make it quick, George. I want to find the mission before dark."

They examined a chalkboard menu. The waitress announced that the chili was fresh today, ladling up iced tea without request then returning to her conversation with two grizzled octogenarians.

"Excuse me, Ma'am?" Maggie asked. "Could we order now?"

She looked at them disinterestedly and then walked over.

"Ma'am, is the Soccoro Mission out this way?" Maggie asked politely.

"It took all four a youse to come in here to get directions?" she responded in a mixed western–North Jersey accent.

"You're a long way from home, I'd say," Doc said. "Bayonne or thereabouts?"

"Perth Amboy. Then Rahway. You heard a Rahway, cowboy?"

"A prison," Doc said, not breaking eye contact with the woman. "Harsh place, I hear."

She snorted. "Harsh. Yeah, that covers it all right. And I'll save you the trouble. He was the cellblock bull, the only male guard in the women's House a Detention, a big old Texas stud. After I done my bit we packed up our stuff in his '64 Olds convertible and lit out for the 'Promised Land.' This here's the Promised Land," she said. "He stayed almost a whole year. I been here for almost thirty five. Now what will it be, chili or chicken?"

"They must call this place Horizon City," Junior said, "cause that's about all its got–a horizon in every direction. And I'll have the chili, ma'am."

"I see your boy got your gift a gab, cowboy," she said to Doc. "Why'nt you leave him here with me while youse go check out that old mission. I can help with his higher education."

Maggie started to respond, lurching up off her barstool, the color rising, but Doc laid his hand on her arm and eased her back down.

"This family unit likes to stay together," Doc said. "And I'm not sure the boy's ready for that amount of knowledge just yet. Maybe in a year or so."

"Damn, Doc, your about as no fun as Ma," Junior laughed.

They ordered and she was back in a minute with four bowls of chili, a basket of biscuits and a plate of butter.

"Everything all right?" she asked a few minutes later.

"Damn if it ain't about the best chili I ever ate," Junior said. "Who'd a thunk it, way out here."

"In the middle of nowhere," she finished for him. "It's alright, I know it. You're his mom, ain't ya, honey," the waitress said to Maggie. "I didn't mean nothin', you know? I'm just havin' some fun with youse. I don't get too many young bucks in here no more."

"That's alright," Maggie answered. "Motherhood. It makes you protective."

"Like a she bear, with cubs," George said.

"So where's that old dog?" the woman asked Doc. "I thought he came with that crazy lookin' motor home."

"What?" Maggie said. "You've seen the motor home before? Where? When?"

"Calm down, Missy. Unless I'm makin' a big mistake, that old bus a yours used to come through here a couple times a year. I figured youse borrowed it from the cowboy's little brother or somethin'. Y'all look enough alike to be brothers. He was younger and a little darker. I thought he was an Eye-talion from the old neighborhood the first time he come in, with that big smile and those gorgeous teeth, sweet as cherry pie. Where's he at anyway?"

"We don't know," Maggie answered. "We're looking for him. Can you help us?"

"No more than I just did. Couple times a year. Sometimes comin', sometimes goin'." At their collective blank looks she continued, pointing first up the road, then down. "From either direction. There ain't a lot a business here, I usually get to see which way my customers are comin' from." After a pause she added, "The Mission's that way about a mile," pointing up the road. "I guess that's where he was goin'. It's the only thing up there. So where's the dog? I'd always fix him a couple burgers."

The Soccorro Mission was a large, adobe structure surrounded by a litter of frame and shingle out buildings strewn about the feet of the imposing old castle, a smattering of battered vehicles scattered amongst them. As the motor home rumbled down the dirt drive and entered a clearing in front of the mission, people began to emerge from the shacks, first staring silently at the vehicle, then walking and finally running from all directions. Before the travelers could disembark, the double doors of the mission proper swung outward and three robed monks appeared, smiling and waving at the passengers. In another second the mission's bells began to gong and Doc wondered if they hadn't inadvertently arrived just at the start of some festival or an evening devotional ritual.

They were soon surrounded by fifty villagers of all ages, all grinning, the children shrieking and running about, the monks wending a path through the crowd as they attempted to reach the motor home. When Doc climbed down from the passenger's door, he was immediately embraced by a fat old friar who crushed him against his ample stomach, shouting, "Arturo, Arturo. We thought you had left us forever!"

"Look at me, sir," Doc said quietly to the old man. "Look at me," he repeated. "I'm not Arturo. But this is his wife and that is his son," gesturing toward Maggie and Junior emerging from the side door. George was enveloped by the crowd on the other side. The old priest squinted up at Doc for a long moment then looked over at Maggie and Junior, then surveyed the motor home again.

"No, I see now. But this is his, is it not?" he said indicating the vehicle. "And this is his family? Where is he then?"

"We don't know," Doc said. "We had hoped that you could tell us."

"Forgive Brother Maxwell, sir," another, younger monk said to Doc, placing his hand on Brother Maxwell's shoulder. "He is old and his memory plays tricks on him sometimes. Welcome to Mission Soccoro. What brings you to our home?"

"As I said, we seek information regarding Arturo. Can you help us?"

"I'm sorry, but we know nothing of this man," replied the younger monk, guiding the old man back to a third monk and gesturing for them to return to the mission.

"You know his name, you know his vehicle, you were delighted to think he had returned but you know nothing of this man. Why am I not convinced, Brother . . . ?"

"Brother Horatio," the monk replied.

"Brother Horatio. You are protecting your friend. That is admirable. But you are protecting him from the wrong people. Maggie, Junior, this is Brother Horatio, Arturo's friend. This is Arturo's wife and son. They would like to know what happened to him. That is why we are here."

"Please help us, Father," Maggie said. "My husband left us four years ago and I have no idea where he went, if he's dead or alive."

"I am sorry for your loss, my child." Then after a period of silence he asked them to follow him and they trooped through the crowd toward the mission. George remained behind, fielding a host of animated questions from the crowd that encircled him.

They were led through a stone and tile vestibule then down the center aisle of a vaulted sanctuary, cool and dark, then into an anti-chamber fitted out as a small office, ancient wooden desk surrounded by several rickety chairs of wood and hide. The monk asked them to sit then did so himself before folding his hands on the desk top and looking intently at his assembled guests.

"What is it that you think I may know?" he asked.

Maggie answered. "Anything you can tell us about my husband would be appreciated. There are so many blank spots, things we aren't sure about. Do you see?"

"I am afraid I do not," he replied.

"Look, Brother Horatio," Doc said. "You are either a lousy liar or a simpleton. I think it's the former. Do you need proof of identification? What could our motives possibly be if not what we told you?"

"Maybe we should show him the dog, Doc," Junior said. "People seem to remember Pop's dog."

"You have the dog?" Brother Horatio said. "Yes, of course you do. That is the only one of God's four legged creatures that has ever crossed the threshold of this old monastery, at least to my knowledge. He followed your father and I right up the front steps and down the aisle to the altar. He waited behind us while we performed the sacrament then came in here and sat down next to Arturo as if he was just as interested in what I was going to say. I never saw him until I was sitting here looking across at the two of them. I could only laugh, he was too well behaved to be angry with."

"You will help us then?" Maggie asked.

"I will try."

She told him about Arturo's many absences, their timing and duration, her fears and her suspicions, their preparation for the trip and their itinerary, ending with a question.

"Are you familiar with the Elixir?"

The monk looked away.

"I sense a reticence to respond, Brother Horatio," Maggie said. The monk finally returned his eyes to hers.

"You have brought up a topic of some . . . sensitivity, misses . . ?"

"De la Madre', Father. Margaret. Maggie, please. Was that a test?"

"No, Maggie it was not. Arturo never revealed his last name to us. He said it was not necessary and I had to agree. But I was curious."

"And the Elixir?" she asked.

"Yes, the Elixir. He gave us some. Several gallons. On his first visit. After we had talked for many hours."

"And he told you what?" Doc asked. "How were you directed to use it?"

"As a tonic. For the old or infirm he said. Sometimes for others who were ill. There were several . . . variables involved. It was somewhat discretionary, on my part, who would benefit."

"Thank you for talking with us, Brother Horatio," Maggie said. "I appreciate your help, I truly do. But there's more, isn't there? You are not being completely forthright."

After another lengthy pause Brother Horatio got to his feet and said, "Please come with me." He led them out a door in the back of the office and down a flight of stone stairs. They emerged at ground level, blinking into the setting sun, and he gestured across a vegetable garden toward an acre of small, blossoming fruit trees.

"Pears, Ma," Junior said.

"Where did you get the stock?" Maggie asked the monk.

"From Arturo. He gave us seedlings."

"He was teaching you to make your own Elixir," Doc said. When the monk did not respond, Doc continued. "How far did you get? Please Brother, this is very important."

"We have the still, a little one. And we got a small crop of fruit last year."

"And?" Doc said.

"We boiled it to syrup and put it up in barrels. That's all we can do. Arturo said he would show us the rest of the process when we got this far. But of course he has not come back."

"Did he tell you . . . no you all ready said you didn't," Doc said. "Did he give you anything? Anything that might have to be added in the next step?" Again the monk looked away from Doc. "The seminary must not be a very good place to learn to lie, Brother. You really are terrible at it."

"We're Franciscans, my son. You must be thinking of the Jesuits. I'm sure they are much more accomplished." Doc laughed but Maggie was not amused.

"And the additives?" Maggie pressed.

"Arturo said to collect the fruit of a local cactus and dry it which we have done. Much more than I think he would require but we had nothing else to contribute. And the Elixir has helped so many people. We hoped it would be a gesture of our gratitude."

"Peyote," Doc said, turning to Junior. "Do you think? Were you kidding?"

"I had my suspicions, yeah, Doc. But I didn't know for sure."

"I guess that explains jar number five," Doc said.

"When was Arturo here last, Brother Horatio?" Maggie asked.

"In the spring, four years ago. He came to see if the pear trees were growing. To make sure they were okay. He said he would be back in a week, that he would spend the night. He was such an excellent guest, very entertaining. So animated. And so knowledgeable. He helped us with many projects. The windmill–it came to us on a truck one day, in a huge box. We had no idea what to do with it. Then Arturo returned and in two days we had our own electrical power plant! Then we got computers, for the children. From Arturo we suspect but he would never say. And seeds and rootstock for the gardens. Our crops doubled. Where did he get these things?"

"We don't know, brother," Doc said. "But we hope to find out."

"What is the mission of your, ah, mission?" Maggie asked Brother Horatio. "I'm sorry, I don't know how else to ask, I know it sounds silly."

"Not at all, my child. The Soccoro Mission was founded by Spanish priests in the seventeenth century for all the usual reasons, convert the heathen Indians and enforce the power of Spain. The Franciscans received the charter about one hundred years ago. We work with the Hispanic and Indian peoples of limited economic where with all, which means about every non- Anglo in the area. We teach the children, tend the elderly and try to help all of them with job training, language skills and of course we tend to their spiritual needs."

"And Arturo tended to your special needs," Doc said. "Did he ask you to harvest the peyote in quantity?"

"You are looking for a quid pro quo where there isn't one. No, he did not. Unless there was something to be revealed later which I do not believe to be the case."

"Nor do I," Maggie said.

They promised to stop again on their return trip and tell the monk what they had learned of Arturo's fate. They found George sitting on a log, strumming a beat up guitar with a dozen villagers accompanying him on an assortment of instruments, hide drums, stringed sticks, even a wash tub base, all of them singing Mexican folk songs, two bottles of mescal circulating.

"Looks like we're campin' here, Ma," Junior said as he headed over to join his uncle.

"Home sweet home," Maggie said to Doc. "Want to help me whip up some trail grub, cowboy?"

"Maggie, tell me what you're thinking?"

"I'm thinking it *is* the Elixir, the motivation for everything. But where'd the money come from?"

"Sixty-four million dollar question," Doc said. "Certainly not from these folks. This was money out, not money in. And he was going to make them Elixir producers. Not something you would be in a hurry to do if you were selling a scarce commodity. You would never give up your monopoly."

"Maybe we'll learn more tomorrow."

Maggie and Doc were asleep in the bedroom compartment, fully clothed, Maggie's head resting in the hollow of Doc's arm, the dog entrenched on the bed's bottom half, when George and Junior crashed through the side door. Doc jerked awake instantly, his movement waking Maggie.

After they were all seated around the dinette, Maggie told George what they had discovered.

"So." George summarized when she was done. "It don't look like dope so much anymore. That's good. We know the whole mission thing is important so we've got some immediate goals, places to check out. You got jar number five pegged. That's pretty damn good progress for one day I'd say.

"And I picked up a few tidbits too," George continued. "Gossip mostly. They sure did love Arturo. And they were real excited seein' you, Mags. He must a talked you up some. They're kinda awestruck by Junior, almost a Christ thing. Son of Arturo! And they think Doc is Arturo's father, come down off the fiery mountain to avenge his son's death. Don't ask me how they come to these conclusions but nothin' I said made a damn bit a difference. They just sorta smiled at me like, yeah, we know you can't reveal the truth but that's okay cause we already know. There's some kinda superstitious preconceptions mixed in. I don't understand it but I wasn't gonna shake their beliefs, that's for sure."

"Part Indian myth, part Christianity," Doc said. "That's pretty common, mixing the old and the new. It allows them to cover all the bases so to speak, appease the priests and all the gods because who really knows which god will prevail if it comes down to a fight."

"Yeah but how did they get Pop mixed into it?" Junior asked.

"A prophet figure, I imagine," Doc said. "A mysterious stranger appears, bearing gifts, possessed of wisdom. That they would attempt to fold him into their religion makes perfect sense."

"Yeah, I guess you're right, Doc." Junior said. "Saint Arturo. Hell, I like that a lot better than gangster pop."

"I think we all do, Junior."

Chapter Sixteen

Junior pulled on the air horn several times as they sped past the Horizon City diner the next morning. They turned onto I-10, continued west through El Paso and crossed into New Mexico just as the sun cleared the horizon behind them.

"Where to, Ma?" Junior asked Maggie who was seated beside him.

"Take I-25 toward Albuquerque," she said. "We're going to the *town* of Soccoro. To another mission."

One hundred and fifty miles later they exited at the Soccoro sign and came to a stop at the bottom of the ramp. Junior pointed out the windshield.

"Look it, Ma. There it is right there."

The San Miguel Mission looked more like a cheap restaurant then an old Spanish Mission but the huge, gaudy billboard erected in the parking lot left little doubt that this was in fact their destination.

Junior parked in the back of the lot and they all gazed at the strings of snapping flags strung above the cluster of life size plaster

Indians and Conquistadors, robed priests, horses and donkeys that flanked the brightly painted entryway.

"I wonder who says mass in this joint," George said. "Liberace?"

"It doesn't look much like a cathedral does it?" Doc said.

"More like a whore house," Junior said. "You sure we ain't in Vegas, Ma?"

She laughed then suggested they at least check the place out. "How about walking the dog, Junior. A little more shit won't make any significant difference in this dump."

Doc and Maggie went inside while Junior, George and the dog wandered the grounds. The inside was scarcely different from the exterior in decorating style and resembled a south-west tourist trap more than a church. The conquistador theme was predominant throughout.

They walked up behind a chubby little man who was in the process of unlocking a door marked private, fighting to return a large ring of keys to his pants pocket through a slit in the side of his robe which was crudely embroidered across his shoulders with 'The Mission at San Miguel.'

"Excuse me, could we talk to you for a moment, sir?" Maggie asked.

"Just one moment, my dear," he responded, glancing over his shoulder at Maggie then scurrying into the office.

"High strung little guy," Doc said.

"Maybe he thinks we're going to rob him," she grinned.

"How may I assist you?" the little man chirped as he slid backwards through the door. His smile vanished as he turned and saw Doc and he made to step quickly away but he was already fast up against his closed office door.

"A moment please, that's all," Maggie said. "We didn't mean to startle you so."

"I, ah, I, um . . . you *did* startle me. Goodness! I think I, ah . . . I thought you were someone else," he said, glancing at Doc.

"Who might that be?" Doc asked.

"Oh! No one in particular. Just a face from the past. Never mind that old business." He began to edge away from Doc but Maggie blocked him, holding her position.

"Just a question or two, kind sir," she said.

"I'm very pressed for time this morning, young lady. Perhaps on another occasion. You could make an appointment with my, ah, with Fredda, at the checkout counter."

"We only need a minute," Doc said. "I'm sure you can accommodate the lady for that long."

"What then?" he snapped, again trying to slide away from Doc.

"Is this mission associated with the Church? Do people worship here?" Maggie asked.

"Ah, no. Not formally."

"Are you a priest?" Doc asked.

"I am . . . a spiritual advisor to many, of my people, my flock."

"I see," Doc said.

"How do you minister to your congregation? What services do you provide?" Maggie asked.

"I, ah, fail to see how this is any of your concern. Now if you will–"

"Is there another San Miguel around here?" Doc asked. "Another mission? Perhaps we're in the wrong place?"

"Yes! Yes of course you are," the man said. "Why just up the interstate and then east on highway sixty there are *three* missions that I'm sure you'll find most interesting. Very holy places, very old. Go up the access road, then–."

Maggie and Doc turned to see what had caused the man to stop speaking. Just inside the double doors stood three figures. The little man began to produce a keening sound then swiveled, turned the office knob and flung himself against the door but it was still locked and he bounced off with an audible grunt.

"Easy, Brother Rat," Doc said. "You're going to hurt yourself. It's alright. They're with us."

"Get away from me!" he shrieked. "Keep that dog away from me! I told him I wouldn't do it anymore and I haven't! I swear. Please. Leave me alone!"

"What haven't you done anymore?" Doc said.

"Sold the pear stuff! The brandy," he said as he cowered against the wall.

"You have five seconds to explain yourself," Doc said, "and then my hairy friend here is going to ask you a few questions."

"The other man, the one that looks like you, I told him I'd stop selling the brandy. I swore."

"Clarify," Doc said.

"I heard about the brandy he had, rumors, from some of the Indians. Big medicine, they said. So I made my own. It was just store bought stuff, cheap schnapps. I sold it in mason jars with my own label, under the counter, you know? I wasn't hurting anybody!"

"But you sure as hell weren't helping anybody either, were you," Doc said. "Except yourself. You sold to the Indians, didn't you. For how much?"

"Fifty. For a pint jar," he responded, head down.

"You piece of shit. So then you got a visit. Tell me about that."

"He came in one morning, just like you two. I said I didn't know what he was talking about. He told me to stop. I didn't. He came back, a couple months later, not nice this time. With that dog. He said stop or else. When he left I thought, maybe I should stop, maybe he meant it. Then I heard this horrible crashing sound. I ran outside. He had this big motor home and he had run over all my statues! And he was driving back and forth across them! They were destroyed, rubble.

"He got out of the thing and said 'Gee I'm sorry, my foot must have slipped off the brake.' He told me to give him the name of my insurance company, he'd take care of it. Then he said, 'This thing gets away from me all the time. It's a wonder I haven't run somebody over.' Then he winked and said he'd stop back in a month or so, see how I was doing. I stopped selling the schnapps but he hasn't been back."

"How long ago was this?" Maggie asked.

"About six years, maybe seven."

"Do you still hear rumors about pear brandy from your customers?" Doc asked.

"No! I don't want to hear anything about anything from anybody! I'm out of that business!"

Doc leaned toward the man. "I strongly suggest you stay out of it. Do you understand?" They all turned to leave but Maggie had to drag the growling dog most of the way to the door before he turned and walked out on his own.

"You two are some tough customers," Junior said with a grin as they walked across the parking lot. "That ole boy's liable to get out of the plastic Jesus business completely after this." When Junior glanced back at the building he saw that the open sign in the small front window had been flipped over and as they reached the motor home, the flashing neon billboard shut down. "I think y'all probably ruined his day."

"Good. What a loathsome creature," Maggie said.

"Fifty bucks a pop," Doc said. "From the poorest people. Preying on their fears. Arturo should have run *him* over. I'm tempted to do the statues again just as a reminder."

"Let's just get away from here, please," Maggie said. "It makes me feel dirty. Junior. Go north on 25 to Route 60 east. Let's move!"

"How'd we get on to that dump, Mags?" George asked her as they sped away.

"A post card. It's here somewhere," she said and began to rifle through her knapsack.

"Well," George said, "it's either a red herring or Arturo was makin' a joke. He sure as hell never did any business with that creep."

"I certainly hope not. Here it is." She handed the card to George.

He glanced at the front then read the handwritten inscription on the back aloud. "'The Mission at San Miguel. My spirits were much improved upon leaving here. I'll sure miss those statues!' Postmarked September. Almost six years ago. He must have been laughin' his ass off when he wrote this."

"An inside joke," Maggie said. "That bastard! He never said one word about it. God, he must have laughed all the way home. Squashing Cortez. How delightful."

"There's more," George said. "'When visiting this area, be sure to experience the wonderful mountain air.' What the hell does that mean? How do you experience air, other than breathin' it?"

"Wait a minute," she said flipping through one of her guidebooks then consulting the map. "Mountainair. It's a town. One word. It's also where the Salinas Pueblo Missions National Monument headquarters is located. There are three old mission sites in the vicinity of Mountainair. They've been combined into one National Monument. That's what our slimy friend was talking about. 'East on highway 60, three old missions.' Oh, yeah," she said to George. "You hadn't arrived yet. Doesn't matter. The town is what Arturo was referencing and that's our next stop."

The town of Mountainair was aptly named. The topography was ruggedly mountainous and the remoteness of its location kept the air crisp and clean. They had no trouble locating the headquarters building and as Junior was maneuvering to park, Maggie suggested that they keep a low profile.

"I'll go in," she said. "You guys stay here with the four-legged animal."

"Now Mags," George responded. "I ain't the one that's been threatenin' the local shopkeepers and if you recall, I didn't throw nobody out a no restaurants either so I think I'll join you here. Besides, I need to stretch myself a little. I'll be good, I promise."

There was only one park ranger on duty and she proved to be well informed and forthcoming, first giving them a thumbnail sketch of the area and the former inhabitants both Spanish and Native American and then asking if she could direct them toward any specific point of interest.

"Are there any active missions in the area?" Maggie asked. When the ranger said there were not, Maggie was at a loss.

"Anything like a mission?" George asked. "An order a monks or somethin'? People who work with the natives?"

"Nothing church sanctioned, to my knowledge," the ranger replied. "There is a sort of commune down toward Grand Quivira, South on 55. I guess you could say they 'work with the natives' although this isn't exactly a desert island or darkest Africa so our natives don't get real restless."

"Pardon my brother's politically correct deficiencies," Maggie said. "I think his euphemism is a result of his ignorance of who the local people might be, by ancestry I mean. We were at a mission in El Paso yesterday that worked with Hispanics and Native Americans and I think the lines are somewhat blurred in his little man brain."

"Jesus, Mags, you make me sound like a damn hillbilly," George said.

"I told you not to be such a redneck all the time. Now you can't help yourself." Turning back to the uniformed woman she continued. "You should see what he's done to my son. You would swear the boy was raised in a tar paper shack with no readin', writin' or rithmatic."

"I hate to break up this here ERA meeting," George said, "you two havin' such fun at my expense and all, but perhaps the ranger would be good enough to tell us some more about the kindly hippies who are so helpful to all our down trodden brothers. And sisters."

"I certainly will try," the ranger said. "First of all they aren't hippies like you probably mean, long hair and flowers. I believe the founders were former Vista workers who liked the area and the people and sort of stuck around after their year or two, I'm not sure which it is with Vista. There were five or six of them. This was way before I was transferred here. I was in Philadelphia for two years. At Independence Hall. That sucked. The historical part was okay but I'm an outdoors kind of girl.

"Anyway, somehow they leased a few hundred acres from the government, I don't know which branch but they are next to the Cibola National Forest so it could have been the Parks Bureau. They put up a bunch of back to nature looking buildings and started taking in indigent families, orphaned kids, people like that.

"There's a big group of them out there now. They grow their own food for the most part, run some cattle. They get some federal grants too and some state aid, I believe. They're a real nice bunch, real friendly. Always doing stuff for the community, Adopt a Highway, helping with fundraisers for the school, you know what I mean."

"Sounds like hippies to me," George said.

"You might be right," the ranger said. "But go see for yourselves. They'll be happy to talk to you."

They followed the ranger's directions south out of town on state road 55 then turned on a narrow, county road. They wound up and up through the heavily wooded terrain, finally turning onto an even narrower road marked by a small wooden sign with an arrow that said Soccoro– Mountainair Camp.

"What's Soccoro mean, Doc?" Junior asked. "Is it Spanish or Indian?"

"It's Spanish. It means succor, to aid or help, usually in terms of serious need as opposed to giving somebody a hand. It's more a rescue."

"Interesting, ain't it?"

"Yeah. I've been thinking the same thing."

After a quarter mile on the camp road, they came to a large clearing, an Alpine meadow, two-hundred yards or so in diameter, the circumference defined by a tree-line of mature aspens and pines. Inside the tree line, on the edge of the clearing, completely encircling the open area, were structures of all sizes and styles from rough lean to's to fully evolved log homes. Beyond the driveway was a larger log and stone building, a covered porch extending across the width of the cabin. By the time Junior brought the motor home to a stop, unsure of exactly where to park, three people were descending the steps off the porch and several more were staring at them from the railing.

The person in the lead, a gray bearded man in his early fifties, was smiling broadly. When he reached the driver's door, his smile was suddenly gone, replaced by an expression of wary neutrality. "I'm sorry," he said. "I thought you were someone else."

"No," Junior said. "We aren't him. Just his kin. And dog." They disembarked and the dog did a giddy dance, prancing around the man who had spoken to Junior, nuzzling him, demanding attention.

The man stared at them individually for several seconds and then said, "I sure did miss this damn dog. Where's Arturo?"

"It's a long story," Maggie said. "Where can we talk?"

He led them past the big cabin without introductions to the others gathered there and then up the steps to the adjacent house. He turned at the top of the steps and indicated a grouping of branch and twig chairs placed around a slab of sawn log balanced on a stump. As Doc reached the porch deck they exchanged a long look, Doc stopping as he searched the man's face, their expressions mirrors of each other's puzzlement.

"You look like him," the man said.

"I've been getting that a lot lately. You remind me of someone as well. Let me chew on it for a bit. It may come back. I'm Doc," he said and extended his hand.

"Al Tekniquco. I'm one of the charter members of this alternative society. A pleasure, Doc."

"The Technician!" Doc said. "That's it! You're the Technician!"

"Al Technico. Spanish for the technician. Yes, that is correct," he stated, looking away from Doc.

"You want to leave it at that, it's okay with me. Al. Maybe we can talk some more later."

"Yes. Thank you," Al said. "How about some introductions, Doc. You guys have caused quite a stir."

They exchanged names and handshakes and Doc explained the kinship to Arturo, then Maggie started the questioning.

The Soccorro Camp, Al explained, accepted anyone in need as long as they were willing to follow the rules and work with the others. Their funding was derived from a smattering of grants, state aid and charitable donations augmented by the sale of crafts and country furniture. They were self sufficient in food products. They operated a retail store in Mountainair and a medical clinic. The camp members were ethnically diverse and the medical clinic was free to those in need and the needy in the vicinity tended to be Hispanic and Native American. They operated a foster care program supervised by the state and typically had between ten and fifteen children on hand. The children went to public schools. They were currently building a small nursing home beside the clinic but it was slow going, mostly because of financial shortfalls. Arturo had been very interested in the nursing home, helping with the planning from both the architectural end and the administrative.

He knew the state and federal requirement for the building and directed them through the bureaucracy from the initial Certificate of Need to the application for permanent license. Unfortunately, they were three years behind schedule and Arturo was no longer around to help.

Doc asked how Arturo had found them.

"Arturo just drove up the access road one day in a beat up, Toyota Land Rover. Eighteen years ago? Seventeen maybe. I'd have to count back through benchmark events to be sure but we hadn't been here more than a year or two.

"I remember the day clearly enough though. We were working on the big cabin, trying to. It was our first permanent structure and none of us had any real experience with log homes. We had read the books of course and we were a cocky bunch. We had this tripod contraption with a chain hoist on it and that's how we were trying to raise the logs. It looked easy enough in the pictures but it wasn't very stable and when you'd swing the log to try to lay it up on the one below, half the time the tripod would shift and the log would slip off. It's lucky no one got killed.

"We had just lost a log down the backside, the tripod fell completely over, and it was hot too and we were all yelling at each other and cursing and I started to just walk away, till I calmed down, you know, and I look up and there's Arturo, sitting on the top of the seat of that Jeep thing and he's *laughing*! Really laughing his ass off. At us!

"He was just a kid, early twenties I guess and I got pissed. Who the hell does he think he is, laughing at us? So I stomped over there and I'm going to chew this bastard a new one. I got right up to the jeep, had my finger up ready to start shaking it at him, had my damn mouth open, ready to just give him hell!

"And he looks me right in the eye, still grinning like a lunatic and tells me we needed a different style of log hoist. The one we were using was only designed for dead lift, not lift and pivot. He whips out a tablet and a pencil and within about thirty seconds I knew he was right. Then he says he can help us build one.

"By that evening we were swinging logs faster than the saw guys could notch them and it was real clear that boy knew exactly what he was doing. We invited him for dinner and the rest is history."

"How often did he stop?" Maggie asked.

"He stayed almost a week that first time. Worked like a dog. And he asked a lot of questions too. What were our plans, who were we going to help, philosophical issues. He didn't seem to care about our financial problems or our spiritual bent. He was back again about six months later, stayed a few days. Then a couple times a year on average. Some years only once. He never spent more than a night or two after that second visit."

"Did you do any business with Arturo," Doc asked.

"Business like what?"

"Did he sell you anything? Did you barter for . . . I don't know, goods and services?"

When the other man shook his head, Doc tried a different tract.

"Did he give you anything?"

"Well, he always had that excellent pear brandy with him and he'd always leave us a few gallons. And he was always very helpful with technical advice. Especially with the nursing home. The last couple years, before he stopped . . . stopping. Are y'all going to tell me what's going on here? I think I've answered all your questions, do I get to ask a few?"

"Maggie?" Doc said.

"Yes, of course, Al," she replied. "And I really appreciate your help. It sounds as if Arturo was very fond of you and admired what you were trying to accomplish. I'm glad he could be of help to you."

"But you're disappointed somehow. What were you expecting to find?"

"Let me jump in here a second, Ma. Did Pop, Arturo, ever give you any plants or seeds, ask you to grow stuff?"

"Oh, yeah, sure. He seemed to take a lot of interest in our gardens. He brought us seeds and cuttings all the time. He said you had the green thumb, Maggie, that you were the source. My wife, he would say, is amazing."

"How about orchards, Al," Junior asked. "You grow any fruit?"

"We tried. We planted apples, cherries and Arturo's pear trees. The trees do okay but the weather is so unpredictable that most years a late frost gets the buds. They rarely produce much fruit."

Maggie and Doc exchanged a look as Junior sank back in his chair.

"A failed experiment," George said.

"Sounds like it to me, Unc."

"Would you folks like to bring me up to speed on this?" Al asked. "I'm really curious now."

"How about I take this one, Mags," George said.

"Think of Arturo as a philanthropist slash Johnny Appleseed. He had a little money and he liked to help people. And he had this pear thing, thought they had all kinds a health promotin' properties. So he spent about half his time drivin' all over the south west, buildin' things for folks he thought were worthy, helpin' 'em to improve their food production. And plantin' pear orchards. Sounds like they didn't take real well here but he liked y'all enough to keep comin' back anyway. You see what I'm sayin'?"

"Yes, I believe I do," Al said. "The pears, the nursery stock he brought, little trees, they were handled very reverently. He personally picked the place to plant them, took the whole thing very seriously. And the brandy. There was a, oh, almost religious aspect to that as well. It wasn't like knocking back shots of tequila, you know."

"Ritualized," Doc said.

"Yes, exactly. Let me get Doctor Barker over here. He and Arturo were close and the brandy was mostly given to him directly."

Al walked across the porch till he was closest to the big cabin and hollered for someone to ask the doctor to join them. Several minutes later a big lumberjack of a man climbed up on the porch and Al made the introductions.

"Paul, what did Arturo tell you about that brandy he always brought?"

"The Elixir? Potent stuff. 'Use it sparingly.' That was the main thing. We kept it for the elderly mostly, terminal patients. It seems to block pain signals going to the brain, that's my guess anyway. I treat depression with it and it works really well on chronic fatigue syndrome. It's an amazing tonic. Why do you ask?"

"We're curious about its, ah, health benefits," Doc said, "and how Arturo directed people to use it. We seem to be getting similar responses from everyone. So in your opinion, it does have some medicinal properties?"

"Without a doubt. I don't know how it works but it most definitely does."

"Did you ever try to analyze it," Doc asked. "Check its chemical composition?"

"No. Arturo requested, adamantly I might add, that we keep the Elixir … to ourselves. And I had no desire to kill the golden goose, so to speak. It works and he kept me supplied. I was not interested in upsetting that balance. And Arturo was such a . . . benefit to us. Such an excellent friend. I did not want to cross him. But I'm almost out, down to seeds and stems. It only goes to the most needy now."

"We can help there, Doctor," Maggie said. "At least for the short run. We brought a little along."

The doctor smiled hugely and said, "That would be most appreciated," then added, "Arturo said that when the nursing home was completed he would need to get us a better source of supply. I remember the conversation distinctly but I don't think he knew exactly how he was going to do that. Do you know what he meant?"

"No," she replied. "But we're trying to find out."

Al told them they were staying for dinner and spending the night and showed Junior the camp site that had been cleared years before specifically for the motor home. After George and Junior had gone off to settle them in, Al asked Maggie if she would like to explore their village. When she said yes, she'd be delighted, he turned and addressed the dog. "Your old girlfriend still lives over there, buddy," he said pointing across the meadow. "Take Maggie over and introduce them to each other. Go on!"

The dog jumped up and let out a whoop then leaped off the porch and began to caper on the grass, barking up at them.

"I guess I'm being paged," Maggie said. "This ought to be interesting. Are you going to join me, Doc?"

"This looks like a mother-son thing to me Maggie," he grinned. "I'll catch up to you in a bit."

She hopped down the steps, kicked off her shoes and took off at a run after the dog, her hair sailing out behind, long skirt flapping and the sound of her musical laughter echoing across the valley.

"What a marvelous woman," Al said watching her sprint through the wildflowers, gamboling playfully with the dog.

"Yeah, she sure is that," Doc said.

"How long have you two been together?" Al said. "Not that it's any part of my damn business."

"We're not. Not like you mean."

"But you'd like to be," Al said.

"Yeah, I would. What's your point, Al?"

"They're big shoes, Doc. He isn't going to be easy to forget."

"I don't need her to forget him. I don't want her to. I just want to be part of her life. Even if we don't get any closer than we are now."

"You are *not* going to be content to sit on the sidelines of her life, watch her with another man, say. Friendship be damned."

"I hear you. And I know you're right but I have no choice at the moment."

"Ah, love. Ain't it grand."

"Not so far. But. You didn't arrange for us to be alone so we could discuss my unrequited love life, Mr. Technician. Have you placed me yet?"

"Not to the exact op, but that probably doesn't make a lot a difference, does it?"

"No. They were all pretty much the same in the long run. It was in early '67. You were attached to my team for a cross-border drop in Laos. The target was a hardened bunker that supposedly was the province HQ. Intel had a big senior officer pow-wow taking place there. Sort of R and R with some 'kill the Yankees' seminars thrown in. The information allegedly came from a top-shelf French call girl who was going to be there. Along with a couple dozen of her closest friends."

"I remember the initial briefing vaguely. It never happened."

"They tried to do it with B-52's. Sent in a three man team of Air Force Black Berets to spot. I have no idea how it came off. But I remember you. My CO told me I was getting 'the Technician' as a demolitions 'consultant.' I was honored. You were supposed to be the best. That afternoon they scrubbed the mission. We hung around my hooch all night getting shit faced on warm Bud and Jack Daniels. You remember?"

"Oh, hell yes! That was you? The captain with the thousand-yard stare and the nastiest bunch of fucking outlaws I ever saw. Anywhere. And I went on a lot of ops. With some very nasty boys.

But your team, they were the scariest, real stone killers. Any of them make it?"

"Three negatives. Our last mission together. One MIA later, one possible. I never heard otherwise."

"And you."

"Yep. And me," Doc said. "I, ah, I take it your history is not common knowledge."

"No. I don't lie about it but I don't exactly brag either," Al said.

"You're concerned that your present mission statement doesn't collate so well with blowing the living shit out of our little yellow brothers?"

"That's close enough."

"It's okay with me, Al." After a couple of minutes Doc said, "You want to show me this place or is it all right to just wander around."

"Go," he said with a grin. "Find Maggie. Take a walk in the woods. Hold her hand. You never know, this is a very romantic place."

Doc found her lying in the tall grass at the edge of someone's garden being overrun like Gulliver by a herd of miniature bear hounds.

"Doc! Look at the puppies!" she said, adolescent hounds climbing on her, gumming on her clothing, hands and feet.

He sat down beside her, the big dog rolling in the grass then jumping to his feet and cavorting around her and the puppies, the mother off to the side. Doc rolled over on his side and they lay facing each other. He put his hand out and brushed a strand of hair off her cheek, then met her eyes, as green and luminous as the spring grasses surrounding them.

"I want you," he said. "But my whole existence tells me that it can't happen."

"Doc, you beautiful man," she whispered, laying her palm on his cheek. "You are so full of shit."

"What?" he said. "I tell you I'm falling hopelessly in love with you and you tell me I'm full of shit? You're a hard woman, Margaret Marone."

"I'm a bitch! Mean as a hellcat. But only when someone is trying to spoon feed me crap from a can. And that's exactly what you're doing–serving crap. Doc, I know you're infatuated with me," holding her hand up when he started to protest. "Okay. You love me. And just so you know, I love you too. But don't tell me you'll never find love, you aren't deserving of it, that you wasted fifty years of your life. That's crap."

"The whole 'I am a rock' thing starting to disintegrate around me. Is that what you mean?"

"Precisely. Your island had a seven point eight earthquake and it knocked you down, shook the foundation. Hard."

"Yeah, well, in your metaphor I'll be living in a grass shack on the beach now, looking for air-sea rescue to come get me out a there."

"It's time, Doc. You have to get out of there."

"I'm afraid," he said. "And don't interrupt, I know what you're going to say. 'Better to have loved and lost' blah, blah. That *is* what I mean but it's so much more intense when it's not hypothetical, when it actually hits you in the face, like a rifle butt. It fucking hurts, Maggie! I'd almost rather take another round. At least you know if it didn't kill you outright, if you made it on the slick, they'd probably save your ass. You'd heal eventually."

"So let me make sure I understand. Loving me is like a bullet, in the groin perhaps. It hurts like hell but eventually some medic will stitch your dick back on and everything will be okay. How romantic!" He was laughing but she only smiled slightly.

"Doc, you are missing the entire point. Falling in love can be traumatic sure. But *being* in love, that's the brass ring, baby, the jelly in the donut. Life is so fine anyway, but alive and in love? Doc, you just have to let it happen. Let yourself be happy for once. You deserve it, you've earned it. It's okay."

"Even if it only lasts a week or a month?"

"Even if it only lasts a day." Doc reached for her with both hands and hoisted her up and on to his chest then eased her down until their lips met.

By the time they walked hand in hand back across the field, the sun was well down behind the crown of trees atop the rim of the valley and the temperature was beginning to drop. They could hear music playing by the halfway point and they recognized George and Junior singing a country song, accompanied by an orchestra of assorted instruments.

Al and two other men were tending a slab of meat spitted over a fire pit as big as a pool table, alternately slathering on sauce and giving the meat a quarter turn. As they entered the circle of light cast by the campfire, they were met by Al's genial greeting.

"Yo, Doc! Looks like you took my advice. It must be the mountain air."

Doc just grinned and after a few seconds they walked on toward the big cabin and the festivities taking place on the steps and porch.

"What was that all about?" Maggie asked.

"Al and I met once before, in Nam. He was a demolitions expert, the best they say. We were talking and your name came up. Quite a coincidence, isn't it?"

"That you know Al or that my name came up during your boy talk?"

"Both, of course."

"Un hunh. I guess I should be flattered, the object of so much manly conversation. Are you going to elaborate?"

"Nope." When she stared at him, frowning, he continued. "Okay. He said you were a magnificent woman. I said I knew that.

He said you love her, I said yes. He said I should . . . what did he say? He said I guess, if I love you, I should tell you and, um, hope it works out? Something like that. Don't be afraid may have been the simplification."

"Wise man, that Al."

"Yep. He's a real blast. Ha! I made a joke."

"You think?"

"Maybe not."

The song ended and all fifty plus souls broke into hollering applause and as it died down, Maggie called out 'Rose of San Antone,' George, which led to some murmured conversation between the front man and the band. They began to play, Junior's voice carrying the melody of the ballad and Maggie said to Doc, 'Dance with me, cowboy' and he took her in his arms and they danced in the flickering light.

As the song ended Junior leaned down to his seated uncle and whispered something to him. George looked up in time to see Maggie's smile as she finished her spin and leapt into Doc's arms.

"How'd you feel about sleepin' under the stars tonight, boy?" George asked his nephew.

"Sounds like a plan, Unc," Junior replied, watching Doc carry Maggie up the steps toward them.

Chapter Seventeen

When the aluminum side door of the motor home clanked open the next morning and George and Junior climbed in, arms loaded down with sleeping bags and shelter halves, Doc was standing in the galley in a pair of ratty U. of G. Macon gym shorts trying to assemble a pot of coffee.

"Mornin', Doc," George said cheerfully, trying to squeeze by in the narrow corridor. "Jesus, Doc. You really are beat up some," he said, stopping to inspect Doc's back. "Junior said you had some bodacious battle scars but I didn't realize how intense they were. There's even a few fresh ones here," he said poking Doc lightly on the shoulder blade.

"War is hell," Doc said.

"Yeah and life's a beach," Junior added. "Y'all want a spread out a little so I can stow this gear? The coffee's up there Doc and the water's down yonder. Ma still sleepin'?"

"Not since you two yahoos got back," she answered, coming out of the bedroom compartment wearing a silk robe cinched tight at the waist and decorated with gold and emerald dragons coiling around themselves from hem to hood.

"Whoa, Ma! Where'd you get that robe?" Junior asked.

"What, this old thing?" she said, spinning around. "Beautiful, isn't it. It's Doc's."

"I thought Doc might need it on our trip," George said, "so I included it when I pack up his stuff for the adventure."

"I think I'll get dressed," Doc said moving toward the back.

"Ol' Doc's blushin' like a school boy, Mags. What do you think's got him so uptight?" George said as Doc closed the bedroom door.

At Al's request, they met for breakfast at the main lodge.

"Where's the next stop on your journey, Maggie?" Al asked as they lingered on the porch after eating.

"We're going to look at a couple more missions then probably head down to Mexico. The itinerary is fairly fluid, depending on what we find."

"Al, something's been gnawing at me," Junior said. "Your pear trees don't produce much, correct? But you get some fruit, occasionally?"

"Yes we do. Almost every year there are at least a few pears that mature. They're wonderful. Why?"

"What do you do with the seeds?"

"We save them, of course." He looked at their expression, then continued. "I assumed you knew, from other friends of Arturo. He was very specific. Save the seeds. All the seeds. We have, oh, maybe a quart jar of them. Why?"

"You might have a cold weather pear there, Al," George said. "That's what you're thinkin' ain't it, boy?"

"Yep. The strong ones survive the frost. You might want a try plantin' some of them, Al. You want, I can give you some tips before we go."

They reversed their arrival route back to Mountainair and then followed Maggie's directions.

"We takin' the scenic route, Ma?" Junior asked, looking over at his mother who was brushing out her hair, still wearing the kimono.

"Are we in a hurry?"

"Nope, I guess not."

"Then enjoy the ride. When you get to Interstate 90, go toward Santa Fe then 285 North. We're going to Chimayo."

They cruised through Santa Fe, enjoying what they could see of it from their cramped quarters, and admiring the mountains visible to the north and east. They wound through a beautiful narrow valley before beginning an ascent into the highlands they had seen from Santa Fe, the road lined with a bounty of fruit trees in the lower elevations, orchard after orchard awash in white and pink blossoms.

The high country was dominated by red rock cliffs and gorges accented by gnarly pinion and cedars and the view from the pinnacle of the mountain was so spectacular that Junior parked the motor home on the narrow shoulder so they could gawk at the snow covered mountains shimmering in the distance, the next valley spread out below them.

The town of Chimayo was tucked into the sides of the valley, clutching at the rocky foot of the mountain, an impossibly quaint little community of adobe and stone houses and shops.

Just to the east of the town, Maggie explained, was the Santuario de Chimayo and a few hundred feet beyond that, the chapel of Santo Nino de Atocha. When Junior found a large enough spot to park their vehicle, Maggie gave them a brief history lesson starting with an admonition.

"I want you rowdy men folk to understand something," she began, looking at George first, then Junior. This is a very sacred place and I expect you both to show it the respect it deserves. Understand?

"There are two churches here, both famous for their well documented abilities to heal. Miracles have been taking place here for hundreds of years and Arturo was fascinated by the stories. I have two different post cards about each of them, from two different visits, and a long letter. For Arturo it's long, more than one page. He talks about the history of course, the glowing earth and buried cross at the Sanctuary and the boy saint that the chapel is named for. I assume you all read this stuff?" They all nodded and she continued. "Then you are aware that the earth itself here is where the alleged healing power comes from. The dirt beneath the churches. Which you are allowed a sample of. Anyone see where I'm going here?"

"Jar number six," George said.

"Yes, that's about it. Is this stuff in jar number six? Speaking of which, should we call Doctor X while we're here, Doc?"

"Yes, I think we should. Y'all want to go ahead, I'll find a phone."

The Santuario de Chimayo was a humble church, a small adobe building with a modest parapet and short bell tower with a plain white cross above it. But the alter inside was outrageously carved and wildly colorful.

There were a dozen worshipers inside but no sign of a priest or guide. They admired the eccentric display for a few minutes then George began to walk around the perimeter seeking an office. There were several closed doors and one which was open to a small ante-room.

"Maggie," he whispered. "Come here." The ante-room was decorated, overwhelmed, by hundreds upon hundreds of canes and crutches, pictures, drawings and letters stacked, pinned and pasted on every available surface.

"Doc should see this," Maggie whispered. A minute later, Doc joined them.

"I couldn't find a phone. Y'all find the head man?"

"Do you see this?" Maggie asked, gesturing into the room.

"Yeah. It's the pozito room, where the dirt can be handled. Oh, you mean all the tokens? It's customary to leave a symbol of one's past affliction, a thank you note, something to memorialize the event or experience. Why?"

"There's so many!" Maggie said.

"Well, think of the time frame," Doc said. "It was almost three hundred years ago, the first miracle. That's a lot of time for a lot of disciples to come calling. This place is the Lourdes of the Southwest. It's famous. Why are you staring at me? I did my homework," he said.

They entered the room finally and Doc sat on his haunches beside a small hole in the floor, reaching in and down almost to his shoulder, coming up with a small pile of reddish dirt and holding it out for them to inspect.

"Looks about right, don't it," Junior said.

"Sure does," Doc said, sniffing and even repeating his taste test from the gunroom, this time not spitting out the few grains he had placed on his tongue.

"It is customary to touch the sacred soil, not to eat it," an authoritative voice from behind them said. "I am Father Truchas. What affliction has brought you to this holy place?"

Doc studied the rigid figure, seeing no hint of mirth in his face and nothing but disapproval in the downward cant of his lips.

"We seek only information, Father," Doc said, carefully dusting his palm back into the hole. "And we are prepared to reward those who provide it."

"The church is always in need of contributions, my son. That is how we are able to help so many. But perhaps the police might be better able to provide you with information."

"A friend of ours passed this way several times," Doc said, ignoring the thinly veiled threat. "He would have wanted to speak to a priest. Have you been here long, Father?"

"The church sends its servants where they will be most useful. I serve here until called to my next mission."

"Do you know Arturo de la Madre', from your service at this facility?" Doc asked.

"No."

"You're certain? Mid thirties, dark-hair and eyes, handsome, well spoken. He may have been traveling in a motor home with a large dog."

"No. I am certain."

"Father," Maggie said, but Doc cut her off with a gesture.

"Do you mind if we walk around, observe your staff in the Lord's work?" Doc asked.

"The public areas are well marked. Nothing else is available to you."

"I see," Doc said. "And the other mission, the Chapel of Santo Nino, it is also part of your parish?"

"They are one and the same. Now if you will excuse me, I have God's work to do. Allow me to show you the way out." There was no doubt that the interview had ended.

As they marched up the side aisle, Junior spoke over his shoulder to the priest.

"Hey, Father. Do you have a brother that runs the mission down in San Miguel?" When the man did not respond Junior continued. "There's a guy down there that reminds me a whole lot a you."

"What a fuckin' shit heel," Junior said as they walked toward the motor home. "That asshole couldn't be more uptight with a mesquite log stuck in his butt."

"I ain't sure you handled that boy just right, Doc," George said. "I don't think he liked the whole reward idea."

"That man hasn't liked anything in a long time," Maggie said. "I think Doc's approach was all right, there's just no way to get through to someone like that. But there's more than one way to pull the beard of a billy goat."

Doc suggested they split up and look around the grounds. "That pompous prick can't watch all of us at the same time, even with that extra eye in the center of his forehead," he said. George and Junior went off to Santo Nino while Maggie and Doc went into the shops that were an adjunct to the Santuario.

The first shop was staffed by a pretty girl in her late teens, black hair neatly braided into a long rope that hung nearly to her waist. Maggie complimented her on it and they were soon engaged in conversation. Doc wandered the shop, a tasteful and understated assortment of religious nick-knacks and mementos commemorating the miraculous events of the two churches. When he returned to the counter, the girl was whispering in Maggie's ear and he immediately veered away, then exited the shop. Maggie came out a few minutes later, smiling broadly.

"You're going to love this," she said. "I got the dirt on laughing boy," cocking her head toward the church. "No wonder he's so bitter. The Cardinal from the Albuquerque archdiocese banished 'the Fish' to this backwater for allegedly getting a little too touchy feely with an altar boy."

"The Fish?"

"Yeah. Father Trout. Truchas is Spanish for trout. I thought you spoke the language."

"I speak some Spanish but I'm not exactly a bilingual biologist. 'The Fish', hunh. Sounds like your new friend was more forthcoming than the Father."

"Oh yeah. She hates the bastard. They all do, the other staff members. Even most of the other priests from what she said. The Fish thought he was going to be the next Bishop of Santa Fe. Took the fall from grace real hard."

"Too bad for him. Did she say how long he'd been here?"

"Only a year or so, so he can't help us anyway. But I know who can," she added.

"I had no doubt. What's the plan?"

Maggie and Doc were sitting on the grass on the shady side of the motor home when George and Junior returned and stretched out beside them.

"You're going to love what we found out," George said. "It seems the esteemed Father Truchas is a legend in his own mind. Nobody likes the son of a bitch and he ain't been around long enough to know nothin' anyway so we just have to stay out of his way."

"No news so far," Maggie said. "We got all that."

"I ain't done yet. They got another priest here, he's sorta retired. He's been around since like 1812, knows everything about everything. That's who we need to see."

"Father Francis. Yeah, I know. What else?"

"God damn it! Junior, we could a sat in the damn shade all day drinkin' beer all the good our expedition done. Alright. So where do we go to see Father Francis?"

"The parish house is down that lane over there about a quarter mile," she replied.

"Yeah, but where is he in the house? You can't go drive down there and knock on the door askin' for him can you?"

"I don't know," she said. "Where is he in the house?"

"Ha! Second floor rear. His bedroom looks out over–get this–the orchards! Pear orchards no less. See, it pays to make nice with the janitor. They know all the dirt. No pun intended."

"Do you have a battle plan, George?" Doc asked.

"Nah. We figured that's your department. But we did find out when Truchas ain't around, from Bob, that's the maintenance engineer that was so helpful. The Trout does an evenin' mass on Tuesdays. Tonight."

At Doc's suggestion they got the motor home out of sight of the churches. George drove it into the parking lot of the Hootin' Holler, which, he assured them, per Bob was the best country western bar in the area.

"Damn," George exclaimed. "It ain't open yet."

"George, it's three o'clock in the afternoon," Maggie said. "Of course it isn't open yet."

"Yeah, well. I was hopin' they served dinner before the music started. I should have asked ol' Bob where to eat instead of where the music was at."

They gathered around the little dinette to discuss their approach to Father Francis.

"I don't think we can just walk up there," Doc said. "But I do think we can approach the parish house from the rear, use the orchards for cover. I think I go in alone and you all stay here. I even think this bar can work for us. We go in when it opens, before the crowds, so the staff remembers us. Then if anything unexpected happens, we at least have something of an alibi."

"You oughta love that 'un, Unc. You get to be the designated drinker."

"Beats the shit out a crawling through some field. I like it," George said.

"I like it too," Maggie said, "but I'm going with you, Doc and here's why before you start all that macho stuff. I like the bar part. That's good. At some point you and I can walk out together, holding hands maybe, like we're going outside to, you know. Then we can slip away on one of the bikes, come up behind the parish."

"That was essentially my thought," Doc said. "But I suggest we park the bike somewhere a little ways from here for the noise. And you can stay here in the motor home."

"I'm not finished. With me along we can simply stroll through the orchard, lovers out for a walk, if anyone stops us."

"Helpful but not critical. It would just save me some crawling."

"Lastly and most important, if you climb through the window of Father Francis' room, he's liable to either stab you with a crucifix or drop dead from the shock."

"All right, all right. Maggie and I go. We're probably making this more complicated than it needs to be anyway. We could probably all walk up to the front door as soon as Father Trout swims away."

At seven o'clock they went into the bar, nursed bottled beer and watched the band set up.

"I had a thought," Doc said. "Do you think you could convince the band to let you sing a couple songs, George?"

"A diversion?" George asked. "I sure can give it a whirl."

"Take Junior," Maggie added. "Everyone will remember."

George ordered another round from the buxom redhead who was waiting on their table then walked over to the stage and began speaking to a cowboy clad musician.

The cowboy stuck out his hand to George and gave him an assist onto the band stand then stepped up to the lead microphone, flicked it on and gave it an experimental tap.

"Ladies and Gentlemen. Welcome to the Hootin' Holler. We're Hell Fire and we're gonna be playin' for y'all in a little bit but as an added bonus, live from Llano County, Texas, I'm proud to present…." After a whispered word to George, he continued. "George and Junior! Let's give 'em a big hand, folks."

George was handed an electric guitar. He spoke a few words to Junior who stepped up to the mike beside his uncle and without a word of introduction they sang 'Whiskey River', George the opening verse and Junior soaring with the chorus, his clear tenor hitting each note perfectly. The band's bass man joined in before George was off the first phrase and the drummer was in on the second, two more guitars and the harmonica player there for the last verse. The band's front man stood on the side shaking his head, grinning like a schoolboy.

As George played the last chord, the house erupted in applause. The front man took the mike and shushed them and said, "There ain't no reason for me to sing tonight, I sure can't top that." He pulled George back a bit and began an animated conversation.

"He wants them to join the band," Maggie said. "I've seen it a dozen times."

"They sound pretty damn good together. They could do worse," Doc replied.

"Honestly? Those two could make a third grade string quartet sound like the Philharmonic. They should at least cut a couple tapes, for posterity."

As George, Junior and the front man approached the mike, Doc said, "We should go, during this song."

"At the end," she replied, "while everyone is clapping."

Chapter Eighteen

Doc and Maggie walked out unnoticed. They climbed in opposite sides of the motor home's driver's compartment then, after a minute, out the side door away from the restaurant.

The smallest dirt bike was chained to a lamppost a hundred yards up the street. Doc unlocked it, wrapped the chain around the handlebars and kicked the bike to life. Maggie climbed on and they puttered off. A gravel access road led past the back of the mission property. A field of pear trees in full bloom occupied the one hundred yards between the road and the rear of the parish house.

Doc coasted to a stop and they laid the bike over in a drainage ditch. A wire fence defined the property line but the nearest house was barely visible a third of a mile farther up the road. They hopped the fence and then walked hand in hand under the canopy of blossoms toward the house. As they came to the edge of the orchard, they looked over the back of the building. The rear porch was unoccupied and the second floor windows were unlit.

"We could just knock on the door and ask to see him," Maggie said.

"But if they say no what do we do? Let's eliminate the middleman and go right for the window. From what George's buddy said, the man is basically under house arrest, so there has to be a warden, even when the Fish is away."

There was enough cover, flowering shrubs, small ornamentals and mulched beds of flowers, to make an undetected march from orchard to rear wall a good possibility. Maggie followed Doc as he glided silently from bush to shrub to tree to house.

"Up on the porch roof," he whispered, cradling his hands and hoisting her up over his head. He took the porch post in both hands and climbed up after her. They crawled across the roof to the side of the closest window then popped their heads around the edge of the sash. The room was empty. They repeated their maneuver at the second window with the same result. The third window was casting a faint illumination onto the roof and Doc held his palm up for Maggie to stay, then crawled over and peeked in. He pulled back quickly but as Maggie crawled up beside him, the lower sash slid up and a white haired head leaned out and stared at them.

"Father Francis, I assume," Maggie said. "A pleasure to meet you."

"The pleasure is decidedly all mine, my child," the man replied. "And who is your rugged friend?"

"This is Doc, Father. And I'm Maggie."

"Would you two like to come in and perhaps explain yourselves?"

"That is exactly why we're here, Father," Maggie said as Doc helped her to her feet.

"This could be the most entertainment I've had since the Fish arrived," the old man said. "But we're not going to talk about my troubles."

"Actually, we may have some of the same troubles," Maggie said.

"How is that, child?"

"We're here at your beautiful sanctuary hoping to find out what happened to my husband. I think you knew him. Arturo?"

"You're Margaret? The incredible Maggie? Oh, child, you are every bit as beautiful as he said you were. I'm so sorry for your loss. I loved that boy like my own son. Why, he would talk and talk to me about you and Junior."

"Father? Father Francis? What loss? Is Arturo dead, do you know for sure?" she asked, clutching his fingers in both her hands.

"Why yes, my dear. Didn't you get my note, in the big box?"

Maggie looked from the priest to Doc, her eyes wild, her questions starting to spill out. Doc shushed her, put his arms around her shoulders and pulled a chair up behind her so she could still be in touching range of the old man.

"Sit down, Maggie," Doc said. "Father Francis, I think we have an awful lot to talk about."

"Son, I'm locked in here. I have all the time the good Lord leaves me."

"You're a prisoner in your own house?" Doc asked. "Why?"

"Father Truchas doesn't like the way I do things. Did things. He's in control now."

"But that's not legal," Maggie said. "He can't just lock you up. How does he get away with it?"

"He fired my staff, brought his own people with him from Santa Fe. I'm an old man. I can't fight them. I can't jump off the roof. Well, I could but I don't think it would turn out so well. I can't call out. I'm stuck."

"Father Francis," Doc asked, "if we can get you out of here, can you tell us what happened to Arturo? And can you expose this bastard Truchas, go to the bishop or something?"

"Oh, I should think so. Father Truchas is no longer respected by his holiness the Cardinal. He did something heinous, I'm afraid."

"Played grab-ass with an altar boy, we heard," Doc said grimly. "I'm surprised they didn't send him to jail."

"The church believes in forgiveness, my son. And second chances. If Father Truchas had repented his sins and returned to God's merciful embrace, I'm sure he could have been a powerful servant of the Lord."

"You mean he hasn't?" Maggie said.

"I'm afraid not. Not from what I saw. That is why I got locked away. What I saw."

"Which was?" Doc said.

"Which was a mortal sin best left unspoken."

"Father? We can help you," Doc said.

"He is still doing it," the priest said after a long pause. "Molesting the children. Can you help me get away from here?"

They stayed with the priest for an hour, slipping out the window at the sound of heavy footsteps on the stairs, retreating in the dark through the orchard, pushing the dirt bike for several hundred feet before starting it and returned to the motor home. Doc and Maggie entered the bar near the end of the last set and George and Junior soon joined them. They quickly reviewed their conversation with the priest, leaving out the confirmation of Arturo's death.

"Y'all work up a plan to spring the old guy?" George asked.

"Not yet," Maggie said. "Some ideas. Can we get out of here now? There's a lot of things to talk about."

"I, ah, kinda have a date, Ma," Junior said. "Is it okay if I catch up with y'all a little later?"

Maggie stared at her son without expression for a few seconds, then said yes, it was okay.

"All right!" Junior said with a grin to George. "I'll check y'all later."

"Be careful!" his mother shouted at his back as he strode away. He acknowledged her with a backwards wave. They watched him approach their waitress who slipped an arm around his waist and spoke a few words in his ear, grinning over at their table and winking as she finished.

"Don't say one word, George," Maggie said, catching him with his mouth open. "Father Francis says Arturo is dead. He sent the note, in the box. There's a whole lot more but we'll wait for Junior. He should hear it first."

"Mags, I'm sorry. We didn't know. I'll go get him," he said, starting to get up.

"No. Let him have some fun. This is his big adventure too. And we knew Arturo was dead so another day to hear it confirmed won't change or hurt anything."

"Well, tell me about the priest at least," George said.

"When we get out of here."

"Are we all right to stay parked here?" Doc asked George.

"Christ, yes. The owner practically begged us. He wants to book all of us indefinitely. Offered to provide hook ups, deliver meals, anything. He even said he'd put us up in a fancy bed and breakfast up on the hillside, a spa joint, if we'd stay. He wants to put a big banner on the motor home, advertisin' us. Said it wouldn't violate the zonin' code. Apparently they're real touchy about tacky signs around here. But you can park a tacky motor home as long as you want."

"I doubt if Junior would object too much," Doc said.

"Depends on how it goes, I expect," George grinned.

Maggie drummed her fingers on the table top, looking from one to the other.

"Do you want to hear about the priest or not?" she said. When George said yes, she told him what they had learned.

Father Francis had been at the Santuario for twenty years. It was his life and he strenuously resisted all attempts to move him to other parishes. When he turned seventy, his bishop warned him that the archdiocese would be forced to retire him soon. They negotiated a compromise. Father Francis could stay on, essentially retire in place, if he would immediately, and graciously, accept a little help. It would create a smooth transition for the church and, unbeknownst to the old priest, provide an innocuous dumping ground for the wayward Father Truchas. When Doc had asked, 'Why here,' Father Francis had explained that the congregation at Santuario and Santo Nino were largely transient, either tourists interested in the historical aspects of the buildings or supplicants hoping for a miracle of their own. Most of the local Catholic's worshipped at a more modern facility in Espanola in the next valley over.

Santuario therefore had no Sunday school, no choir and no revolving stable of altar boys, no youth programs at all. The priestly functions were largely ceremonial, two masses a week and an occasional wedding. How could Father Truchas get in trouble? And his constant scheming and political maneuvering would be mooted. Father Francis had only learned these last things after the arrival of his taciturn and disgruntled 'assistant', when he made some discreet inquiries about the man. The bishop apologized for not preparing him but insisted that neither of them had any choice in the matter. The orders allegedly came from the Cardinal himself.

Father Fish, anointed as such unanimously within hours of his arrival, wasted no time in first undermining, then neutralizing the old man. He fired those staff members who did not quit in disgust at this heavy-handed administration and brought in two of his former assistants.

The Guppy was an administrative assistant by title, gopher by scope of work. A distant cousin of the priest, he was dim and pliable and more than a little mean spirited. The Shark was a fellow priest and Father Francis, in his prior naiveté', would not have believed it possible for one such man to have been sanctioned by the Holy Church let alone two. They had eliminated Father Francis' duties, deleted his staff and cut him off from his friends, eventually simply locking him away, his medical condition, they explained to all inquirers, too grave to allow visitation.

"And they totally fucked with the Elixir program," Maggie said in conclusion. "We'll explain that tomorrow. I want Junior to be here."

It was the next day before they saw Junior again, his arrival announced by a guttural rumble as he pulled up next to the motor home on a purple Harley, bare-chested, the redhead in cut-off's and a tube top behind him, her arms wrapped around his chest.

Junior carried the girl to the door. He stopped and let her down and they were talking quietly, forehead to forehead, when Maggie slid open the window and said, "Junior, bring your friend in so we can meet her."

"Ma, this is Kate. Kate, my mom Maggie," Junior said, his head on an angle looking around her mane of windblown, rusty hair. "And that's my Uncle George and this is our friend, Doc." She took two strides into their midst, clustered as they were around the dinette and stuck her big hand out to Maggie and said, "A pleasure to meet you."

"Morning, Doc," she said, shaking his hand and inspecting his face. "I bet you've got some stories to tell.

"And Uncle George. You stand up here and give me a hug. You two ought to take your show on the road. You guys are great!"

"Thank you very much, Kate. You look pretty great your own self. You kids have fun?" George asked.

"You bet!" she said. "How long y'all gonna be in town?"

"We ain't sure just yet but I'll bet the boy's gonna want a stick around some."

She slid her arm around Junior's waist, Doc thinking they made a striking couple, both big and buff, Junior bulky and tanned bronze with white-blond hair, Kate full bodied but muscular, definition in her arms and legs, complexion white and luminous in sharp contrast to the dark red hair. He thought they would have fabulous children, then glanced at Maggie hoping she couldn't read his mind.

"How long have you been working at the restaurant, Kate?" Maggie asked.

"A couple nights a week for about two years. The tips are fair to good and I like the music."

"Can you survive around here on two nights a week? I would think the cost of living would be fairly steep this close to Santa Fe."

"Ma," Junior said, a note of warning in his voice.

"Junior," she said right back in the same tone.

"Kate has an internship at Los Alamos. She's a physicist."

"Whoah!" George exclaimed. "Pretty *and* smart. Good for you, Katie!"

She said how nice it was to meet them but she had to get to work and Junior walked her out, kissed her and then she swung herself up on the chopper, kicked it to life and roared off.

"I'm in love," Junior said with a silly grin when he rejoined them.

"I can't imagine why, boy," George said. "That's a fine lookin' hunk a woman."

"Very self assured," Doc added.

"She seems nice, Junior," Maggie said. "I like her."

"But?" he said.

"No buts. She's lovely. She has a great personality, smart, educated," Maggie said shrugging. "What's not to like?"

"And built like a brick shit-house," George added. "That don't hurt none."

"We didn't do anything, Ma," Junior said. "I know what you're thinking. We just laid out on her star gazing platform looking for shooting stars and talking. Mostly about you all and our quest. She knows Father Francis real well. She offered to help any way she could."

"Sit down, Junior," Maggie said. "We found out some things from Father Francis. We need to talk about them." She summarized their conversation with George regarding the priest and then launched into the personal matters.

"Father Francis says Arturo is dead. He's who sent the note and forwarded the box to us."

"You think he's tellin' the truth?"

"Junior, when you see this man," Doc said, "I think you'll agree that he's probably incapable of telling a lie. He looks like a little old white-haired cherub."

"There's more I assume," Junior said.

"Lots," his mother answered.

Chapter Nineteen

"Father Francis told us that Arturo first arrived at Santuario in a beat up Jeep, probably the old Toyota that he was driving when he first stopped at Soccoro Camp. It might even have been the same trip. He found Father Francis and they struck up a conversation. Father Francis took him to the parish house and they had dinner. Arturo spent the night.

"They spent the next day together and Arturo stayed over again. He was there a total of five nights Father Francis thinks. Arturo opened a bottle of Elixir the first night and they had some after dinner every night. Father Francis was in his late fifties at the time. He does not remember the exact year but he was not in the best of health, he said. By the morning of the fifth day he said he felt as if he had been transplanted into a younger man's body. When he commented on this to Arturo, your father asked him if he would like to know why he felt so much improved.

"After Arturo explained the Elixor to Father Francis, they reached an agreement. Arturo would provide the nursery stock and hire the workers to till the fields owned by the church and Arturo would supervise the initial planting and return at least twice a year to assist with the spring pruning and the fall harvest. Once the orchards were producing enough fruit, Arturo would build them a still and teach Father Francis how to distill his own Elixir.

"In return Father Francis promised that the Elixir only went to those in need. What you need to understand is that the missions had no social programs at all at that time. They were known for their miracles but didn't really have a congregation, the same as now. They had to change the whole structure of the operation.

"Father Francis had a problem there because nothing could be done without the blessing of his superiors. In a place as well known as these two landmarks, the Cardinal and maybe even the pope might have had to bless any changes. So they put in the orchards without asking. Your father paid all the out of pocket expenses.

"Over the next couple years, Arturo wrote proposals for Father Francis to forward to the Bishop. None of them involved a contribution from the church. Arturo guaranteed the seed money.

"The daycare center and alternative school they proposed were rejected flat out. So were the Native American Seminary and the nondenominational nursing home. The gift shops were approved provided that the Archdiocese in Santa Fe got seventy five percent of the net prior to any funding being used for social programs.

"Eventually they were authorization to do a geriatric daycare program and a 'meals on wheels' service. Once they had one program sanctioned, they could manipulate the system. At least that's how I took it. Sort of like holy money laundering. The meals on wheels vans were used as school buses to bring local people to a day program. Volunteers taught things like beginner's English and citizenship.

"In the summer the geriatric folks 'sponsored' a camp for poor kids. They brought thousands of them from all over the state to the Sipapu Ski Area. The children spent a week or two in tent villages, learning nature skills, Native American culture. The Indians from the Taos Reservation were the teachers. The counselors were the geriatrics. It was their vacation too."

"Where did all the money come from?" Junior asked.

"We don't know yet," Maggie answered. "We had to leave when Truchas came back."

"So when are we going to spring the old guy?" Junior asked.

"To be determined," Doc said. "We need to gather a little more information first. Not tonight."

"Pop was a missionary, wasn't he, Ma," Junior said. "He was all over the damn place helping people. Not a damn dope dealer at all. Ever. Jesus. I don't know what I'm….what to think. It's kind of fucking me up."

"But in a good way," George said.

"Hell yes, Unc. I'm feeling a whole lot better about my dad. I mean, we knew he was dead. Should I feel bad about that now that it's been confirmed?"

"Of course you should, Junior," Maggie said. "But you're right. I feel a lot better about everything too. Better then I did when we didn't know anything for certain, just had suppositions."

"Ma, we're going to be here for a while, right?" When she nodded he added, "I'd like to go tell Kate my dad wasn't a drug dealer."

"Yes, of course. Go call her." Maggie smiled as he bolted out the door and sped off on the Kawasaki.

"Let's make some plans," Doc said.

They agreed that Doc should re-infiltrate the parish house that night, alone, to get Father Francis' input on an escape plan and that George should look up Bob to see if he could shed any more light on the Trout and company's schedules. They also agreed that it would not hurt any of them to spend a couple nights in a mountainside spa and dispatched George to talk to both Bob and Carl, the owner of the bar, to see if Carl's offer was still available.

George was back in an hour at the wheel of a Cadillac convertible with 'The Hootin' Holler' painted on both sides. "We're all set," he exclaimed. "Grab your gear and I'll chauffeur you up the mountain."

"George, what exactly did you commit us to?" Maggie asked.

"Oh, nothin' more 'en we talked about. We stick around for a few days, he puts us up, plus he gets to hang a sign on the Winnie."

"How long, George? How long are we committed?"

"Just through the weekend, Mags. Hell, it wouldn't be right to pull Junior out a here before then anyhow, right Doc?"

"He may have helped solidify the plan, Maggie," Doc said. "Sunday with the Fish and company at mass might be the easiest time to get Father Francis out. You need to find out if the Shark is in the church with him, George."

"I'm on my way," he said. "I'll be back in an hour. Be ready. I'm takin' the dog."

"I can hardly wait to meet Carl," Maggie said as George pulled out of the parking lot trailing an oily cloud. "He must be a real piece of work. Do you think it's okay for us to stay here that long? Or stay up there," meaning the bed and breakfast, "that long?"

"It's like you said to Junior, are we in a hurry?"

George was back in an hour as promised. They loaded a few things in the car and he chauffeured them up the mountain. Their arrival at the Casa de Chimayo was obviously expected as the elegant couple who stood on the front steps of the hacienda smiled and waved graciously as they turned into the sloping driveway. The woman, however, turned stone faced as the car lurched to a smoking stop at her feet.

George bounced up the stairs, shook their hands and welcomed himself to their lovely home and then ushered them back inside. He soon had all of them signed in to two adobe cottages remote from the main house, each with beamed ceilings, antique furnishings, kiva-style fireplaces and hot tubs on their secluded patios. After securing a menu and a six pack, he led Maggie and Doc through the intricate landscaping that surrounded their bungalows.

"You leave a note for the boy?" George asked as they entered the first cottage.

"Of course," Maggie said. "Now get your butt off my bed and get out of here."

It was an hour and a half before Maggie and Doc wandered back to the main lodge, still damp from their shower and freshly clothed. George was seated in a rocking chair, feet on the rail, strumming a Martin twelve-string guitar, accompanied by their male host on a mandolin, trading off on the verses of a folk song from the sixties.

"You have a beautiful place here," Maggie said to the man.

"Thank you. We're very pleased to have settled here and to be able to share our good fortune with our guests."

"For a price," George added, slapping the man on the back.

"A damn hefty one too," the man said laughing. "But Carl can afford it. That dive of his is a gold mine. And I'm still a child of the sixties, despite what I did in the seventies, eighties and nineties," he said winking at George.

"'Ol' Ben here was a corporate raider," George said, "before he saw the light and retired to this here mountainside."

"Saw the SEC is more like it. You must be Maggie and Doc. My pleasure. Please join us. Can I get you a refreshment?"

They were all seated on the porch admiring the view over the village below, across the valley to the Sangre de Christo Mountains, when the sound of distant thunder began to intensify, soon becoming a staccato roar.

"Here comes my nephew I bet," George explained to Ben.

They heard the Harley downshifting then watched it appear between the dry stacked stone columns that marked the Inn's formal entrance, Junior driving, the fan of red hair behind him looking like a curly helmet.

"Nice bike!" Ben shouted as the noise intensified. "Ruth Ann will shit when she sees this."

Ruth Ann was on the veranda at her husband's back before Kate and Junior had dismounted and it was extremely clear that barbarians in her home was not what she anticipated when Carl had called to book the rooms.

"Ben," she demanded imperiously. "May I speak to you in the foyer, please?"

"Hold your horses, Ruthie. I need to welcome our new guests," he said, his eyes fixed on the leather clad Valkyrie with the flying crown of red tresses that was striding across their porch arm in arm with the reincarnation of Thor himself.

"What a magnificent couple," he whispered to George.

"Ain't they a picture?" he answered. "Kate and Junior, our hosts Ruth Ann and Ben. Welcome to Casa de Chimayo," as proud of them and the inn as if he was the proprietor of it all.

"This is wonderful!" Kate exclaimed to Ruth Ann. "Could you please show me around?"

"Ruthie gets a little flustered if anything disrupts her sense of order," Ben said after his wife had gone off with Kate. "She doesn't like surprises and I must say, you are one very surprising family. How about lunch, George?"

Ben took their orders himself after seating them at a linen covered table on the corner of the veranda, the view outstanding, the service from two livery clad young women impeccable and the food as extraordinary as any of them had ever eaten. They thanked their host profusely after the meal, then retired to the patio of Maggie's cottage.

"Kate," Maggie began, "I assume Junior has explained our, ah, reasons for being here?"

"I told her everything, Ma. If that pisses you off I'm sorry but it was my choice and I made it."

"I agree with you, Junior," Maggie said. "Sometimes you have to go with your instincts and yours have always been pretty good."

"Thanks, Maggie," Kate said. "I won't do anything to hurt you or your 'quest.' And especially not him," she said, placing a hand on Junior's knee. "I might even be able to help."

Chapter Twenty

They left the inn at seven, coasting both the Harley and the Cadillac down the driveway before starting them in deference to their hosts and fellow guests. They parked by the motor home, now adorned with a thirty-five foot, hot pink banner, 'Hell's Fire' in eight foot blue letters accented with yellow flames, 'Featuring George and Junior,' the letters smaller but just as blue and also flaming. They all stood on the shoulder of the road staring at the sign.

"Wow," Kate said. "That'll get your attention."

George and Junior went in to change for the show and the others ambled along the edge of the parking lot with the dog.

"Did you play hooky this afternoon, Kate?" Doc asked.

"I'm on flex time. When Junior called, I packed my gear and said so long. He met me at my place, then we brought the bikes down here and found the note."

"Here they come," Maggie said pointing at the motor home. "Should we go on in?"

"Might as well," Kate said. "It'll be nice to have someone wait on me in there for a change."

Carl himself was the MC, issuing a nonstop patter from the moment he took the microphone till the front man pushed him off the stage. He eventually found his way to their table, by random chance Doc thought, having watched some of Carl's wandering voyage around the room.

"Are you familiar with chaos theory, Doc?" Kate shouted into his ear, nodding toward the approaching owner.

"You're saying he found us by sheer happenstance."

"Close enough," she said.

The three of them, Maggie, Kate and Doc, slipped out at the start of the second set, stopping at the motor home to check the dog and gather some equipment. Then with Doc in the lead on Maggie's 175CC Honda, the girls on the Kawasaki, they made their way to the intersection of the highway and the gravel access road. Doc quickly applied some camouflage face paint and adjusted the wireless radio. Maggie heard his voice clearly in her earpiece as he climbed back on the Honda.

"Stay close," he said. "I'll check in every ten minutes to make sure you're still in range. I'll meet you here in one hour." Then he turned and jogged up the road, stopping to take a look around near where they had left the bike the night before.

He crossed the fence and wove through the orchard, crawling the last fifty feet. He surveyed the rear of the house for several minutes, settling into the role of hunter-killer, letting the adrenaline surge through his system, his instincts taking over, tasting the air, hearing the insects in the grass around him, seeing the texture of light and shadow, then inching toward the house.

There were occupants on the lower level. He could feel them walking across the floor when he pressed his hand to the wall, heard murmured conversation through the wood and plaster. He slowly raised his head till he could peer onto the back porch, verifying that it was unoccupied, then stood and silently scaled the corner post onto the roof.

He paused there for another minute, listening for sounds from the upper rooms, then glided from window to window until he could peek into the priest's bedroom which was illuminated only by a small night light.

He slid the window open a foot then slipped though the opening onto the floor and crept up to the bed. He gently pulled the covers down off the old man's shoulders and touched his arm, whispering in his ear, hand poised to clamp over his mouth if he woke with a start. Father Francis opened his eyes, stared silently at the green and black faced creature that loomed over him, then slowly smiled.

"Have you come to take me away?"

"Not tonight, Father Francis," Doc replied.

"Are you two having fun," Maggie spoke in Doc's ear.

"Maggie says hello, Father," he said pointing at the radio wrapped around his head. "And Kate," he added.

"Kate, the luscious red head?" the priest asked. Doc nodded.

"Are the two of you going to start telling ribald stories next?" Maggie said in his ear. "He's a priest, for God's sake. He shouldn't even notice things like that."

"Father, let me bring you up to speed," Doc said quietly, then proceeded to tell him what they had done and learned in the past twenty four hours. Father Francis confirmed the Shark's roll in Sunday service. He said mass at the Nino while the Fish did Santuario, the Guppy doing the setups for both and helping them count the take after.

"So we're going to get you Sunday morning," Doc said. "Did you write the letter to the Bishop?"

The sound of footsteps in the hall outside brought Doc around in a crouch and, at the keying noise, he glided over to the door, flattening against the wall on the hinge side. The door swung open and a robed figure stepped into the room and flicked on the light. Doc saw him through the crack between door and frame and smelled him at the same time, body odor and garlic.

"Bed check, old man. Did I wake you?"

"Go fornicate with a horn toad, you evil creature," the priest responded.

"I'll fornicate in your ear old man," the Guppy said in a malevolent voice as he stepped up to the bed and pulled the covers completely off the priest. He raised his arm, fist cocked, but Doc caught it on the down swing, pulling it wide of the priest and up behind the man's back, hard, simultaneously running him head first into the carved post of the massive bed. Doc checked his pulse then scooped him up and plopped him down beside Father Francis, hog tying him quickly with the priest's vestments.

"Change of plans, Father. You're leaving now. Grab a few things," his voice low and urgent. "Don't forget the letter." Doc eased his head out the door, listening for any sounds of assistance but the other occupants of the house seemed unaware of the problems above them, classical music wafting up the stairs from below.

"Maggie," he said into the microphone. "We had a small problem. I'm bringing him out tonight. Do you copy?"

"Yes. What do you want us to do?"

"I'll get back to you. Stay close."

Father Francis dressed quickly then pulled out a small knapsack and began to stuff papers and notebooks into it. "The dirt on the Fish," he winked at Doc, "is in here," he said, carefully opening a hidden compartment beneath his ancient desk and removing an accordion file. "And a little mad money. And this," he said, holding up an ornate golden flask.

"Elixir," the priest said taking a good pull and handing it to Doc. Doc did the same then returned it, feeling the liqueur hit his system with a jolt.

"Okay," Doc said. "We're going to go out on the roof and I'm going to carry you down. Put your arms around my neck and your legs around my waist. And hold on. And don't choke me. And be quiet!"

"Should we thump that thing again to make sure he stays put?" the priest asked in a hopeful voice, pointing at the Guppy.

"I think I thumped him hard enough, Father."

They made it to the ground more easily than Doc expected, the priest calm and nearly weightless and surprisingly nimble as they crept away from the house.

"Are you okay to walk a bit, Father?"

"Oh, I'm right as rain, my son. I haven't had this much fun in eons! I could even run for a bit if you need me to."

"I hope we won't need to. Maggie," he said into the mike. "Come in slowly and meet us on the access road, where we started the bike last night, okay?"

"We're already there. We pushed the bikes in from the road."

"Good girl. We'll be there in ten."

They returned to the motor home. Maggie and Father Francis walked in the last one hundred yards ahead of the noisy bikes.

"Kate, can you take the Father to your house and hide him?" Doc asked.

"Not till this old leprechaun gives me a great big hug," she said enveloping the smiling priest. "I sure have missed you, you reprobate. How could you let those slimy fucks lock you up? You should have kicked their asses!"

"I was biding my time, child," he said.

"You probably napped all day and slept all night. Well, vacations over, Frank. We're going to bust those creeps. You ready to ride?"

"You bet!" he said. She peeled him off and they climbed on the Harley, Father Francis snuggling in behind her, wrapping his arms around her waist. He looked over at Doc as she revved the bike, and mouthed 'Thank you' as they sped away.

"He's having the time of his life," Maggie said as they watched them roar up the street. "Tell me what happened," she continued as they climbed into the motor home. "I could only make out part of it."

"We got busted by the Guppy. I assume it was the Guppy. Just bad timing. I had to pop him. He was going to punch that sweet old man. Can you believe that? But he didn't see me, so that's good. And we got away clean so we have a little time. I suspect they'll go directly to the police, hope to get him back before he can do any damage. And I'm just as sure the cops will come looking for us. We need to stonewall them long enough for Father Francis to make contact with the bishop, which he will attempt tonight. He'll go to the cardinal if he can't get to the bishop. And he has the proof, the goods if you will, on the Trout, but there's going to be a time lag. And we'll be vulnerable."

"So we need to hide him out for a couple days but ideally, *we* need to be around."

"That's about it. I thought of Mountainair Camp. Kate and Junior could run him down there or just Junior. I know Al would help but it's a little far and they will be a bit conspicuous on the road."

"You don't think he can just stay at Kate's?"

"Tonight probably. It'll take a while for the cops to trace us, talk to people, make the connection between her and us but if they take it seriously enough, they will. They'll get on to the Inn quickly as well and no one up there is going to forget us all leaving together."

"She's pretty unforgettable, on the Harley."

"With Junior. They make a hell of a package."

They were silent for a minute.

"Why don't we run him straight down to Santa Fe, tonight, to see the Bishop in person?" she asked.

Maggie pulled Junior off the stage as the song ended, giving him a quick summation of the situation and handing him over to Doc who continued to talk to the boy as they headed toward the exit. Carl tried to block their path, appearing beside them at the door but Maggie grabbed his collar and pulled him inside telling him to shut up or the deal was off. George joined them as Maggie finished talking, her fist still clutching Carl's silk shirt and goat suede jacket.

"Hello, boys and girls," George said. "Do we need a time out here?"

"Junior needs the rest of the night off. I was just explaining the unfortunate necessity to Carl. But he understands now, don't you Carl."

"Yeah, sure," Carl said. "Shit happens, but come on, man, the show must go on, right?"

"And so it shall, my friend," George said. "It shall indeed. Now calm down, little buddy, leave this here problem to me."

Carl trotted off and George led Maggie toward the stage, hand clamped firmly on her elbow, an easy smile on his face, oblivious to her stream of invective laden complaints.

Doc got Junior in the Cadillac and was admonishing him to be careful and not to leave the priest alone and to make sure they didn't give the bishop originals of anything and to keep in contact and he probably would have added an additional dozen ands but Junior finally just waved and drove off.

When Doc re-entered the restaurant, he headed straight to the bar, thinking cold beer. He had changed out of his fatigue pants and washed his face and hands and was now dressed in jeans and a flannel shirt. When the band began to play again, George's alto filled the room. He had the beer in his hand, almost to his mouth when the vocals were taken by a woman, the voice sky high and sweet as summer rain. He knew immediately who it was but turned to see anyway, the sound giving him goose bumps.

Maggie sang three songs, George having to drag her back for an encore after the second and she promised the audience that she would return during the next set and sing a couple more.

"Why aren't I surprised that you can sing too?" Doc said to her as she rejoined him.

"I'm not as good as they are," she said "but I enjoy it. Or I used to. I'd forgotten what a rush it is, the crowd, the applause. Can we go outside for a minute?" They walked out the door into the cool night air and Maggie threw her head back and shook out her hair and Doc thought she was going to howl like she had at her ranch.

"Easy, wolf girl," Doc said, pointing toward the motor home. "We have company." There was a police cruiser parked beside it and two uniformed officers were walking in opposite directions around the vehicle.

"Give me your hand," he said. "We're lovers. You're with the band. Be happy, maybe a little drunk." They ambled over to the police car, seeming to notice it at the last minute.

"This thing yours, bud?" the first officer asked.

"Nope," Doc said pleasantly. "It's hers."

"There's someone in there, Jake," his partner, a stocky, plain woman, called out from the side door.

The first cop pointed at the door. "Open it, lady."

"It isn't locked, officer," she said. "But unless you have a warrant, I don't have to open anything. That's my house."

"Maggie, let them look around," Doc said, then turned to the first cop and whispered, "She's a hippie without the pot. Sings with the band. Activist type, you know?"

"Off the pigs. Yeah, I read my history books. You gonna open it or not?"

"Sure officer. What are you looking for?" Doc said.

"A missing priest, possible kidnapping."

"No shit! Who'd want to kidnap a priest?"

"Just open it, pal," the male cop said. "We can yuck it up another time."

"Okay. I've got to get the dog, though. That's what she's hearing," Doc said. He opened the door and called the dog outside, then made a sweeping gesture with his palm. "She's all yours, officer." The male cop was inside for thirty seconds, the female officer outside.

"Sorry for the inconvenience, folks," he said when he emerged.

"Come back and catch the show when you get off," Doc said. "They're mighty fine."

"Another time," the female said as they got in their car and drove off.

"Ain't you just the good 'ol boy," Maggie said.

"Just trying to fit in which is more than I can say for you. What was the warrant bit all about?"

"I don't like being told what I'm going to do in case you hadn't noticed. He pissed me off."

"I'll remember that," Doc said. "You ready to be a superstar again?"

The next morning Doc heard the shuffling of feet and murmured voices outside their cottage before the loud knock and he was up and in his jeans before the authoritative 'Police! Open up in there' rang out. He checked to make sure Maggie was awake and decent before he opened the door.

"Good morning, Officers," he said. "Y'all havin' a long shift."

The male officer started forward as if to muscle past but Doc didn't step aside and as they came chest to chest, his partner hooked a hand on his upper arm and pulled him back a ways, eyes fixed on Doc's bare torso. When she got the male cop out of range, she whispered in his ear, then he turned to inspect the damage to Doc's upper body. Stepping back toward the door, the first cop looked up into Doc's eyes.

"What the hell happened to you?" he said.

"A bullet here, a mortar there. Why? You think I've got a priest tucked away in there somewhere?" Maggie stepped up beside Doc before the cop could answer.

"Well, good morning, Officers. Do come in, please. Doc, you're being rude to our guests," she added, clad in the dragon robe and turned him into the room, giving the officers a clear view of the damage to his back.

"Sorry to disturb you again," the female stammered, stepping through the doorway, "but we have a few questions."

They first requested ID which was supplied without question, Doc's for Dr. Robert E.L. Beaumont of Macon, Georgia, then they asked about their reason for visiting the churches and their encounter with Father Truchas.

"All I can tell you," Doc said, "is that is one miserable excuse for a man of God. Is he the priest that's missing, cause that would be no great loss."

"I can't release that information," the male cop answered. "Did you meet a Father Francis?" The questioning went on in that vein, Did they meet the Shark? Did they see the Guppy? Real names used but the answers the same–no. When did they get to the bar last night and did any of them leave at any time? A little after seven and only to get some air or walk the dog.

"Where are the other members of your party?" the male asked, consulting a small notebook. "A large, bald man and a muscular blond, younger man?"

"That would be my brother, George, and my son, Junior. They're most likely next door."

"They're also in the band?" the woman asked.

"They're the headliners," Doc said. "Didn't you see the pink banner?"

"How could you miss it?" the female officer answered, smiling for the first time.

"I think we're about done here," her partner said. "So, you have no knowledge of Father Francis and you only saw Father Truchas the one time at the church, is that correct?"

"Yes it is," Doc answered. "You want me to roust the boys? They probably got in later than we did."

They went to the next cabin but no one answered their repeated knocking. Maggie had a key to their room but neither of them was there although one bed showed signs of a recent inhabitant.

"Knowing George," Maggie said to the officers, "they either aren't home yet or they're having breakfast," which proved to be half correct. George was on the veranda having steak and eggs with Ben. The cops made the same inquiries of George, declining Ben's invitation to breakfast, then asked where Junior might be.

"That rascal took off with a new acquaintance about, oh, midnight or so I guess," George said. "Ain't seen him since. Don't really expect to till tonight. Y'all want me to have him come find you?"

"That shouldn't be necessary," the male cop said. "How long will you be in town?"

"Till Monday at least," Doc answered. "You can reach us here or at the Holler."

The cops thanked them for their help and then drove off.

"Well, Maggie," Ben said. "Is your life always this exciting?"

"No, thank God. And I'm so sorry for causing you this inconvenience. We must be quite a spectacle in your peaceful Inn."

"You guys are the main attraction. I'm thrilled that you're here. Truthfully," he said, "most of our guests are pompous bores. Ruth Ann likes it like that but they drive me crazy."

"Glad we can help you out, Ben," George said. "You name the time and I'll bring the whole band up here."

"Ruth Ann would run screaming into the night," Ben replied with a grin.

By mid-afternoon there had still been no word from Junior and Maggie was getting worried. Doc told her that there was nothing they could do but wait and suggested they have an early dinner and then go down to the bar. George said they could rehearse a little in case Junior didn't get back in time to go on, which got her pacing the cabin again.

"How about if we call Doctor X again, Maggie?" Doc suggested. She agreed and they took the dirt bikes down into town to find a pay phone. They found a phone booth at a Quick Stop not far from the center of town and Doc dialed up the number for the lab, calling collect from Bob.

"Bob is it," the chemist chuckled. "I'm surprised you didn't say from Shit Bag."

"I was afraid you wouldn't accept."

"I wouldn't have," he said. "So how goes it so far? Life is good?"

"Life is grand, Eugene. I couldn't be better. Did you receive my package?"

"Days ago. I was beginning to wonder if you got derailed somewhere. Everything going all right?"

"For the most part. We got waylaid in New Mexico but it seems to be working out. What do you have for me?"

"Patience, lad. Let me find my notes." After some paper ruffling and some muttering he returned. "Ah, yes. Interesting items you sent me. You may wish to be careful around certain, ah, authority figures with some of these."

"I thought as much. Number five is peyote isn't it?"

"Actually nearly pure mescaline. I took the liberty of doing some personal research with the sample, after testing it of course. I'd like to run some more tests if you have another sample or two."

"I'll see what I can do, Eugene," Doc laughed. "And number four is coke?"

"USP one hundred. Pharmaceutical grade, not street shit and it *is* a hundred percent. I'll need more of that to test as well."

"You're on your own there. Get it from one of your little lab assistants. How about number six? Is it dirt?"

"Yes. A sandy soil, very low in organic matter. From a desert perhaps."

"Nothing else odd about it?"

"Just sandy dirt as far as my instruments can tell. No unusual trace elements. It tells me it's not from an urban site."

"Okay. And the others?"

"One is, ah, well, a multi-vitamin. High concentration of C and E relative to the others and a fair percentage of beta carotene but basically it's a powdered vitamin heavy on anti-oxidants. Two is a hormone, a powdered form of DHEA. You want the full name? It's dehydroepiandrosterone. It's sort of a synthetic blend of testosterone and estrogen, a neutered version if you will."

"Interesting. Is it readily available, over the counter?"

"No, but it's not exotic either. It's used to restore vitality. Supposed to increase muscle mass, reduce fat. And give you a big woody from what I hear about it."

"Do you need more of that too, Eugene?"

"Not yet. I'll get back to you in a few years. Now number three is an odd cocktail, I have to tell you. There's a bunch of minerals in it, magnesium, phosphorous, iron, some copper, like an over-the-counter supplement. But there's also a significant proportion of something I can only describe as an antibiotic, similar to penicillin. I don't have the background in virology to give you a better answer. I could send it off to Atlanta, to the Infectious Disease Center, ask them what it is if you'd like."

"What would your exposure be?"

"Depends on what it is. Worst case? Where did you get this, Eugene? We've never seen anything like it in which case I'd make something up. An anonymous submittal from a former student. Maybe an alien life form! What do you think?" the chemist asked.

"It's probably not necessary at this point. Let's wait and see. It may turn up on its own. The peyote did. What did you think of the pear brandy? That's where all the samples end up, as a tonic that may have some significant powers. Life sustaining."

"It has a monster kick, I can attest to that. I ran it for toxins than tested it personally," he said. "What is in it is what we talked about. But the accumulation produces a chemical reaction. In other words, the whole is greater than the sum of its parts. Whatever your tonic does, the how is a mystery to me. I'm still working on it."

"Use it sparingly, Eugene. Like a shot a week, okay?"

"Okay, but don't forget your friends at Christmas, Doc. That was some mighty fine feel good."

"Thanks, Eugene. I won't. I'll call when I've got news. Thanks again, buddy."

Maggie had been puttering up and down the street in front of the convenience store while Doc was on the phone, pulling into the lot as he hung up. Doc got on his bike and pointed up the hill towards the Inn.

George joined Maggie and Doc on their way to the cabins. Doc briefly explained the contents of the jars, none of them sufficiently motivated to discuss it in depth.

"Nothing from Junior?" Maggie asked George.

"Not a word, Mags, but don't fret, the boy's fine. He'll be back soon, I promise." She didn't say more and they went off to wash up, agreeing to meet at the bikes in a half-hour.

They drove down to the motor home, Maggie behind Doc on the 350, George on the 175 and they let the dog out. They were all subdued now, sitting in lawn chairs outside, when the dog picked up first his ears, then his head and then got to his feet, his attention fixed on the main road south of the restaurant. George turned in time to see a black limousine slowly making the turn onto the side street that the bar fronted on followed immediately by another and then a third.

The first limo stopped directly opposite them and two men in black suits, sunglasses and earplug radio receivers stepped out, scanning the motor home, parking lot, bar and surrounding roof tops. Two more emerged from the third.

"You think the President come to hear us sing, Mags?" George said.

"Maybe the president of the local Grange," she replied, "but I doubt he could afford the transportation."

The men in black approached the second car and opened both rear doors simultaneously. Laughter spilled out of one followed immediately by Kate and Junior. Out of the other climbed first Father Francis, then another priest, and finally a robed figure, one hand on the arm of the second priest, the other clutching a carved staff, a massive hat perched on his head.

"Jesus Christ!" George whispered. "I think that's a fuckin' cardinal!"

"Sure as hell isn't a robin," Doc said.

"Shut the fuck up!" Maggie hissed at them. "Are you both idiots?"

Father Francis spotted them in the shade of the motor home and called out a greeting.

"There they are, your Holiness! There's my rescuers!" He gave first Maggie than Doc an enthusiastic hug, his head barely coming up to their chins, and then tried to wrap his little arms around George's belly.

"Your eminence, this is Maggie and Doc," he said. "This is Cardinal Garcia of the Archdiocese of Santa Fe, a good man and an old friend. And this must be brother George and, of course, the Dog."

The cardinal shook their hands, the dog giving the ringed hand a sniff and a lick which caused the cardinal to laugh aloud and scratch the dog's floppy ears. "He obviously knows the protocol," Cardinal Garcia said. "I cannot thank you enough for helping this fine man," he continued. "The Church owes you a debt of gratitude which I will not forget. If there is anything you need, please do not hesitate."

"Thank you, Cardinal Garcia," Maggie said. "There is a favor I might ask. Could we borrow Father Francis for a couple weeks? Would he be allowed to travel with us for a bit?"

"My child, that is not a favor I can grant," he said. "That is strictly up to Father Francis," he continued, laughing now and turning to the old priest. "What do you think, Frank, road trip?"

"Hell yes! These people are more fun than an Irish wedding."

They had a reunion with Kate and Junior after the cardinal and his bodyguards departed, leaving Father Francis behind with his rescuers.

"They're going to collect the Fish and company," Father Francis said. "Those creeps have no idea what a shit storm is about to descend on them. I wish I could be there to see it," he said, "but I expect to have a better time here! When does the music start?"

"Father, do you go to country western bars often?" Maggie asked.

"I wasn't always a priest, child. And call me Frank for God's sake. I'm off duty."

There was a lot to talk about and they only had an hour before the band was scheduled to go on so Maggie had to referee the conversation.

"Junior. You and Kate go first. What happened in Santa Fe?"

"Yo, Ma, it was so cool! You should see the cardinal's crib! It's a castle, man. Bigger than any church you ever saw."

"You should probably start at the beginning," Kate said when Junior took a breath. "For continuity."

"Yeah, you're right. Okay. I picked up Kate and the padre about one. Actually we took Kate's car, her Range Rover. It's a little less obvious," he said. "The horn mobile's still at Kate's. We can get it tomorrow. So we all jump in, Kate's driving and Frank, he's all fired up, weren't you Father, showin' us the evidence on the Fish. Pictures, Ma. You wouldn't believe that scumbag. He's got his hand on this little guy's ass. It was . . . never mind, you get the idea."

"Infrared film and a three hundred millimeter lens on my Nikon," Frank said. "I used to be quite the photographer."

"So then Frank starts tellin' me about Pop, all the shit they did together, places they went. He knows Grandma de la Madre', Ma. Can you dig that? From Mexico!"

"You traveled with Artoro?" Maggie said. "Wow. He never took us anywhere near his business."

"There was a reason, Margaret. He didn't want either of you at risk and Junior wasn't old enough. His long-range plan was for Junior to . . . take over, when the time was right, after the operations were established. I was mostly just a good cover. A man of the cloth, sort of a token of sincerity. Who could doubt the truth of the words coming from this face?" he said smiling at them.

"So let me get back to the Pope real quick," Junior said, "then we can move on to the Elixir business."

"He's a cardinal, Junior," his mother said.

"I know, but he looks so grand in that get up I gave him a promotion. Anyway, we yack it up all the way to Santa Fe and we go to the bishop's place but he's got this cranky old caretaker broad who answers the door after about fifty rings and she ain't lettin' us in for nothin'. That ol' boy was getting' his Z's no matter what, nuclear war, it didn't matter.

"So we kissed her off and went to the cardinal's. Ol' Frank knocks on the door and one of the cardinal's boys opens up right away and says, 'Father Francis, how can we help you', not what the fuck are you doing here at like three in the morning?"

"Johnny and me are like this," Frank said, holding his hand up with two fingers crossed. "Seriously. We went to seminary together. I'm older because I came late to the priesthood but I was a mentor to the boy, particularly in worldly matters where I had more experience. He could run rings around me in the scholarly pursuits."

"So we go on into the castle and in about two minutes Johnny's downstairs and we're all drinkin' coffee and shootin' the breeze. It was way cool, he's laid back."

"You addressed," his mother said, "a Roman Catholic Cardinal as Johnny?"

"Yeah. He insisted. I told you he was cool. So Frank lays out the gig, the Fish, the whole bit and Johnny starts gettin' redder and redder. Reminded me of you, Ma, when you get your temper up."

"I don't have a temper," she said.

"Yeah, right. Eventually Johnny sort a held his hand up like that's enough, I get the picture, then he grabs the phone and starts makin' calls. He calmed down some after that but you could see he was still way pissed. Then he says let's have breakfast, and we all sit down and about ninety servants bring us a banquet, six hundred courses on solid gold plates, forks carved out a diamonds, it was a little over the top but the food was great." The whole table was laughing by then, especially Father Francis.

"We Catholics can be a tad ostentatious," he said, "but it isn't every day you get to eat with the Pope, eh Junior?"

"Yep. After we ate Johnny says he's got a bunch a meetings this morning that he can't blow off but this afternoon we're going to 'get the Fish'. That's what he called him. Then he says we can all chill in some bedrooms, take showers and shit if we want and he takes off. The secret service guys woke us about two, we had lunch–only about a hundred courses–and here we are."

"Damn," George said. "I'm sure sorry I missed those meals."

"Oh, you'd a loved it, Unc. All you can eat and then some."

"Father Francis," Maggie said, then added "Frank" when he started to protest, "there is so much I want to ask you, I honestly don't know where to begin."

"Allow me, my child, please. As I told you, I loved that boy like a son, and when I heard he was dead, I just ached. I so wanted to write to you, tell you the whole story, but I had to honor Arturo's wishes, that our business together remain strictly between us. Now, I think . . . now it's all right. The boy is old enough. And you are here, looking for solace, answers to those questions. So. I think it's time.

"After Arturo found me, we planted and planned and finally succeeding in getting some of our programs approved. After about five years the orchards were ready to bear a crop worthy of rendering into Elixir. Up until then, Arturo had supplied me with 'an inferior product'– Arturo's words–and we had used it sparingly, almost exclusively for those suffering from the symptoms of terminal illness.

"In the summer of the first harvest year, Arturo arrived in that motor home with a load of vats and pipes and tools and the two of us built a small still in the basement of the parish house. That fall he returned and, with the help of the day program clientele and other volunteers, we harvested the crop and crushed it in an electric press. And of course we saved the seeds, always save the seeds.

"Then it was just the two of us. We worked at night. We boiled the pear juice to syrup then started making Elixir. The first crop produced about sixty gallons which we aged in stainless steel barrels that Arturo brought. The next year we got almost a hundred. The next year one hundred and fifty and each year thereafter, two hundred on average.

"When the second crop was in barrels, we began to bottle the first, but only as much as we thought we'd need soon. Arturo said it got better with age, don't bottle it unless you have to. Three years is sufficient, five is better, ten is ideal."

"Are you familiar with the trace additives?" Doc asked.

"Do I know what they are? I do now. I didn't at first. Do I have or did I have a stockpile of them? No. Arturo always brought them along. Except the Holy soil, of course, which comes from here."

"Do you know why he didn't leave you with a supply?" Doc asked.

"At first it was to maintain control I suspect. Insure that no one could duplicate the formula. Later, when I found out what all was in it, I knew why. He was protecting me from the authorities. Bad enough I'm making bathtub gin without a narcotics charge thrown in. But that was really secondary, a risk I would have taken gladly. No, the real fear was, oh, the establishment I guess you could say. Having someone discover the Elixir, try to monopolize it. That was the nightmare. Until he could get enough production generated in enough places to guarantee its survival, he was paranoid. And rightly so I might add. Distributed by prescription, assuming whoever stole it had any intention of mass production, it would be a gold mine. Hoarded for an elite few, it might be truly priceless."

"The rich man question, right, Doc?" Junior asked.

"Precisely. How much," Doc repeated for the others, "would a rich man pay to extend his life twenty years?"

"I don't think that's what it does, Doc," Father Francis said. "At least not as a matter of course. I think it more adds to the quality of life. And it certainly eases pain. That is unquestionable."

"Wait a minute," Maggie said. "Before we get into that, I want to clarify something once and for all. Arturo's paranoia was the fear of having the Elixir stolen? Not dope, not drug dealing at all?"

"Margaret! I am surprised at you. Of course not dope. The only 'drug dealing' he did was for the additives in the Elixir and that was mostly done through me. Hold on," he said as they started to ask questions, "we will get to that in a minute. *I* want to clarify something now. Arturo was terribly paranoid about the Elixir, afraid for his family. But even more than that, as much as he adored the two of you, and you too George by the way, he was afraid that someone would suppress the Elixir. Discover it, covet it, steal it and keep it out of the hands of those it could most help–the old and the ill, the weak of spirit. That was the biggest fear. That's what made him cautious."

They were all quiet for a time, digesting this revelation, one of the two Holy Grails of their quest now in hand. Maggie asked, "Father Francis. Do you know how he died?"

"Yes, child. I do."

"And," she said.

"And I will tell you in good time. But this is neither the time nor the place. Patience, Margaret. It will not be much longer."

Maggie stared at the priest for fifteen second, the sparks fairly shooting out at him, all the others holding their breath, then she pushed her chair back, slowly stood, and without a word marched out of the restaurant. Doc started to follow but both George and Junior put their hands up to stop him.

"Give it a minute, Doc," George said. "Then go to her. She needs to fume in private for a bit. Make it two minutes to be prudent," he added.

Doc eased back down and turned to the priest. "Why won't you tell her, Frank?"

"I will. But not here and not now. You will understand but you must trust me for a little while. Please try to make her see that this is not a capricious decision, Doc. Better yet, *I'll* try to make her understand. Wait here, Doc, all right?" he asked as he got to his feet and followed Maggie out the door.

"Well, boy, looks like it's about time for me and you to sing for our supper," George said as the band members began to tune their instruments. "You ready?"

Junior gave Kate a kiss and whispered something in her ear and she nodded her head and then kissed him back.

"All right, Unc. Let's rock and roll!"

They were just finishing the first set, the songs more mellow than the night before, more emphasis on George and Junior's vocals, when Doc felt a hand on his shoulder and looked up into Maggie's smiling face. He snaked an arm around her hips as she bent down and kissed him lightly and he murmured, "I am so in love with you", which made her smile wider. Then he asked, "Did you work it out with Father Frank," and she kissed him on the ear this time and whispered, "I'll tell you later."

She was still standing behind him, hands on his shoulders, Kate seated to their left, when two black-suited men circled their table and began to scan the room. A few seconds later Frank joined them, sitting next to Kate and throwing an arm around her shoulder. A minute after that they were joined by two other men, these without suit jackets or microphones and also without their distinctive white collars.

"Johnny!" Kate said when the cardinal sat next to Frank. "How nice to see you again. And out of character yet. Can I get you a beer?"

"Hello, Kate," the cardinal said. "Still working on the next big bomb?" he asked, winking at Doc and Maggie.

"They haven't done weapons research at Los Alamos in twenty years, your Eminence, as you surely know," she said.

"So they say. And hold off on the Your Eminence crap, Kate. We're undercover. And I'd love a beer. Thomas," he said to the other priest, "get us a round," indicating the whole table. "Kate's off duty tonight."

Father Thomas returned just as George and Junior rejoined the group, between sets now, and Johnny promptly ordered him back to the bar for two more beers and a round of tequila shooters. Father Thomas had time to actually sit for a minute when he returned the second time before being dispatched again for more beer.

"Father Thomas is going to look after the missions," Jonny said, "while Frank is on vacation with you folks. Then, if he meets with

Frank's approval, and I apologize again, you should have called, I would not have let Cole dump these bad eggs on you Frank, despite what he told you. Cole is the bishop that sent the Fish up here," he explained to the group. "Wait until I ream that boy a new one. He's going to wish he was running a soup kitchen on skid row, which is not a bad idea, eh Thomas? Anyway, Thomas is going to help Frank, if it's okay with Frank. And I want to get those programs of yours up and running again ASAP, Frank. That is your first priority, Thomas. That son of a bitch Truchas shut down all of Frank and Arturo's human services! Can you believe that idiot? Yes, Maggie, I knew and respected your husband. A great deal. I can see by the look on your face that you did not know that. Thomas – another round, shooters too.

"He was a great man, a true humanitarian. He would have made an excellent priest, selfless more than any lay person I ever met. And that Elixir, sweet Lord is that stuff a miracle."

Johnny and his entourage stayed till closing, at one point all three of the priests on stage doing a wildly out of sync dance routine while Carl sang lead. Kate and Junior returned to Santa Fe with Johnny to get the cars and the cardinal promised Maggie that they would spend the balance of the night there with him and he would send them back in the morning after brunch. Maggie, George and Doc doubled up on the dirt bikes and drove back to the inn.

"How about a moonlight dip in the hot tub," Doc suggested as they undressed. "It'll relax you and you can tell me about your conversation with Father Frank."

"Go fire the thing up, I'll be right out," she said.

He was up to his chin in hundred degree bubbling water, the relaxation part working so well that he was nearly asleep, when he heard the French door to their room swing open and turned lazily in that direction. Maggie stepped out onto the patio, the light from the half moon creating a dappled pattern of shadows across her body, enough light for him to see the bottle in one hand and the two glasses in the other, more than enough light for him to admire the subtle tautness of her legs and belly, the gentle swaying of her breasts, full and firm, nipples budding in the chilly night air.

"You are magnificent," he managed as she reached the tub.

"Thank you. You ain't so bad your own self. I brought us a nightcap," she said, pouring them each a little Elixir.

They sipped the sweet, copper liqueur, its fiery burn heading straight to Doc's crouch. He gulped down the remainder of his glass and reached for her, wrapped his hands around her waist and pulled her onto him, her breasts squeezed against his chest. His hands caressed her butt and thighs, then slid up and along her labium as he guided her down. He moaned as she engulfed him, head back and tears flowing. Maggie started a gentle rhythm, kissed his neck and chin, cheeks and lips and flicked at his tears with her tongue.

"You're pretty good in the sack, cowboy. Anybody ever tell you that before?" she whispered up to him, her head on his chest.

He had his head back and was staring up at the stars, a dopey smile on his face, lost in a state of bliss so complete that it took his semiconscious mind a full minute to process her words.

"What?" he asked. "Was that a serious question?"

"Nope. Just makin' sure you hadn't gone to sleep on me. I'm not through with you yet."

Chapter Twenty-one

Maggie and Doc slept till noon, made love once as the first light of the sun creped into the room around the edges of the pulled draped and then again before surrendering to the necessity of going out to greet the day. Doc still had no idea what Frank had said to her the night before and really had not cared as long as he had her in his arms. But when she finally rolled off his chest and kissed him, announcing her intention to take a long, hot bath, he broached the subject.

"I'll tell you while I languish in the tub. You can be my handsome man in waiting, massaging me with scented oils," she said as she strode toward the bathroom, head up in a regal pose.

"Did he tell you how it happened," he asked once Maggie was nearly invisible in a quilt of bubbles, the tub large enough for both of them, Doc kneading the muscles in her neck and shoulders as she reclined against him.

"A little lower," she sighed. "Oh, this is divine. Nope," she answered finally, groaning under his hands. "The little bastard was nice about it, but he said it was important for me to have patience.

He even had the audacity to say 'all good things come to those who wait', like I was an impetuous schoolgirl. He did say that we needed to go to Mexico for the answer. And he told me some nice stories, inconsequential stuff, about Arturo, things they had done together. He was very sweet. I should not have called him a little bastard."

"Did he tell you about the drug business? He said the drugs were purchased through him didn't he?"

"Yeah, we touched on it. They had the vitamins and the hormones shipped to their day program. I think that's all he meant, unless he was just playing dumb about the coke. The antibiotic stuff is in Arizona. That was his response."

"I suspect there is a good deal more to Father Francis than his cherubic exterior would lead you to believe. He's made reference to his past history a couple times, almost like he's giving us hints. Did you notice that?"

"Yes. 'I wasn't always a priest' and, ah, 'worldly matters' regarding his student days with the cardinal."

"And 'coming late to the priesthood'. I wonder what he did before. I imagine there's a good story there."

"Let's go ask him," she said.

"Okay. In a bit. I may not be through with *you* yet this time."

"Oh, you are an animal," she said as she spun around and climbed up his soapy body, growling as she bit him on the neck.

George was strumming a guitar, sitting on the veranda with Frank, Ben and Ruth Ann. Maggie took Frank by the arm and asked him sweetly if he had seen the view of the mountains from the other end of the porch, tugging pointedly when he said why yes he had. Finally she fairly dragged him up and away when he made no attempt to rise on his own. Doc followed and Maggie sat the priest at a small table around the corner from the others before she started her interrogation.

"Frank. We need to talk. Is this a good time for you," she said, smiling at his look of absolute innocence, his eyes as round and blue as sapphires.

"Certainly, my dear. I am at your disposal."

"Good. I wouldn't want to interrupt your music appreciation class here at Ben and Ruth's vagabond's spa."

"You already have, child," he said.

"Sorry, but I need some answers and I think you have them." He started to protest but she hurried on. "We will be leaving here tomorrow. You are going with us aren't you?"

"Yes, of course, Margaret. Unless you would prefer that I did not."

"No! I want you to come, you're important to us, you…"

"We need you, Frank," Doc said. "You have a unique knowledge of Arturo and his plans, and we need to understand what that entailed. We need your help."

"I understand. I will help you all that I can. But some things cannot be explained. They need to be discovered, witnessed first-hand if you will. All I'm asking, Maggie dear, is that you allow me to *show* you what I know instead of trying to tell you that which I cannot adequately explain. Do you see, sweetheart?" She nodded her head without looking at him and he took her hands in his.

"Why didn't he tell me about the Elixir?" she asked. "I thought he was a drug dealer, for God's sake."

"I told you, child. He was afraid. With good reason. There are nefarious people in the world and some of them would have killed you, and Junior, certainly Arturo, anyone, to have control of the Elixir. But you must also realize that the secrecy was not permanent. It was his way of protecting his family for a time, until there were so many producers that no one could find them all, destroy or control them all. He had almost reached that goal."

"How many operations are there?" Doc asked.

"A dozen or so I think. Arturo rather pointedly explained that I did not know about all of them."

"The money, Frank?" Doc asked. "Where did it all come from?"

"Do you mean the money in the box or seed money for the programs?"

"Both," Maggie and Doc answered together.

"Well, there is money in Arturo's family. That's how he got started, that was his seed money. I assume that is how he funded our programs initially, until we had an abundance of Elixir."

"And then?" Maggie asked.

"And then we accepted donations," the priest said.

"For Elixir?" Maggie asked. When he nodded she continued. "How did you solicit for donations? I can't picture it."

"Let me try to explain," he said. "You know that the Santuario and the Nino are healing places and that people come here from all over the world seeking a miracle. Some of them actually receive one. Most do not. Why is this so? Why these two places and not other houses of worship? Is it some confluence of magnetic waves or electrical impulses? Is the soil itself somehow magically infused? I honestly do not know. But I do know, have seen it with my own eyes, that miracles *do* occur here. And the existence of miracles, the possibility, lifts the spirit. Even for those who don't walk again, who are still blind or ill when they leave.

"I've studied these people for twenty years. When Arturo taught me about the Elixir, I knew how it could be used but I also knew it could not help everyone.

"It is not the Fountain of Youth. It's a tonic, a medicine, and my job was to dispense that medicine to those who would benefit most. Thousands have. And many of those thousands have been grateful enough to contribute to the expansion of our program.

"The box served two purposes. One with a corollary actually. To make sure that you and Junior were financially secure. Arturo's wishes. And also to guarantee a source of supply, to make sure that someone could continue production, had the wherewithal to keep making Elixir in a worst case scenario. You are the well head, Maggie, the spring from which the waters first flowed. Arturo wanted to be sure that you would not abandon the home place, that you could afford to stay there indefinitely, growing the pears and making the Elixir, not be forced out because you went broke."

"Life insurance," Maggie said.

"In a sense. But much more as well."

"And teaching Junior the process," Doc added, "was also a form of insurance."

"Precisely. But again in two parts. Knowing how to make it but also having a reverence for the Elixir itself, what it does."

"What about when we ran out of the additives?" Maggie asked. "What were we to do then?"

"Exactly what you did. Come looking. You're just a little ahead of schedule. Actually, I think he felt you would come anyway, if something happened to him. You should have perhaps three or four more years worth of additives, yes?" They both nodded. "There was a certain hedge factor built in I'm sure. A margin of safety? Certainly he did not expect to die, but he planned for the possibility. We would send you the post cards, always having such fun with the cryptic messages. Did you like the one from San Miguel? That was my favorite even though it had nothing to do with a legitimate mission. We laughed and laughed when he destroyed those awful statues, seeing that miserable huckster put out of business."

"You were there?" Maggie asked.

"Oh, yes. One of our instructors at the summer camp came through there with a load of kids. They needed a rest room and that charlatan tried to sell Jack Littlefoot some bogus Elixir. Arturo and I drove down to check into it."

"All that money came from donations," Doc asked, "from here?"

"From all over, Doc. This was just the clearinghouse, the last stop if you will. And not all our donations were a dollar here and a dollar there, not that anyone was asked for any set amount. Not that anyone was asked for *anything* for that matter. An example. A man came here once, by himself. He was weary, Doc. I tell you this poor man was bone tired, down in his soul. He went into El Nino and prayed on his knees for hours, then he asked me if he could have a pinch of the Holy soil, to take home for his wife. I took him back to Santuario, to my office, and he told me his story. His wife was terminal, breast and liver cancer I believe. Her final wish was to live to see their daughter graduate from Notre Dame. It was October as I recall and the doctors had given her a month, two at most. Graduation was in May. There was no way she was going to hang on. I gave him two bottles of Elixir and told him to have faith. Miracles do happen. In July we got a check for fifty thousand dollars. From her! She had made it and wanted us to use the money to help other people. She said she was close to death now but it was okay. Now she was sure that there was a God and she knew he would be waiting for her. I could tell you a hundred similar stories."

Maggie was crying when she rose from her seat and circled the little table, knelt beside the priest and put her arms around him. "I'm so glad we found you, Frank."

"Hush, child. I *sent* for you."

Junior and Kate returned to the inn from Santa Fe just as they were all being seated for dinner. Ben had prepared a celebratory feast in honor of their last meal together, an extravaganza served to all the guests in the inn. The instruments were carried out with dessert, as the tables were being bussed. They played for an hour, moving from swing to big band to 'Great Balls of Fire' as a closing number. When Maggie's group headed down the hill to the night-club, the entire patronage of the inn followed along, Ben, Ruth

Ann and all their staff included. The bar band played nonstop for two hours, took a ten-minute break and played for two more, the song selection fast and happy, the crowd loud and appreciative. At the first set break, Junior brought in the dog who lapped up a beer supplied by Carl personally then curled up at Doc's feet and slept through the entire second set, his ears bouncing on the wooden floor when the music got loud enough.

At closing time, Carl bolted the doors, shut down the registers, piled ten cases of cold beer on the bar for the remaining crowd, then stripped off his embroidered cowboy shirt and screamed "Let's Party!" at the top of his lungs. The band played raunchy, high-speed rock and roll for another hour, Carl whirling and stomping on a table top the whole time.

Chapter Twenty-two

They got off to a late start the next morning, a combination of sleeping in and eating brunch and as a result, didn't get down to the motor home till nearly noon. They had to wait a half hour more for Junior and Kate to arrive on the Harley, Maggie surprised to see a large backpack strapped on Kate's shoulders. Junior went straight to his mother and announced that Kate was going to join them, not a question, and Maggie took his cheeks in both her hands, stood on her toes and kissed him on the nose.

"Good," she smiled. "I'm happy for all of us." Then she took Kate's hand and led her inside saying, "Let me help you stow your gear."

The boys loaded her Harley on the lift gate, Junior checked the motor home's vital fluids, then they drove over to the rectory so Frank could get a few belongings and give Father Thomas some advice on the missions. Frank emerged from the house carrying a knapsack and a lidded brass pot with ornate handles. "For the holy soil," he informed them. They marched over to the Santuario and the priest squatted beside the small hole in the floor. After a short benediction, he blessed himself and began to scoop dirt from the hole with a long handled ladle. They repeated the procedure at Santo Nino, Frank blending the soils together reverently with his fingers.

"Why are we taking the soil, Frank?" Junior asked.

"For those in need, grandson. One must always be prepared."

"Grandson?" Junior said.

"It's ah, a metaphor, Junior," Frank said

They were finally on the road by two, backtracking through Santa Fe, then on south to Albuquerque where they turned west. They crossed into Arizona about seven, running parallel to the Painted Cliffs in the southeast corner of the Navajo Reservation, reaching the Painted Desert just in time to watch the sun come crashing down behind the red and cream and yellow carved sandstone hills, the valleys already in full shadow, the temperature falling rapidly.

"We're at something of a crossroads here, Maggie," Frank said as they watched the colors of the setting sun overwhelm the pallet of desert hues. "The scenic route would take us south from here through pine forests and mountains that are worth the extra time from a site seeing perspective but it's sort of pointless in the dark."

"Or we stay on the interstates and drive all night," she said.

"That about sums it up."

"Personally, I'm anxious to get on with it," she said. "We've already agreed to skip the Ganado Missions. They're north of us now?" she asked.

"Yes. Up in the Navajo Reservation. A small operation, a one-man show so to speak. Brother Chee. He was in pretty good shape when we spoke last. A year or so ago."

"And the people in San Carlos, the Apaches?"

"The same. Okay for now."

"And the friars in Sedona? Are they also all right?" she asked smiling.

"They are dilettantes!" he said. "They spend more time being photographed with the tourists, posing in front of their chateau than they do helping those in need."

"They certainly have a lovely monastery," she said. "The views of those red mountains are spectacular."

"Pah. You read Arturo's cards from that place? They make just enough pear brandy to keep themselves intoxicated most of the time. It is *not* Elixir. Not after Arturo found out and cut them off. No more additives. He said they were a waste of seeds."

"So you feel we could safely bypass the good monks of Sedona. For now," she grinned.

"Forever. Do you know for a while they were watering down their already worthless product and selling it over the counter to the tourists? As magic wine or some such nonsense. The only good that came out of that experiment was the 'donation' I extorted from them, oh, seven or eight years ago. They wrote me. They needed Elixir and they wanted holy soil, in quantity. I called them, told them five thousand a bottle and I'd throw in the dirt but they had to send cash up front. Twenty-four hours later a courier brought a big envelope full of hundred dollar bills. A hundred grand! I sent them two cases of rebottled Jaquin's pear brandy and a bushel of dirt from the town dump. I never heard from them again. They probably wrote it off on their taxes! Do you know they gross almost a million a year on trinkets and mission tours? They charge ten bucks to have their picture taken! It's preposterous!"

"I'm sorry, Frank. I didn't mean to get you all worked up."

"I know, child. It's all right. We put their money to good use though. And Arturo said the pears are there if we ever need them."

"Where should our next stop be then, in your opinion?"

"The mission San Xavier del Boc on the San Xavier Indian Reservation. We must go there. It's south of Tucson."

"Junior," she called out. "Are you okay to keep driving for a bit?" He said yep and she said, "Stay on Forty to Flagstaff. We'll change drivers there."

Junior made the turn on I-17 south and George took the wheel when they gassed up in Mountainaire, the Arizona version. They drove through Phoenix in the early morning, picking up I-10, still heading south, finally stopping at a 'No Facilities' rest area just below Picacho. Doc was the only other person still awake.

"Did you see that sign back there?" he asked George as they parked in the truck side of the lot. 'Prison Area. Don't pick up hitchhikers.' Gives you a warm and fuzzy feeling about stopping here at night, doesn't it?"

"The poor escaped convict that wanders into this nut mobile's gonna wish he was back inside," George laughed.

By sunrise, the women were up. Maggie walked the dog, encountering only a trucker urinating beside the tire of his rig. The coffee was brewing when she returned and Kate was quietly harassing Junior, tickling him and kissing his neck in an attempt to wake him. George was snoring in the aft bunk, Doc asleep in the rear cabin. Frank emerged from the bathroom looking as well rested as if he'd slept in the stateroom of a cruise ship.

"Can I drive, Maggie?" he asked, adding, "Arturo used to let me, when we were on the freeway. It scared me a little on the back roads."

"Be my guest. I'll bring us coffee and sit up there with you. We'll be the king and queen of the road."

It was less then fifty miles to Tucson and then another twenty-five to their exit, Frank needing neither map nor road sign to find his way. They drove slowly down a narrow, dusty road bordered by drainage ditches, a few scraggly pinion trees the only substantial vegetation, clumps of cactus emerging here and there amongst the desert grasses.

"Kind'a harsh country, isn't it?" Maggie said.

"Yes it is. We left the woods behind above Phoenix. It's mostly desert from there south. This reservation, these Indians, are a poor lot. They have so little to work with in this country, the desert. Their mission church is quite fascinating though and there is another building here that I think will interest you as well. We're almost there."

They made two turns and entered a parking area across from a long, white adobe structure, the center of which was apparently the church itself, a tall bell tower with the ubiquitous white cross above. Surrounding the lot on the other end were flea market style stalls and tents, some complete with roofs and doors, others simply sawhorses and planks with a tarp staked above.

"Some of the locals ply the tourist trade," Frank explained, seeing Maggie reviewing the open air market. "Let's go in and roust Brother Odham. We can let the boys sleep a little longer. Would you like to take a walk, Kate?"

The three of them crossed the street between the parking lot and mission and climbed the limestone stairs leading to the church. "This is the oldest Catholic church in this country," he explained to them, "and quite beautiful on the inside. Very ornate. Shall we?" he asked. The church was breathtaking, wildly colorful painted walls, dozens of extravagant life sized figurines, carved columns and beams, even the ceiling a tapestry of intricate religious symbols in every hue imaginable.

"Wild, isn't it?" his said as they stood in the back. There were a few worshippers in the front pews and a priest setting up for morning mass. They tiptoed down the aisle to the priest.

"Excuse me, Father. Is Brother Odham about yet?" The priest turned from the altar, recognition simultaneous and they embraced, slapping each other's backs heartily.

"Frank, how have you been! I haven't seen you in, what, four years? And you stopped calling a year ago. Shame on you for not returning my calls," he said.

"I had a bit of trouble, Paul, but things are back on track now. Kate and Maggie, Father Paul Odham, the big cheese in this mousetrap. Paul, Maggie is Arturo's wife."

"Oh my God! Oh, sweet merciful Jesus," Father Odham exclaimed, taking Maggie's hands in his and bowing before her. "Bless you, bless you, dear Margaret, can we ever repay your kindness? My people owe you so much."

Maggie looked at first one priest, then the other. "Ah, you're welcome? But I don't–"

"Hush, child," Father Francis said placing his hand on her arm and winking to her. "I'll explain later. Well, Brother Paul," Frank said. "Do you have time to give us a tour of your operation? It's been quite a long time since I've been here and I'm sure Margaret would like to see what you have accomplished."

"Certainly, certainly. It would be my greatest pleasure," Father Odham replied. "Please, Margaret, allow me," he said offering his arm to her and leading them through a side door.

"What's going on, Frank?" Kate whispered.

"Patience, lass. A few more moments will tell the tale," he said.

They walked along a maze of dark corridors, leaving the church proper judging by the change in wall construction, going from adobe to concrete block to frame and drywall, and then back to block, the last section clearly a recent addition. They stopped in front of a freshly painted steel door and Father Odham looked back at them and smiled, then threw the door open and led them out into the daylight, all of them blinking, briefly blinded.

As Maggie's vision adjusted, she found herself looking up at an angle at a multi-colored stucco building, three stories of green tinted windows staring back. A circular driveway led up to and under a canopied entry pavilion. Mounted on the leading edge of the lower roof of the pavilion were a series of flags. The US, Mexico, and Texas she recognized, the other six or seven she did not.

Beyond the flags and above them, on the face of the building itself, there were sparkling letters which she could not read because of the angle at which the group faced the structure.

"Come with me, my dear," Frank said. They walked out into the driveway and he turned them all to face the building.

"What do you think, child?" he said to Maggie.

'The Margaret Marone Wellness Center' in two foot copper letters emblazoned the painted façade of the building, stripes and swirls of color racing across every vertical surface, the polished letters glinting in the morning sun.

"What is it, Frank? What is it for?" she asked.

"Just what it says, Margaret. A center dedicated to making people well. A hospital, a nursing home, outpatient rehab, daycare, head start. Paul has it all here, don't you Paul?"

"We are blessed indeed, Brother Francis. And we owe it all to you, Margret and your magnificent husband. Thank you, my dear. Thank you, thank you."

"Show us around, Paul," Frank said.

"The medical center," Father Odham explained, "includes all that Frank said it does and much more. We have a trauma center, an x-ray unit, pre and post natal care areas, a drug and alcohol treatment facility, fitness center, all arranged around shared core areas. The operations overlap but are independent. Your husband designed it, Margaret. He showed us how to get the approvals and he helped us to build most of it. Not that we paid much attention to the damn government. One of the few advantages to reservation life," he said. "We can tell the city and state to go screw themselves. But the Bureau of Indian Affairs, we had to let them think they had some oversight. A remarkable facility, isn't it?"

"Like nothing I've ever seen," Maggie said.

"Well, there's two more operating and three under construction to my knowledge," Father Odham said. "If you get a chance to stop and see them, I know their proprietors would be as glad to see you as I am."

Maggie smiled for the first time since seeing her name on the front of the building. "I love the colors, Paul. It's so… un-institutional, I guess. Cheerful, you know?"

"Arturo said you wanted it to be bright," Paul said. "And uplifting I think was his exact word, so when we had the scaffolding up for the stucco work, I turned the children loose, told them to make it happy. I think they succeeded."

"Indeed," she said. "Thank you for the tour. If you have time later, I'd like to talk some more but I need to get back to my companions now. I'm sorry."

"It's fine, Margaret. I am at your service."

Father Paul went back the way they had come and Frank led Maggie and Kate around the end of the church buildings, the motor home visible in the parking lot now two hundred yards off.

"Well, Frank, are you going to make this easy or do I have to beat the truth out of you," Maggie said. "What's it gonna be?"

"I suspect you have a few questions," he said. "Okay. Let's get everybody together, then I'll fill you in. You have to admit it was a grand surprise though, wasn't it?"

Maggie shook her head and kept walking.

The boys were awake when they returned, Doc and Junior showered and changed, George reclining in his bunk with a cup of coffee. Maggie announced that Frank had a story to tell them, that it involved The Margaret Marone Wellness Center which, she explained, was just on the other side of the church and she had no damn idea at all how it came to be.

"Let me see if I can give you the background, Maggie," Frank said. "Where to begin," he mused. "Alright. Once there was Elixir production, there was Elixir income, from donations usually although there were some outright sales, especially early on. More on that later. The goal, as I'm sure you have all ascertained, was to help the needy. The wellness centers are the final product if you will."

"Centers?" Doc asked.

"Father Paul, the director of this place," Maggie explained, "said there are two more built and three being built. Where are they, Frank?"

"There's a little one on the Apache Reservation and a bigger one on the Navajo. I was sort of glad we didn't go there. I wanted you to see this one first. It's the flagship. There's one in Gila Bend that isn't done yet and two in Mexico. One of them is near Magdalena in Sonara Province. Our next stop."

"So Arturo designed these facilities," Maggie said, "and Elixir funds paid for them. There must have been a hell of a lot of donations."

"There are. Or were. Current production figures I don't have, with Arturo's death and the Trout problem. But bear in mind, the costs were nowhere near what you would have in the private sector. Between labor from the local people and the assistance of volunteers, the cost was greatly reduced. We mostly had only material costs. And Arturo was amazing at soliciting product contributions. These facilities are all legitimate, non-profit corporations so all donations are tax deductible. And the Elixir made a powerful bargaining chip when there was a need."

"Why didn't you want Father Paul to know that I was not aware of its existence?" Maggie asked.

"Ah, that's a metaphysical question, child. You are like a mythical creature to these people. A good fairy if you will. Arturo they could see and talk to, but you were an abstract. He would talk about you, but of course they never met you. And the implication was that you were the source of funds. He did not want the Elixir to be viewed as a product, especially not a valuable product. Do you see?"

"Sort of. But certainly Paul must recognize reality."

"Yes and no. The power of any myth resides in the minds of the believers. Father Odham chooses to believe in the magic, his follower's believe in him and the magic is therefore enhanced. The center would be no less useful without its patron saint, but the spirit of those who work there would be reduced and so would their effectiveness. And let me make sure that you understand something: you *were* his motivation. If he had never met you, none of this would exist."

"Wow," Kate said. "You're practically a deity. Should we avert our eyes in your presence?"

"Kiss my divine butt," Maggie said. "I'll settle for blind obedience."

"Hell, Mags, you already got that," George said.

"Then no back-talk. That might be nice."

"Nah," Junior said. "That'd be no fun at all."

"Christ on a crutch, even a goddess gets no respect around here."

Maggie took George, Junior and Doc on a tour of the church and hospital, all of them impressed by both the colorfully ornate church and the wildly imaginative wellness center. Father Paul found them as they were exiting the center and the introductions were made beneath the array of flags.

"Is there a specific reason for the flags, Father Paul?" Doc asked.

"They represent the origins of our constituents basically. The US, and Mexico, Arizona, New Mexico, Texas, tribal flags from here, the Apache and Navajo Nations, and of course the Catholic Church. Arturo thought they added a nice touch."

"Paul, I need you to explain something to Maggie," Frank said. "The Elixir ingredient that you produce here, the what and the how."

"The antibiotic," Doc said.

"Certainly," Father Odham said. "And yes, it is a form of antibiotic. A scientifically improved version of an old folk remedy, generally attributed to the Anasazi, the ancient ones. The Hopi are their closest direct descendants although all the southwestern tribes are related to some part of that rootstock. We're talking about thousands of years ago."

"I assume it's made from indigenous flora," Doc said.

"Correct. And then enhanced with various vitamins and minerals. Processed of course, for purity and consistency. I'll be glad to give you a print out of the ingredients, directions on how to cook a batch," he said.

"I think we should have that information," Doc said. "Don't you, Maggie?"

"Yes, please, Father Paul. Did you provide this medicine to Arturo or was it the other way around?"

"Anasazi Aloe? That's our nickname," he laughed. "The primitive form is more or less common knowledge amongst the Native American population, in this area anyway. Arturo had an improved version and he asked us to produce it in quantity for him. For the Elixir. We were only too happy to oblige. I have quite a stockpile on hand. You're welcome to as much as you need. Is there anything else I can do for you, Margaret? Anything at all?"

"Not that I can think of, Father. Not now."

"I got one," Junior said. "Where are your orchards? You do have pears, don't you?"

"Oh my, yes. Our orchards have been producing for fifteen years or more. They're on the other side of the interstate on this side of the Santa Cruz River on land your father leased from the state. A ninety-nine year lease for a dollar a year. The State Agricultural Agent told us that land was worthless and that we were insane to waste the dollar. Arturo brought in big earth moving machines. Pots? I forget what they were called."

"Pans," George said.

"That's it. Pans. And we built a reservoir. The Santa Cruz is intermittent. We divert to the lake when we can and irrigate the trees. We get wonderful fruit. Each year we send a half- bushel to the agent with a check for the dollar. Arturo thought that was hysterical."

"Sounds like Ol' Pancho, don't it, Mags?" George said.

"Yes it does. I'm surprised he didn't deliver them personally."

They took their leave of Father Odham, returning to the motor home to discuss their next move.

"How far is it to Magdalena, Frank?" Doc asked.

"A little more than two-hundred miles, most of it in Mexico."

"And the roads?"

"Fair. About like a US state road. Two lanes. We'll be okay, especially in the daytime."

"Are you suggesting we spend the night here, Frank?" Maggie asked.

"I suggest we cross the border in the morning, yes. And we may want to take stock of our belongings. We will be very carefully searched when we return."

"Meaning?" Maggie asked.

"Meaning I traveled sufficiently with Arturo to know that this vehicle has certain hidden assets, shall we say, and depending on what you folks have stored therein, we could face potential problems if one of those assets were to be discovered."

Doc and Junior exchanged a look.

"Do you think Father Paul would look after a few things for us?" Doc asked.

"I thought as much," Frank said. "Of course he would and we can get them on our return."

Chapter Twenty-three

They purchased insurance for the motor home and bikes and acquired travel visas in the Nogalas on the Arizona side of the border, then crossed into Mexico without incident, maneuvering through the narrow streets of the other, much larger, Nogalas before emerging on Highway 15, south of town. The topography was similar to the desert terrain they had driven through around Tucson until, as they got further south, the cactus and grassland began to give way to oak and pines, visible on the hillsides to the south and east of the highway.

The town of Magdalena was quaintly bucolic, the town square dominated by a church of impressive proportions, far out of scale compared to the little shops and offices that surrounded it.

"Big church," Junior said as he carefully cornered around the manicured parkland that marked the town square.

"Santa Maria Magdalena de Buquivaba," Father Francis offered. "A monument to its founder, Father Eusebio Francisco Kino. He's buried here. There are a couple dozen missions in Sonara and southern Arizona that trace their origins to him. Very prolific missionary. Your father was fascinated by him, all that he accomplished in such a primitive environment. Amazing actually. I wanted you to see it," he said addressing the group, "for an historical perspective."

They parked and took a short walking tour of the church and grounds and visited the mausoleum of the founder. When they had circumnavigated the park and returned to their vehicle, Maggie addressed Frank.

"What are we doing, Frank?" she asked.

"Call it what you will, my dear. A respite, a history lesson or mental preparation. This church and its founder are important to your understanding of your husband, his motivation. Do you see, child?"

"A role model," Doc said.

"Correct. *The* role model. Now, my impatient daughter, we go to meet your mother-in-law."

"What?" Maggie said. "She's been dead for twenty years! More."

"Not hardly," Frank said.

They drove out of town on a narrow but well-maintained gravel road, winding gradually uphill. After a few miles they passed a turn-off clearly marked 'San Ignacio'.

"Down there is the original," Frank said.

"Dare I ask?" Maggie said. "The original what?"

"The first of Arturo's missions. The incubator if you will."

"Is it still operating?" she asked.

"Certainly."

"And we aren't going there?"

"I thought you were in a hurry, child," Frank said.

"You take great pleasure in pulling my chain, don't you, Frank?"

"It would be a sin to take great pleasure in the discomfort of others," he said. "I take *some* pleasure in it."

"You bastard," she answered. "I take back anything nice I ever said about you."

"Junior," Frank called out. "Turn right up ahead, see the drive?"

Junior made the turn between two tall oaks with some difficulty, creeping the bus up a one lane cart path, slowly maneuvering between pairs of specimen-sized trees, pine then oak, the pattern repeating out of sight as the road climbed the side of a small mountain, other, larger peaks visible beyond. After twenty minutes of almost continuous assent, Frank told Junior to stop. They were at the crest of the mountain and the view of the hills beyond and the valleys below was spectacular.

"Let's stop here and I'll give you some background," he said. "I told you Arturo's family had money," he began after a moment of contemplation. "This is their land, what we have been driving through since the turn-off and much more there and over there," he said gesturing broadly ahead and to the left. "Some of it has been in the family for several generations, your grandmother's family, Junior, and some of it is more recently acquired, your grandfather and his brother's family. The brother still lives over there," again indicating the left.

"A considerable holding," Doc said. "Old land grant or something?"

"On grandmother's side, yes. From Porfirio Diaz, the last true dictator before the revolution. He offered land grants to thousands of people in an attempt to settle the Sonoran region, sort of take control back from the outlaws by sending in the citizens. It worked well enough that the combination overthrew him eventually," Frank said.

"Your great-grandfather fought in the revolution, Junior. He was a champion of the people. A true Renaissance man, a soldier, a doctor, trained at the University of Texas by the way, botanist, distiller and something of a mystic as well. As he got older he became interested in folk remedies, studying with the medicine men of the local tribes, traveling up into Arizona, and Colorado. You see where this is going don't you?" he asked them.

"The Elixir," Maggie said.

"Yes," Frank said. "He was the originator. Experimented with various fruit stock, different additives. He may have begun distilling just for recreational use, but apparently something he concocted struck a chord because it became his life's great work. And he taught Arturo."

"And where was Arturo's father during all this?" Maggie asked.

"You're getting ahead of the story, Margaret. In the early forties another family moved into the neighborhood, descendants of a French officer who immigrated to Mexico with Maximillian. They were civilized enough as a whole, their plans being to timber and farm, raise some beef cattle. But their sons, oh, they were devils. They wanted no parts of a farmer's life. They squandered their early years smuggling and gambling, whoring and raising hell. And eventually discovering dope. And your grandmother, Junior.

"They courted that poor woman like they did everything else–fast and hard. And in competition. The younger one, he truly loved her and it was no wonder. She was a beautiful girl, a lovely, black-haired senorita, from a good family, well mannered, smart, and a body, ah, it would make you weep.

"The older one, the blue-eyed devil, he wanted her because his brother did. And they fought, many times, but the younger brother won her heart and eventually the doctor allowed them to marry. Arturo was born three years later.

"The other brother started the dope business, buying marijuana grown in these mountains and taking it north to the Gringos. It seemed harmless enough and the younger brother worked with him sometimes, other times working with the doctor, traveling with him, sometimes doing both things at once," Frank said.

"But the pot business, it did not interest the older brother for long. It's bulky, it smells bad, it grows anywhere, the quality is inconsistent. He wanted something more compact and more lucrative. Heroin. Mexican brown tar at first. Eventually he refined his own. The younger brother wanted nothing to do with it. Smoke a little dope? Okay. He did that himself sometimes. Shoot something into your body? No. He would not be a part of that enterprise.

"In 1965, as the Devil brother was starting his heroin business, the younger brother told him he was done. He would take this last load of pot across to Tucson, but then he was out. The Americano drug police busted him not far from San Xavier. Arturo was nine and did not see his father again for many years."

"Tell us about Arturo's childhood, Frank. What do you know of it?" Maggie said.

"We'll let his mother be part of that conversation. Let's stretch our legs and then we'll go meet her."

They let the dog off and he began capering excitedly as soon as he hit the ground, nose up sucking in great lungs full of the sweet, piney air, a high-pitched howl bursting forth several times.

"He's been here before," George said.

"And he likes the place," Junior added.

With one more howl the dog took off down the driveway, loping, head up, tail wagging.

"Dog!" Maggie called but he ignored her, soon passing out of sight around a turn.

"He is fine, Margaret. Our destination is just around the bend. He'll be our emissary."

They drove down a short incline, rounded a bend right on the edge of a wooded slope, then crested another rise and the hacienda came into view below them. Built on a bluff overlooking a valley checkered with fields of various crops, the house was a rectangle of adobe and native stone with a low pitched, clay tile roof. A veranda extended almost from the house proper to the cliff's edge and stone stairs led from a circular parking area to the side of the porch. Standing at the top of the stairs, hand resting on the head of the dog, stood a woman, slightly bent, but still of proud bearing, silver hair coiled in a bun pierced by a golden comb.

"There's your mother-in-law, Margaret." Frank nodded toward the woman through the windshield as they parked.

"She looks like her son. Or vice versa. Let me out," Maggie said.

Maggie climbed down from the motor home and walked directly to the stairs. She began to speak to the woman from the next to last step, making them eye to eye. None of the others could hear the exchange but everyone saw the lady spread her arms and wrap them around Maggie's neck, kissing her on both cheeks. Maggie gestured for Junior and soon the greeting was repeated, the boy standing two steps down and leaning in toward the woman for his kisses.

Then the others were brought forward, Kate, Doc, George, and finally Frank, nearly hidden behind George, the woman's reaction upon seeing him peeking out from behind George's back a mixture of shock, joy and anger, the emotions flying across her face as the priest stared back at her.

Her expression finally fixed on anger and a verbal hurricane of Spanish flew out of her, the onslaught sufficient to move George down two treads, Frank cowering behind him. The woman took a step toward George, screamed 'Francisco!' then charged down the last three steps. George fainted left then lunged right, leaving Frank to face her on his own. She leapt on him and Doc was moving to intercede when the woman stopped screaming and wrapped her arms around Frank's neck and kissed him on the lips. Frank put his arms around her waist and began to mumble something.

"Rosario!" he said eventually. "Calm yourself, woman. I'm a priest, for Christ's sake!"

"You were my husband before you were a priest, you son of a bitch!"

"Frank?" Maggie said. "We need to have another little talk, don't we."

"Yes, child, we surely do and we are finally in the right place at the right time. Rosario, you are forgetting your guests. Come, everyone, we will have coffee and tell stories."

Rosario marched across the patio, dragging Frank along, hosing him with staccato bursts of hostile Spanish, his vocabulary reduced to single syllables as the others gathered at an iron table surrounded by a dozen bull hide chairs.

"So, Ma. You think Frank is Arturo's father?"

"I think *Frank* is the blue-eyed devil whether his brother lives over there," she gestured across the valley, "or not."

"Now Mags, don't be so hard on Father Francis. He's just goin' for maximum dramatic impact in the tale," George said. "That old boy sure knows how to spice up a story, don't he, Doc?"

"I don't think it's all theatrics," Doc answered. "If he would have just come out with it, the parental aspect, it probably would have clouded our objectivity, skewed our understanding."

"So what!" Maggie said. "Would we have not believed him? Left him to rot in Trucas' swamp?"

"No. But we may have assumed that his point of view was prejudiced by their relationship. And George is right–this makes a much more interesting presentation," he said as he put his arm around Maggie's shoulders. "You have to agree with that."

"No arguments there," she said. "He certainly surprised me. It does explain the depth of his knowledge of the subject though."

Rosario and Frank returned, each bearing a silver tray, one with a coffee service, the other with cups and saucers. They were followed a moment later by a woman in her twenties, waist length black hair tied in a long braid.

"Maggie," Frank said, "your sister-in-law, Sinaloa. Introduce yourself, Sin," he added as he fussed with the service of the coffee.

"Frank, for the love of God! I am going to *kill* you," Maggie hissed.

"No, daughter," Rosario said. "*I* am going to kill him. You may beat him though, if you wish."

"With great pleasure," Maggie said as she rose and embraced Sinaloa.

"The famous Margaret Marone," Sinaloa said looking Maggie over head to toe. "You *are* beautiful, he did not exaggerate. And Junior. You look like your Mama, but you're so big," she said as she hugged him.

"This is Kate," Junior said, "and my Uncle George. And this is Doc, my friend and mentor."

"Are you Frank's daughter?" Doc asked.

"Uncle Frank," she laughed. "No, I would be Arturo's half sister," she said. "And his cousin."

"Ah," Doc said. "I see, I think."

"Estiban Gomez Palasio," Rosario said, "Frank's brother and my second husband, after the no good *first* one ran off," she added vehemently, "is Sinaloa's father."

"Curiouser and curiouser," George said. "It's like a bilingual soap opera. Interestin' family you married into, Mags."

"Uncle George?" Sinoloa said to him. "You have no idea!"

"Yet, I hope. I'm expectin' one a you to finish this here story for us."

Frank got them started by giving his niece and ex-wife some background on the journey so far.

"Grandfather's Elixir," Sinoloa said when he was done. "The tonic that could change the world. That's what Grandfather believed."

"Anyway," Frank said, "I have explained the family history up to our marriage, Arturo's birth and my incarceration, but I thought it best for them to hear the rest from you, Rosario, what happened after."

"My first husband was a reprobate in many ways," Rosario said. "Especially in the ignorance of his youth. But he was also a kind man, to me and my father," speaking as if Frank was not there. "My second husband, he was the Devil himself which I did not recognize until it was too late. When this one," now indicating Frank with the jerk of a thumb, "vanished, our only source of information was his brother. Who told us Francis was dead, killed by the Gringos in the drug business. I was heart-broken, my young son fatherless. Who would look after us, who would help Papa run the ranchero? He was too old to till the fields, round up cattle. Not that he had any interest in those things. His head was in the clouds, we thought, fooling with that damn Elixir.

"And the Devil, he was charming. He fooled me. He even fooled Papa. A year later we were married and ten months after that, Sinaloa was born. By then I knew the Devil for what he was, an evil man, a drug smuggler and a killer."

"And a thief," Frank added. "Tell them about Arturo and the Elixir."

"The Elixir," she sighed. "The damn Elixir. Papa started experimenting with his herbs and tonics long ago. He always studied such things it seems. My mother died when I was an infant. Papa raised me," she added. "And when Arturo was old enough, five or six, Papa would take him along on his journeys. Papa would hear about some potion the Navajo used or a Zuni concoction and he would pack up his old Jeep and the two of them would toddle off. It was great fun for Arturo, big adventures. They would return in a few days or a few weeks and they would try to discover what the weed or fungus, awful stuff mostly, actually did. If anything. Arturo was as fascinated as Papa.

"And if Papa found something he thought had some value, he would blend it into his pear brandy. Looking for the 'Fountain of Youth', a modern Ponce de Leon. Everyone laughed at the foolish old man."

"Until he discovered something that worked," Frank added. "That was about '63 or '64 I guess."

"Yes. Until then. By the time this one went away," again jerking a thumb at Frank, "Papa's pear brandy had become the Elixir, a tonic. Papa was very excited about it, wanted to take it to a pharmaceutical company in the U.S. for testing. His disappearance," the thumb again, "put that on hold. Papa was robust, from his magic tonic he claimed, but he was old. Too old to undertake the journey, the negotiations with the Gringos. Too old to stop them from stealing it from him was his biggest fear."

"Ingrained from an early age in his grandson," Doc said.

"Exactly," Maggie added. "That was what Arturo apparently feared as well," she explained to Rosario and Sinaloa.

"Papa should have feared the Devil next door more than the Devil Americanos," Rosario said. "Estiban offered to help. While he was courting me. I did not realize it was courtship at the time, just my brother-in-law trying to help the widow of his only brother. Hah! Help indeed!

"He had his chemists analyze the Elixir. He was a heroin drug lord by this time. We did not know this until later. He duplicated it as best he could. It was not like Papa's but it had a certain power of its own. And he sold it by the bottle.

"After we were married, he took control of our lands, to help Papa he said. But what he wanted was the pears and Papa's Elixir formula. Papa would not help him. Estiban confiscated all his lab equipment and all his Elixir. That was the end for Papa. He died a month later, broken hearted. But the formula survived. In Arturo, up here," she said tapping her head. "Estiban did not know."

"How did Arturo feel about his stepfather?" Maggie asked.

"My son was an unusual man, Margaret. I'm sure you know that. But he was also an exceptional child. It was obvious almost immediately that he was smart. Gifted beyond my experience. Or that of his grandfather. We did not send him off to school with the other children, it would have been pointless. By his fifth year he could read, and write, anything placed before him, in Spanish and English. By seven, his mathematics exceeded those of Papa. We had to send to the University in Mexico City, and in Texas, for text books. By nine, he had absorbed all of Papa's chemistry and botany and all of this medical schooling. Arturo's books had to come from graduate level classes to keep up with his appetite for learning. Then Papa died. I was with child. It was not an easy pregnancy and the father was of no help to me. He had what he wanted, our lands, orchards, me. And a son, he thought, an heir. We fooled him there didn't we, Sinaloa," she said to her daughter.

"Screw him," the girl said. "He is not my father but for a squirt of jisum."

"Sinaloa!" her mother exclaimed but everyone else was laughing. "Truth be known," Rosario continued, "I lost track of the boy almost. I let him run wild. I blame myself. My own needs overcame those of my son. I was a bad mother," she said.

"You raised a fine son, Rosario," Frank said. "You could not control his fate. No one could. Now answer Maggie's question."

"Arturo hid his feelings. He embraced his Uncle Estiban, pretending to love and obey him. He went to work for him, even moved into his home. I would not leave here when we were married and once I found out what Estiban's real motives were, what he really was after, I threw him out. We did not speak again for many years, all information, one about the other or about his daughter was transmitted by Arturo, across this valley. That is his hacienda," she said aiming her finger at a sprawling fortress visible on the opposite side, perhaps an air mile away.

"What were Arturo's motives?" Doc asked. "What did he hope to accomplish?"

"I cannot speak for his deepest emotions. The boy was too complex, too far thinking maybe even for his own good. Whatever plans were in his head, he kept them locked away in there. Certainly his uncle never suspected. I can tell you what I know, what happened.

And I know for a fact that he blamed Estiban, rightly, for his grandfather's death and for his father's disappearance.

"At first Arturo would come home some days, after he moved in over there, and tell me what was going on, about Estiban's business, things he had learned. Then he stopped talking to me about it."

"He didn't want you involved," Maggie said. "He did the same thing to us."

"For your protection, Rosario," Frank added. "He told me that."

"He told me that too," Rosario said. "Later. But it still hurt. He was shutting me out I thought. Or worse, turning into Estiban."

"Never," Frank said. "He was spying, gathering information to use against the Devil. Never like him."

"I know that, Francisco. He was also experimenting with the Elixir, using Estiban's laboratory to tinker with the formula. He resurrected his grandfather's product and improved it. He added the cocaine he told me and other things I did not understand. But he said he had succeeded, that he had an Elixir that could really help people and that he was going to take it away, make sure that it was used for the right purpose, like Papa would have wanted. This was near the end, before he fled." She broke down at that point, weeping silently. Her daughter knelt beside her, comforting her with murmured words.

"Let's take a break here, folks," Sinaloa said. "Uncle Frank, take Mama inside while I get us some refreshments." Sinaloa handed her mother off to Frank then turned to Kate. "Can you give me a hand?"

"Well, Mags," George said. "Who'd a thunk it, eh?"

"My opinion," Doc said, "is that every word of it is either fact or the facts as they believe them."

"I'm with Doc, Ma. This doesn't seem like bullshit to me."

"Amazing," she summarized. "Do you think they really know how he died?"

"Without a doubt. And I'll be very surprised if it does not involve the Devil," Doc said, pointing across the valley.

"Uncle Estiban. Can't wait to meet him," Junior said.

The girls returned with a cooler of beer, a brace of limes and a bowl of toasted tortillas broken into bite-sized pieces, accompanied by salsa and a platter of avocado slices. Frank returned with Rosario. After they had all nibbled and drank, Frank began again, saying he would continue for Rosario as he had heard the story first hand from Arturo.

"Arturo was party to almost all of Estiban's secrets by this point, either having been told them or by deducing them on his own. He was a trusted lieutenant in the drug operations, in the lab work mostly but also in the transport. He was nineteen.

"Estiban was a cocaine middle man by now, buying from the Columbian cartel and distributing in the southwest. More money in it than heroin, much more than marijuana. His forte was still the smuggling, getting the product across the border. And Arturo knew all of his routes, all his methods, even most of the mules. And he needed cocaine for the Elixir. Not a lot, there is very little in it per gallon, but he had long range plans and the coke would be the most hazardous of the additives to procure, in the future.

"And he did not want his uncle to profit from the Elixir. Estiban was selling it to his dope cronies for outrageous amounts, thousands per bottle. Arturo's Elixir would have cost them even more, the improved version that Arturo had been teasing Estiban with, letting him sample it as he developed it. Maintaining his trust and justifying his interest and the lab time. And the cocaine. Estiban is a greedy man. Arturo needed his permission to experiment.

"Estiban had bragged to Arturo that he was making so much money from the Elixir that he could probably get out of the coke business completely if he chose, spend his time watching the orchards grow while Arturo cooked pears. Telling him how good his drug pals all thought it was and how much better their lives were because of it."

"That must have stung him hard," Doc said. "Those kinds of men benefiting from his and his grandfather's work."

"Yes," Frank said. "The direct opposite of Papa's intent. Arturo did not let that happen. Twice a year my brother leaves his home to transact business, face to face, with his Colombian suppliers. They used to meet on a private island in the Caribbean. Arturo stayed behind on this last trip, too involved with an experiment he claimed. There was a load of cocaine going north the next day, from a safe house in Magdalena. Arturo told the mule that he was going to go along. That night he emptied Estiban's safe and booby-trapped the lab and the still and emptied every drop of Elixir in the wine cellar where it was stored. He tried to booby-trap the orchards as well but it rained. Most of the crop survived. The bombs were on timers. Arturo was in the mountains when they exploded. He crossed the border with the drug mule, then told him that he would take the load to its destination himself. The mule could go home. Arturo was the boss, the great man's nephew so the mule agreed. Arturo drove to the mission at San Xavier where his grandfather's old friend, Father Odham," stopping now to smile at his audience, "was kind enough to store some things for him, not unlike a similar transaction you may recall," he said to Doc. "Arturo had a vehicle already there, it had been for almost a year, and Father Odham was only too happy to make the pick-up truck Arturo arrived in disappear. Permanently."

"How much did he take from the Devil?" Maggie asked.

"He would never say exactly but I gather several million, in cash, some other valuables as well. And fifty kilos of pure Columbian coke."

"Uncle Estiban must have been furious," Junior said.

"As a pissed on alley cat. The lab was no big deal. It was replaceable. So was the still. The coke, eh, just business. Not that he would not kill you for stealing it, but the loss itself, small potatoes. But the Elixir, that made him madder than the money. He not only had none, he didn't know how to make any, the new version."

"That is when the Devil came into my home," Rosario said, "and ransacked it. He said he wanted information on the whereabouts of my 'traitorous son', which he did I'm sure, but what he really wanted was my Elixir. He was sure I had a basement full. I had two bottles in plain site which he took and two more hidden which he found and took as well. Arturo had buried a barrel of it under the smokehouse. That he did not find. But that night, that is when he told me Arturo was a dead man. Soon. The Devil would kill him personally."

"Let me continue," Frank said. "Arturo fled to Texas, to Houston, where quite by chance, he met an amazing girl and fell in love. You know much of the rest but a couple more details are relevant. Once Arturo had something other than himself to protect," nodding toward Maggie and Junior, "he tried to, ah, explain what he had done, to his uncle, tried to get him to understand. He wrote him a letter, mailed from Florida or somewhere, it isn't important. He told Estiban that it was wrong to exploit the Elixir and worse to keep it a secret, that it should be used for good. He told him what the cocaine was for, the Elixir, not profit, and he asked his uncle to forgive him, that he did not hate him despite the despicable things he had done to his mother, father and grandfather. And he told the Devil that he would send him enough Elixir for his personal needs. Which he did by the way, every year a few bottles.

"Now the Devil had a problem. He loved his nephew, to the extent he is capable of love, and would have forgiven the transgression if he could. But he could not, not without a huge loss of face. His authority was weakened by the attack. To allow the attacker to walk away unpunished would have meant the end for him. His suppliers would have scoffed at his weakness, overcharged him, cheated him with weight. His own people may have even overthrown him. He had already let loose his dogs, he could not call them off now. Even though he did not want the boy dead by this point. Didn't even want him found. But the orders had already been issued–find Arturo. He was able to add a cravat though. He must be taken alive, brought before the Devil unharmed so that he personally could mete out the punishment.

"After a few years the incident was mostly forgotten and Estiban stopped looking. But the hit was never rescinded, couldn't be, and some people remembered. One of them was the mule from the last cocaine run. After many years he was still in the business, a little bigger fish but still just chum. Chum who saw a man on a motorcycle filling up at a gas station south of Nogalas, the Mexican side, on his way to visit his mother. Chum who followed the man and at an opportune moment, on a curve on a narrow road, came up behind him, at dusk, fast, and ran him off the road. And bad luck for the chum, although he did not know it till later that night, he hit the man too hard, the motorcycle skidding off the shoulder, the man crashing into a tree. The chum put the unconscious man in his pick-up truck and threw a dirty tarp over him, then pushed the bike down into the ravine. Then the chum drove to the house of some friends to show off his trophy, drinking mescal and Tecate till midnight before he delivered his prize to Don Estiban, sure that he would be richly rewarded. He was.

"After the Devil carried his dead nephew into his home, placing him on his own bed and ordering his mortician to come immediately, he took the chum down to the wine cellar where two of the Devil's men tied him by his thumbs to the rafters above. It took the Devil nearly four hours to personally peel every inch of skin off the chum and another two before enough of his fluids ran down the same drain as the Elixir had all those years before to finally expire.

"The next day Estiban brought his nephew home. Half his ashes are buried up the hill next to Papa," Frank said, tears flowing down his face, Rosario, Maggie, Sinaloa and Kate all crying as well, Junior and George both wiping at their eyes and noses, only Doc seemingly unmoved, his face a mask, staring across the valley at the hacienda beyond.

Frank got slowly to his feet. "I know you have questions," he said, "and I will do my best to answer them. In a bit." He walked toward the house and Rosario soon joined him.

"What a friggin' waste," George said.

"Why was he coming here, at that particular time," Maggie asked. "To visit Rosario?"

"Maybe," George answered. "Maybe he snuck down here every once in a while to say howdy. It was gettin' dark, on a back road."

"Doc," she asked. "Any thoughts?"

He turned away from the Devil's house finally and they all saw the expression on this face.

"Easy, Doc," George said. "You got your mad up I can see. What are you thinkin'?"

"I'm thinking that motherfucker needs to pay," Doc said.

"For Arturo?" Maggie said. "Estiban didn't kill him. It doesn't sound like he even wanted him to die."

"For all of it," Doc answered. "For his whole worthless, evil life."

"You're frustrated," George said. "You were expecting someone to be guilty of somethin' tangible so we could get after them. But it ain't like that, it's muddy, right and wrong mixed together."

"You're right," Doc said. "Exactly right. There's a villain but no smoking gun. I've been preparing myself, subconsciously I guess, I'm not sure, for some payback. Once we found out how, I was sure there would be a who."

"And you were workin' yourself up to 'do' him," George said.

"Yeah, pretty much."

"Aren't you relieved?" Maggie said. "There's no need to do anything. And I don't think it's our place to make him pay for his whole life." Doc turned toward her for a second and she saw his grim expression, saw the anger but also something else. Disappointment? A longing of some kind?

"Doc got his game face on, Mags," George said to her. "It ain't so easy to take it off, especially when they cancel the whole thing right before kickoff."

"What were…? Never mind," Maggie said. "Doc, it's not your job. It never was. We didn't 'sign you up'," she said, "to be our avenging angel."

"Yeah, that was just a bonus," George said.

"Shut up, George. Doc, look at me. We had a goal. We accomplished it. Forget Estiban, let's go home and have a life together. I love you, I want to move on and I want you with me. Get it, cowboy?"

He turned away from the valley again and looked at her face, her beautiful smile. The tension blew out of him as he released the air in his lungs, his mind clearing quickly.

"Yes, Maggie. I get it. Thank you."

They went inside after a bit, finding Frank and Rosario on a leather couch, arms around each other, talking quietly. Sinaloa and Kate appeared a few minutes later and they all found places around the old couple.

"Are you ready for a few final questions?" Maggie asked them. They both nodded and she continued.

"Did Arturo visit you often, Rosario?"

"A couple of times a year. Sometimes we would meet in other places. At San Xavier. We were there for the Grand Opening of your hospital, Margaret. He was so excited! He said he could stop hiding now, the Elixir was self-sufficient. He was going to see the Devil next, make his peace so that his family could come out of hiding, so that you could see what he had accomplished, work with him. He was very proud of it all. And very happy."

"Is that where he was going that evening?" Doc asked.

"I believe so. He was coming from San Xavier. He told us he would be here on the evening of that day. Late he thought. We had gone on home before him," she said.

"He was on that crazy Harley, Grandma. Followin' a car would a made him nuts. He could a got here in half the time ridin' alone."

"Junior is right. You cannot blame yourself," Maggie said.

"I wonder if Estiban knew he was coming," Doc said, "had his soldiers keeping watch."

"Why would he do that?" Rosario asked.

"To make sure he was alone, that it wasn't some kind of set up," Doc answered. "A man in his profession doesn't grow old by being careless."

"The Devil would not have told his lackeys *why* Arturo was coming," Frank added. "Just that he might be. The chum may have overstepped his directive, trying to curry favor with his boss."

"We will never know," Rosario said.

"Unless we go ask him," Junior said.

"No!" his mother said. "We've been over this and the subject is closed."

"She's right, boy," George said. "There's nothin' to be gained."

"A man's responsible for the actions of his people, right Doc?" Junior did not wait for an answer. "So that makes him responsible for Pop."

"I think the responsible party paid the price, Junior," Doc said. "Capping the old man won't change a thing. Let it go, son."

"God will settle the score with the Blue-Eyed Devil, grandson," Rosario said. "He will rot in the seventh circle of Hell for all eternity. That is my consolation."

"Yeah, well, we ain't gonna be there to see it are we," the boy answered.

"I surely hope not," Father Francis responded.

They had an early dinner prepared by Sinaloa and Kate, then congregated again around the seating area in the living room. Maggie asked Frank how he had come to the priesthood, almost as an afterthought in the conversation. They were all tired and she did not expect any kind of definitive answer. Frank surprised her with his response, complete and loquacious.

He told them about his release from prison after five years and his voyage home, his discovery of his brother's marriage to his wife and the depths of his despair. It was in the church of Santa Maria Magdalena, he said, that he got the call, while on his knees in front of a bank of unlit candles, asking God to forgive him for what he was about to do which was to kill his brother and take his own life, hoping that eliminating the Devil might tip the scales in his favor when he stood before the Lord. The voice of the long dead Father Kino filled his head, Frank knowing instantly who was providing this divine insight. 'Serve the church, my son', the voice told him. 'You will be part of a glorious enterprise'. Frank got to his feet, making the sign of the cross as he backed down the aisle, almost knocking down the parish priest.

"You have seen God," the man said, awe struck by the glow of enlightenment that radiated from Frank's face. Frank told the Father what had happened, what Father Kino had said. The priest called the bishop, the bishop the cardinal, and in a week Frank was enrolled in the seminary in Mexico City. His first and only posting was to the Santuario because who better to guide a place of miracles than someone who had experienced one first hand?

Arturo had found him there in his first year of service, the same year that Arturo had fled his uncle's home, knowing that Frank was alive from his surveillance of his uncle, hearing the talk amongst the soldiers, confirming the recipient of the miracle that his friends at San Ignacio had told him about, tracking the new priest's whereabouts through Father Odham.

"The start of 'a glorious enterprise'," Frank said.

"I'm goin' to bed," Junior announced. "In the Winnie."

The others soon retired as well, Kate joining Junior, George on the big couch, Doc and Maggie in one guestroom, Father Francis in another.

Chapter Twenty-four

Doc woke with a start, fully conscious in an instant, another before he could place the reason. Howling, loud and sustained, from the dog. He got up quickly, Maggie stirring but not awake, and strode through the living room past the snoring George. The dog was tied to one of the big clay pots, a large bowl empty at his feet. He was pulling at the rope, howling into the night, looking down into the valley below.

"Fuck me," Doc said, unaware he had spoken out loud. He ran to the motor home, pulled open the door and charged up the steps, the bang of the door bringing Kate fully awake.

"Where is he?" Doc demanded as Kate sat up. "Damn it, he's gone. Go get George. Hurry!" He began to rummage through his rucksack, pulling out boots and an old set of tiger stripes.

George came running out of the house a few seconds later. Doc was already dressed.

"What, what?" George bellowed.

"He's gone. To find his uncle, I'm pretty sure."

"How, when?"

"Through the valley the way the dog's acting. On foot. The bikes are still here."

"What do we do?"

"I'm going after him. Maybe you can go around in the motor home, come in the front. Run some interference or something." Doc scrambled up on the roof of the motor home and unlocked the concealed compartment below. "George! See what he took. There should be two Browning autos and the .22-250 in the back of that broom closet." The rest of the household was hurrying onto the patio when George stepped back out of the vehicle.

"One shotgun's gone," he called up to Doc.

"Fuck! He's gonna get himself killed." Doc climbed back down, stopping in front of Maggie. "I'll get him back," he said. "I swear to God I will. George! Keep that dog tied. I've got a headset, I'll keep in contact," he said as he trotted toward the ravine, slapping a magazine home on the AK-47, several others stuffed into his right pants pocket, the left bulging as well.

They heard him stop for a moment just outside the field of illumination from the house, heard him rearranging his ordinance, then they heard him chamber a round and take off down the hill. Then silence.

"Be careful, Doc, please!" Maggie yelled into the night, hoping it wasn't too late for him to hear her. Then she turned to the rest of them, searching their faces, settling on the priest.

"What should we do, Frank?" she asked quietly.

"Help them," Frank said, turning and running back into the house.

Doc took a quick lunar bearing before he continued, the clips now carefully sorted and stowed in separate pockets on this right side, the grenades similarly arrayed on the left, an eight inch combat knife sheathed in his right boot. He lost sight of the house lights from the hacienda as soon as he entered the tree line, several hundred yards of which had to be crossed before he hit the fields in the valley proper. He made no special attempt at stealth this far from his target but his passage through the woods was no more noisy than that of a stalking cat but faster, much faster.

He stopped at the edge of the first cultivated plot, hoping the light of the moon, just over half full, would allow him to spot the boy, hoping Junior's lead was not too great, thinking the dog kept quiet till it was done eating, how long would that take, then jogging across the valley, the Kalashnikov at port arms. No sign of Junior.

At the bottom of the valley a small watercourse ran through a brushy trough and Doc moved quietly along the bank, looking for the spot where the boy had crossed. He found it within fifty yards, several fresh boot prints embedded in the muddy bank, the last one still seeping water, his quarry less then ten minutes ahead, Doc's left hand smearing mud across his face as he watched the tread filling slowly.

"Maggie," he spoke quietly into the headset. "Do you copy?" he said as he moved across the creek.

"I'm here, Doc," she said, voice surprisingly calm.

"I found his trail. He isn't too far ahead. I'm hoping I can get him before he reaches the house. I probably won't be able to talk again."

"Okay, Doc," she answered. Then after a pause, "Please bring him back," followed by, "I love you, cowboy. Be careful."

"I love you. I'll see you soon."

"Doc," she said. "George and Frank are going to come around on a bike. It will take them a while."

"You stay there," he said urgently. "I can't have you…involved."

"I know," she said. "I'm here."

He loped across the next set of fields, the ground starting to rise gradually, then more steeply until he was nearly climbing, right hand on the ground every few steps for balance, his breathing too loud he thought, not in shape for a forced march, glad he wasn't carrying a field pack. He had hoped for another wood line between these fields and the top of the cliff that held the big house, but as the climb grew harder still he realized that the woods had been cleared, stumps cut almost at grade the evidence, underbrush almost non-existent. Fields of fire, he thought. The bastard is cautious. Or paranoid. And he knew that he should be crawling now, inching his way to the objective, silent and invisible, not scrambling up the hill like some berserk Viking storming a castle.

He pulled up behind a stump, lying flat, eyes peering over the top as he surveyed the hill above him, the crest he guessed still two hundred yards away. He could see the glow of the house lights on the artificial horizon, knew they were there because the stars were not and he was just getting into a crouch to push forward when he saw a form silhouetted against the lighter sky. Junior, had to be, something in his hands, moving stealthily up the slope. Get down you dumb shit, he screamed silently, now standing and charging up the hill, caution be damned.

The sound of the gun shot knocked him as flat as if he had been hit, all instinct now, burrowing for cover, rifle pointed out and up, ready to issue suppressing fire.

"Doc!" Maggie's frantic voice in his ear a few seconds later. "Are you alright?"

"Shhh," he hissed. "Yes. Don't talk now."

He began a sniper's crawl, as fast as he could, maintaining only the most minimum evasive protocol, until the slope around him was suddenly bathed in light. He froze, not even breathing, then in tiny increments, ratcheted his eyes up, blinded by three blazing lights perched on the edge of the ravine, flooding the slope in all directions. He seemed to be almost exactly in the middle of the lighted clearing, the center spotlight directly ahead. He began to move forward, calculating the length of time it would take him to move a hundred and fifty yards uphill on a cleared slope in essentially broad daylight. He knew he could be invisible to whoever might be looking down at him, moving so slowly that the human eye could not detect the change even while staring directly at him. But it would take several hours. Too long. If Doc shot out the lights, charged up the hill, and Junior was alive, his captors would probably kill him immediately, thinking Junior was walking point on a coordinated assault. Doc would have.

He crawled. Much faster than he would have on a sniper mission, much slower than he wanted to move. It took him thirty minutes and he came up directly under the center light, the last fifteen yards actually the easiest as the cone of light from the giant fixture didn't strike the ground till it had traveled that far, creating a wedge of shadow at its base.

The searchlights were built into a five-foot high hedge/wall combination and once he was in the landscaping, he slithered silently between the plantings. There was one guard walking lazily along the top of the wall, apparently unconcerned with the possibility of intruders coming up the naked grade. Doc worked up to within six feet of him and as the man took a step forward, Doc shot up the face of the wall, took the descending boot in both hands and twisted the guard over the side into the hedge. He smacked him once on the forehead with his rifle butt and had him concealed in the brush a second later. The man was armed with a 9mm pistol, not too serious, Doc thought, not an Uzi, but also with what Doc was pretty sure was Junior's Browning.

Doc tied him quickly with his own belt, slipped the pistol into the small of his back and tossed the Browning down the hedge line, then smacked the man in the head again to make sure he was out. Doc crawled down the hedge line another fifty feet before periscoping his eyes up over the wall. The far end of the house was about forty feet away, floodlights on the corner, nothing planted between the wall and house. But no other guards either.

He pulled himself up onto the wall, keeping his weapon partially behind him, hoping that at a glance he would pass for the guard, and walked purposely toward the near corner of the hacienda and then trotted down the side of the house away from the hedge, peeking quickly into each window before moving under it to the next, none of them showing lights, all of them locked.

He stuck his eyes around the next corner, head near the ground, and looked across a circular driveway. He peered down the length of the front of the house, saw a wide flight of stairs leading to an alcove and a man leaning against the far wall of the house.

There were some small plantings along the front of the house from the corner right to the steps. Plenty, Doc thought. He waited for the man to turn his head away, look in the opposite direction, and then he began to move from shrub to shrub, on his belly, silently, never taking his eyes off the sentry, closing on him in a matter of seconds. At the last bush, now only ten feet away, he paused. The man extracted a cigarette from his chest pocket and as the flame from the lighter flared in his face, Doc took three easy strides and punched him hard on the side of the head with the butt of his rifle. He went straight down and his eyes rolled up, Doc thinking, too hard, I wanted to talk to him.

He frisked the man quickly, taking another pistol and a small ring of keys then tied his hands with his belt, gagged him with his shirt and checked his eyes. Alive but out. Doc hit him again anyway, not as hard this time. The front door was locked but the third key opened it. The foyer beyond was empty as was the great room that it opened into. He crept down one wing of the house and up the next, the hacienda laid out around an open courtyard with a fountain and small pool in the middle.

The third wing ran parallel to the hedge wall and there were several French doors toward the far end that opened onto a stone patio. There was blood splattered on the glass of the middle door and drops on the floor by the sill. He glided down the hall past the last door, his heart pounding, fear of what he might find making him shiver, more terrified than he had even been in combat. He heard a noise behind a swinging door on his left, at the junction of the third and forth wings of the house. Doc pushed the door open sufficiently to peer within and saw a man, back toward him, sliding a thin bladed knife across a leather strap at the kitchen island. Junior's alive! The realization made Doc almost giddy but the black hatred hit him right after. He slammed through the door and, as the man turned, Doc rammed the barrel of the assault rifle straight into his solar plexus, wishing for a bayonet, trying to shove the weapon *through* the man, wanting to see it emerge from the other side. The man lost all his air in a foul burst, reflex bringing the knife up in a swinging arch even as he was driven back, pinned against the far wall, Doc still charging forward, legs pumping, the rifle barrel now buried eight inches into the man's gut.

The blade caught Doc moving forward in his rage and what should have been an easy blow to avoid or deflect struck flesh on the jaw below his ear and traveled up across his temple and into the hairline, knocking the headset off before the man's impact with the wall caused the knife to fly from his hand. He slid down the wall, hands clutching his stomach and Doc delivered an upper cut with the rifle that caught him on the point of his chin, the sound like sticks breaking followed instantly by the boom of his head striking the wall behind.

Doc was hurt and he knew it but not from the pain–there wasn't any–but from the blood that was flowing down his neck and chest, dripping onto the stock of the rifle and the floor. Doc laid the rifle on the island, leaned down to the unconscious man and with both hands, tore the shirt off his body, the man slumping over completely as the shirt came away. Doc wrapped the shirt around his head and blotted at this eye with a sleeve then tied the bandage tight with a topknot. He turned back to the island and reached for his weapon just at two men swung into the room from an open door, both training pistols on his chest.

"You got a toothache, gringo?" the man on the left said.

"Where's the boy?" Doc asked.

"Where you gonna be. Put yer hands up."

Doc's right hand was still in mid air over the rifle, his left below the plane of the island and as he slowly raised it up for them to see, he flicked the pin of the grenade across the counter.

"H.E.," he said to them, extending the grenade a little for them to look at, the handle down in his palm. "High explosive. Modified a little. Those eight second fuses take too damn long. This one's set for three."

"You a crazy fucker, gringo. You come here to kill Don Estiban you gotta be. But you gonna die, not him."

"We're all going to die, it's just a question of when. And I'm here for the boy, not your boss."

"Sure you are. You just out for a stroll with an AK. Put down your little toy and we can talk."

"I'm here for the boy. He's Estiban's nephew. Arturo Palacio's son.

"And I'm Pancho Villa. You try for Don Estiban, you die. Is simple."

"If I wanted to kill Don Estiban, he'd be dead. And so would you. Where is the boy?"

"You that good, cowboy? You such a big killer, how come I got a gun and you don't?"

"Last chance. Where's the boy?"

"In the wine cellar with his 'uncle'," the man said, nodding toward the door they had emerged from. "We just gettin' ready to see what he's made of." Doc rolled the grenade enough for the handle to pop off, neither of the men noticing that Doc's right hand had been slowly descending toward the island during their conversation.

Doc never made a visible movement, never jerked or flinched, nothing to draw their attention or heighten their suspicion but suddenly there it was, the grenade head high between the two men, their eyes locked on its lazy flight as it descended between them.

The AK sang briefly, Doc never even picking it up, just depressing the trigger and pivoting the weapon on the countertop, the height just right to stitch the men across their mid sections. He took a step forward and soccer-kicked the grenade through the open door, the stream of purple smoke just starting to plume forth as he impacted it. He waited a couple seconds for the smoke to thicken in the room below, then crept silently down the stairs.

The basement room was completely filled with a purple cloud and he pulled a sleeve from his makeshift bandage across his face and took shallow breaths as he crawled toward the sounds of coughing coming from deeper in the room. About twenty-five feet he guessed, surprised the wine cellar was so large. A rasping voice stopped his progress.

"I got your boy here. You come near me, I'm gonna kill him."

Doc knew he was invisible, the man talking to his fear as much as anything else but he altered his course, circling the room. A second later he saw feet, two pair, one in ratty slippers, wizened skin, the other large and youthful but just barely making contact with the floor. The rage filled him again but he fought it down, inching forward on an even more oblique angle to the target, looking soon at worn heels.

The voice came again. "You touch me, I shoot. I know you down here. I got a gun in his mouth, I'm gonna splatter his brains."

The smoke was lifting, being sucked out by an exhaust fan in the ceiling Doc thought, the whir of the motor audible in the otherwise silent room. Part of the climate control system for a wine cellar, Doc guessed. If he waited till it cleared, surprise would be gone as well. If he spoke from the fog, he would mark his position and give the man license to shoot him when he could not shoot back. He inched closer to the legs, took a breath and held it as he slowly stood erect, leaving the rifle on the floor, pistol in one hand, combat knife in the other. Then he waited.

The smoke rose like a stage curtain, slowly revealing the hem of a bathrobe as ratty as the slippers, and Junior's naked legs. Then more robe and genitalia, then waists and chests and finally the face of Estiban Gomez Palacio, thin wisps of greasy, steel hair projecting from the back of his balding head, a three day beard encasing his jowls. The Navy Colt revolver held in both his hands, hammer back, a couple inches of barrel inserted between Junior's lips belied the clownish look. Junior was out but breathing, blood oozing down his face from a gash parallel to the Mohawk, arms thrust straight over his head, thumbs tied off to a large wooden timber.

"You behind me, gringo?" Estiban wheezed. "I tell you what. My arm's gettin' tired. I'm gonna count to three and if you not where I can see you by then, I'm gonna shoot this boy. Okay, gringo? One."

Doc eased the gun up on the left and the knife on the right.

"Two."

Doc took a deep breath, let his mind go blank, let half of the breath out, a sniper poised for the kill shot, muscles tensing for the thrust.

"Three," Estiban said just as his name was spoken from the middle of the stair. Doc's hands froze in mid stroke.

"Are you going to kill another nephew, brother? One should be enough for any man," Frank said. He descended the balance of the stairs, then stopped to adjust the sleeves of his black jacket and straighten his clerical collar.

"What nephew?" Estiban demanded. "I have no nephews!"

"Not since you killed Arturo?"

“That was an accident,” he screamed. “I told you. I told everyone! Fuck you! You sniveling…priest!”

“That is Arturo’s son, Estiban. His nineteen year old only son.”

“What?” the man said, more quietly, looking back at Junior’s face. “He is a gringo, come to kill me.”

“Look at his eyes, brother.”

Estiban hesitated, arms shaking now, then took his left hand off the pistol and lifted one of Junior’s lids.

“Hello, Uncle Estiban,” Junior said.

Estiban jumped back screaming, the barrel coming clear and Doc struck in a blur, the knife hand shoving the old man’s pistol aside, Doc’s gun clubbing him deftly on the left temple. Doc pivoted in and to his right and as the old man dropped, he twisted the gun out of his grasp, then back handed his knife across the ropes above Junior’s head, catching the boy in his arms as he sagged.

“Talk to me, son,” Doc said. “Start talking and don’t stop.”

“I’m okay, Doc,” Junior responded, slapping feebly as Doc checked his eyes and probed the furrow in his scalp. “Ow! Christ, that hurts!”

“Good. It means you aren’t dead, you dumb fuck. What were you thinking, coming over here at night. With a fucking gun no less.”

“Let the boy rest, Doc,” Father Francis said. “We can all beat him later.”

George came flying down the steps before Doc could respond, a shotgun in his hands, face pale, mouth turned down.

“He’s fine, George,” Doc said. “Help me get him out of here.”

“What the fuck happened, Doc?”

“Later. We have to get him gone, then clean this mess up.”

They helped Junior up the steps, walking him carefully around the bloody pools on the kitchen floor and depositing him in the great room then dragged Estiban out and threw him on a couch, binding his hands and covering his eyes.

"Doc, yer bleedin' like a gut shot steer, we gotta git you to a doctor," George said as they looked down at the unconscious Estiban.

"I'll live," Doc said. "We've got to clean this mess up."

"What do we do now, Doc?" Frank asked.

"Damn if I know. Go to the police? Pack our shit and get the fuck out of here?"

"Burn this place to the ground, with him in it," George said.

"Maybe. I don't know how to play it. This is your turf, Frank. What do you suggest?" Doc asked.

"A moment please," he said, walking away then clomping down the stairs. He was back in a few minutes, wiping the dust off a clear bottle. He pulled the cork, sniffed and then took a hefty gulp. "Ah, the good stuff. Fifteen years old, I bet." He slipped his hand around the back of Junior's head and held the bottle to his lip. "Drink," he said.

"Whoa! You ain't shittin'. That's some fine Elixir. What's Devil man doin' with the vintage stuff?"

"Your father was too kind to him. There must be a hundred bottles down there."

Frank passed the bottle to Doc, then to George. "To clear the mind," he said. "Let me bandage your head, Doc."

"Do the boy first," Doc said.

George found clean towels and some duct tape and Doc peeled off the dirty shirt and stripped some tape off the roll.

"George," he said, "there's one man out front and one in the hedges by the right spotlight. Make sure they don't get loose. Or see you." Doc tossed him first the roll of duct tape and then the automatic. "Then turn off those damn beacons. We'll have planes landing here. Junior, are you alright?" The boy nodded his head. "Go in the kitchen and find my headset. Tell your mother we're okay. And don't look at the bodies." Junior came back a minute later looking like he might throw up.

"She wants to talk to you," he said.

"Doc, Doc," he heard as he fitted the head set.

"We're alright, Maggie."

"Thank God. We hadn't heard from you in so long, I was starting to freak."

"Does Rosario have a car?" He heard snippets of conversation, then Maggie's voice.

"It's sitting in the driveway. I couldn't decide whether to come over or stay out of the way. We'll be there in about forty-five minutes."

"Okay. Bring cleaning supplies. But don't come in! Do you understand?"

"Yes," she said. Then after a pause she added, "Is it bad?"

"Yeah. It's bad."

"Frank," Doc said as the priest finished wrapping his head, "what will Estiban do if we let him live? Will he go to the police or will he come after us?"

Frank was silent for several seconds.

"Possibly neither. The police definitely not. They are not welcome here," he grinned, "as you might imagine. To 'come after us', as you put it, he would have to admit that someone violated his home, killed his men. Emasculated him, do you see? He would not wish that to be known."

"What about his other men? Any chance they would act on their own?"

"I doubt it very much. For the same reasons. Plus they will do what Don Estiban tells them to do."

"Then we might be able to clean this up and walk away?"

"Probably so."

"Because our other option," Doc said, "would be to kill all of them, make it look like a drug thing."

"Let me try to talk to my brother."

Doc led George and Junior out of the room, hearing light slapping sounds and Frank's voice saying, "Estiban, wake up," as they departed.

"We need to wrap these three up in something," Doc said, gesturing toward the bodies. "Get them out of here and bury them. Then clean up every drop of blood and wipe down anything we might have touched."

"Be easier to burn the place," Junior said. "Toss in a couple a those willie peter boys and say so long."

"Too much attention," Doc said. "But that might work on the bodies."

They found a mop and two buckets and started the gruesome task, Junior coming out of the cellar with a fistful of body bags.

"Looks like the Devil may a had some disposal problems of his own periodically," he said.

They double bagged the two gunshot men and dragged them to the foyer then used the last one on the chef.

"Five bags," George said. "One for each of his men you think or just a lucky coincidence?" Doc just shook his head and continued to disinfect the countertops.

Maggie and Kate came through the doors and stepped around the black pile, mops and buckets in hand and as Doc turned, about to speak, Maggie cut him off.

"We're in this together. Not a word," then took his cloth wrapped head in both her hands and kissed his lips. "You look like a big Q-tip," she said to him and kissed him again. "Are you really okay?"

"You're going to need to stitch me up but I'm alright. Junior's going to need a few too. The headset kept it from being a lot worse for me."

It took three hours, all of them working, to sanitize the place to Doc's satisfaction. Father Francis had spent the time in quiet conversation with his brother, both of them nipping at the Elixir bottle.

"Frank," Doc called from the doorway, motioning for him to come over. "What's going on with him?" he said indicating Estiban.

"We've been catching up on family history," he said. "He understands now. You can go back, I will stay here a little longer."

"What about the bodies? Should we take them, bury them somewhere?"

"That will not be necessary. Estiban has facilities on the premises. If you could get them down in the cellar, that would be helpful, though."

"You're serious."

"Yes, my friend. Quite."

"You're sure you're okay here? It doesn't seem…right, somehow."

"Go, Doc. We will take care of the rest. Oh, Estiban says thank you for looking after his nephew and for cleaning up the house. He appreciates your kindness."

"Okay. Do you want us to come get you later?"

"No, thank you. Estiban will bring me back. He would like to see his wife and daughter."

Chapter Twenty-five

They got back just as the sun was rising across the valley, almost directly over Estiban's hacienda, the morning air crisp and clear, the light glinting on the distant house, making it sparkle like a castle. Maggie and Doc exchanged a look as they stood on the veranda, Maggie's expression dubious, Doc shaking his head.

"Don't even say it," he cautioned her. "It's just a coincidence. Come on, fix my head."

Maggie had pulled her sewing kit out of the motor home and was heating a heavy gauge needle over a kitchen match, looking none too happy, when Sinaloa came out of her bedroom, looked at Doc and Junior holding bloody rags to their heads and at Maggie's preparations, shrieked, and ran back inside.

"I thought that girl was tougher 'en that," George said. Thirty seconds later Sinaloa was back, towing her mother who was on the receiving end of a string of rapid fire, Spanish dictates. Sinaloa marched up between them, pushed Maggie out of the way and thunked a medical bag on the table.

"Mother of God!" she screamed at Doc. "What the fuck have you been doing? And you," turning on Maggie. "Are you a seamstress or a veterinarian? Get out of my way." She was rooting furiously in the bag, pulling forth syringes, gauze and disinfectant, when Doc spoke to her.

"Sinaloa?" he said.

"Dr. Palacio!" she hissed at him. "Shut up!" He did and she anesthetized and sutured his wound, not gently but with precision and speed. "You are going to have a lovely scar. I can not help that. See a plastic surgeon in the U.S. if it offends you." Then she turned to Junior's wound, now barely bleeding, not nearly as deep, and sewed him up in short order.

"Let your hair grow. No one will ever notice."

"What fun would that be," the boy said and she picked up the syringe from the table and stabbed him in the upper arm, saying "Idiot!" as he hollered.

"Where is Frank?" she demanded as she repacked her bag.

"With your father," Maggie answered.

"The Devil is still alive?"

"Yes. And they should be here soon."

"The Devil is coming here?" she said.

"That's what Frank told us," Maggie said.

Sinaloa slapped her bag closed, tossing her horsetail of hair and stomped out of the room.

"This oughta be interestin'," George said. "I hope I never need any emergency surgery around these parts. That girl didn't look too happy about Novacainin' you two," he chuckled. Maggie was studying the myriad stitches in Doc's head.

"She did a hell of a job though. This might even be an improvement," she added. "Thanks," Doc said.

They had showered and changed and eaten breakfast before Maggie brought up the subject of the evening's events, she and Doc alone at the rail of the veranda sipping coffee, the others resting in the motor home. Rosario was cleaning up in the kitchen, having declined all offers of assistance. Sinaloa had not been seen since her work was completed.

"How about Sinaloa being a doctor," Maggie said by way of introduction.

"Like her grandfather. She's quite a kid."

"Doc?" she continued after a pause, both of them looking across the valley.

"What happened or how do I feel about it?" he said turning to her.

"Both. Maybe just 'how do you feel'."

"Yeah. What happened was pretty obvious. I didn't have a choice though. I want you to know that part. Well, the one with the knife, I hit him too hard. I lost it, seeing him sharpening the blade. I went crazy. I saw them cutting Junior, in my mind, and I just..."

"I know, Doc," she said, putting a hand on his arm.

"I'm sorry. I didn't want to kill anyone, just get the boy back and get out. Did you talk to him? Find out why he went over there?"

"Revenge?" Maggie said. "He wanted to confront the old man, tell him who he was, shame him I think. I don't believe he had any intention of shooting him."

"He's really lucky to be alive."

"He knows that. The immortality of youth, Jesus."

"The stupidity of youth is more like it," Doc added.

They were arm in arm a few minutes later when vehicle noises brought their attention around to the driveway. They watched a seventies vintage black Mercedes sedan roll slowly to a stop next to the motor home, Frank driving, Estiban beside him. No bodyguards.

As the men alighted, Doc was immediately struck by the change in the older man. He was shaved and coiffed and immaculately attired in a dark business suite. Frank walked around the front of the car and took his brother's arm, Estiban's free hand clutching the head of an ebony and silver walking stick. They climbed the stairs slowly, Don Palacio leaning heavily on his cane and shuffling slowly across each tread before scaling the next, pausing for a moment at the apex before continuing across the patio. When they drew abreast of Doc and Maggie, Frank released the other man's arm.

"Margaret Marone, Doctor Beaumont," he said, "I would like to introduce you to my brother, Don Estiban Palacio. Estiban is Rosario's husband and Sinoloa's father." The man looked up at them now, his face as worn and wrinkled as an old paper bag, only the shockingly blue eyes giving any indication of the life forces still burning within. He took Maggie's hand, raised it to his lips and kissed her fingers.

"Buenas dias, Senora," he said, his voice raspy. He placed his hand in Doc's for an instant and then drew it back, offering no greeting. The silence that followed was broken by the sound of doors opening and all of them turned as Sinaloa strode out onto the patio, boot heels striking a cadence as she marched toward them. She was dressed now in a creamy blouse and a flowing, pleated skirt. Her hair was unbound but for silver combs at her temples and it fell down her back in a black waterfall.

"Hello, Father," she said. "How nice of you to come calling."

"Good morning, daughter," he replied. "You are a beautiful child."

"How kind of you to notice."

He went to her and put his arms around her shoulders and kissing her on the cheek, then whispered to her for several seconds. As he finished, stepping back, she smiled faintly at him, turned and ran back into the house.

"I would like to speak to Rosario, please," Don Estiban said to them, bowing slightly. "If you will excuse me."

"What's going on, Frank?" Doc asked. "Can you tell us?"

"I believe the end is near for my brother and he knows what that will mean, for his soul."

"He's afraid he'll go to hell?" Maggie said.

"He knows he is going to hell. He has always known I imagine. But soon now. There is a certain amount of remorse but also some things he can still change, some amends he can make, however too little, too late. Arturo's death started the process, Junior's visit, what almost happened, seems to have broken him in some way. But also to have motivated him."

"Do you know what he's planning, Frank?" Maggie asked.

"I have some thoughts, but no, I do not. He does want to talk to the boy though."

"That should be interesting," she said. "I'll go get him up."

Junior, Kate and George had all joined them on the veranda before the old man returned. Frank made another round of formal introductions, Estiban more animated now, even smiling a little. After a short period of silence, he asked Junior if he would take a walk with him. They went toward the stairs, the old man placing his hand on Junior's forearm as they slowly descended and he left it there as they crossed the parking area and disappeared around the bend in the drive.

"I'd like to be a fly on the wall for that un'," George said as they all watched the little man hobble away on the arm of his nephew.

"And how," Kate added. "Junior has no idea what to make of the guy."

"He is a lonely old man who just realized that he does not have to remain that way," Frank said. "Maybe he can find a little peace before he dies."

They were preparing the motor home for the return trip, cleaning and packing, a number of items piled on the porch to be left with Rosario, when Junior and Estiban returned. Estiban seemed to have limbered up some, walking easier now, laughing as they rounded the bend.

Estiban was gracious in his farewells, thanking each of them individually for their courtesy in visiting with him, pulling Maggie to him and whispering to her for a minute. Kate also got a hug, the old man grinning over her shoulder at Junior as he squeezed her. "I am very sorry for your injuries," he said to Doc as they shook hands.

He held Rosario in his arms for several seconds, his eyes damp when he let go. Sinaloa was last and he did cry when he ended his embrace of his stunning, fierce daughter, again speaking quietly to her, her eyes filling now too. Frank led him to his car and Estiban waved once as they turned around and drove away.

"Are you going to tell us what he said to you?" Maggie said to Junior.

"When Frank comes back," he said, getting up and offering his hand to Kate. "Let's go outside, okay?"

"I think he's correct," Sinaloa said as they left. "When Uncle Frank returns, we will talk."

"I feel very….odd about all this," Maggie said.

"Yeah," Doc said. "Change will do that." She looked at him quizzically. "The quest is over," he said. "We found the Golden Fleece, now we go back to our lives. But they won't be the same. Everything is different now, for better or worse, we don't know. Too soon to tell, but definitely different. It's very unsettling."

"We were lookin' to get some answers for the boy, Mags. And for you," George said. "We done that. But we found him some grandparents, an uncle and an aunt, a girlfriend and a whole new set a questions."

"Such as?" she asked.

"Such as what do I do about my new kin? How do I get to know 'em? Should I even. What about Kate? Are they an item or a fling? How does she feel? I suspect that's what the two of 'em are talkin' about right now."

"There's more as well," Doc said. "Especially for Junior. What about the Elixir? There's a good deal of 'in progress' Elixir work that Arturo could not finish and he had plans, it seems, for more to follow. Junior has to be thinking about that. Is it his responsibility to follow his father, in the family business if you will? If he chooses not to, there's going to be some guilt."

"And if he chooses to," Maggie said, "his childhood is pretty much over."

"I think it ended," Doc said, "around the time he took that shotgun out of the closet."

"The boy made a man's decision," George said. "Right or wrong. He cut the apron strings, Mags, you can't hold him back now."

"Fuck you, George. I don't want to hold him back, I just want him to make the right decisions."

"After consultin' with his Momma," George teased.

"Okay, you're right," she said. "I have to let him figure this out on his own. God, I hope he knows what he's doing."

"It ain't like he's got *no* feminine input, Mags. I don't think Kate'll let him do anythin' too dumb," George laughed.

Frank returned alone in the early evening driving the old Mercedes. Doc, Maggie and George were dozing in the living room. He awakened them as he sat down heavily in an easy chair. The sounds of their greetings brought Sinaloa and her mother out of the kitchen. Frank asked them for some glasses as he produced two bottles of the vintage Elixir from his coat pockets. Junior and Kate came through the veranda door as Frank was pouring hefty doses into tumblers and sliding them across the coffee table.

"Everybody grab a glass," he said. "There's still some business to attend to. When the four of you left Texas, you hoped to find out what Arturo did during his absences and if possible, discover what became of him. So that the boy and his mother could stop being tormented by the past, yes?"

"And move on to the future," George said.

"Exactly. Your journey was toward the future by way of the past. Mission accomplished?" he asked Maggie. She did not respond so he continued. "Yes, it is. Now what? You have the answers, now what do you do with them? For my part, I have to repair the damage done by the Fish. Restoring the social programs will take time. And I have no idea what the financial status of the mission is. Or where I'm going to get Elixir until this year's crop is ready. I have a lot of networking to do."

"We can help you with the Elixir, Frank," Maggie said. "Right, Junior?"

"Oh, yeah, Frank. No problem there."

"What are your thoughts, Bartolo?" Frank asked. "You've been the most impacted by these events. I'm very curious about your plans, how you see your future. Is it too personal a question, grandson?"

"No, not really. We're all family, right, so no secrets," Junior said. "First of all, Kate's going to help me. She's going to take a sabbatical from Los Alamos."

"Help you what?" Maggie asked.

"Help him with the Elixir," Kate answered. "There are a significant number of loose ends that we know of and all the missions that we didn't visit, they may have needs as well."

"And then the expansion," Junior said. "We need to find more candidates for the program. I'm thinking about California and Colorado."

"Tell them about your 'funding stream'," Frank said with a chuckle.

"Uncle Estiban. He told me 'half of everything I own is yours'," Junior said in a gravel voice. "I said I didn't need his money. He said it was for the Elixir. Use it to help with your father's work. You are going to finish your father work aren't you, he asked? I got to tell y'all, that guy's a little crazy.

"He told me you got the other half, Aunt Sin. He said you were going to turn his house into a hospital or a nursing home, I wasn't sure which, but he was going to be the first patient and you were going to run the joint."

"That is correct," she said. "The Palacio Memorial Community Hospice Center. It sounds better in Spanish. He said we could start immediately."

"How much money's the old guy got, Frank?" George asked. "We've built big wings on two hospitals in Houston. You're talkin' major dollars to convert that house, plus it ain't nearly big enough."

"The existing hacienda," Frank said, "would be an administrative area, George, according to my brother. He wants a new hospital, one of Arturo's. We talked about them at some length, last night. And his net worth, in my opinion? Two hundred and fifty million perhaps?

"That's pre-tax, of course," he added after they had all calmed down. "And only a guess. It could be considerably more. And there are some obligations outstanding, associated with the, ah, resignation shall we say, from his existing occupation. That's the bad news. The good news is, there's a hundred and fifty million in off-shore and Swiss accounts right now, in cash, which can be donated to the church, the Santuario Community Development Fund specifically, and then dispersed as its director sees fit," he finished.

"Its director being one Father Francis Palacio I suspect," Doc said grinning.

"Precisely. We will have no further tax issues and it is all quite legal."

"Another holy money laundering scheme," George added with a laugh. "Hey Sin, you need a general contractor, you let me know. I could get used to livin' some place clean and quiet for a spell."

"Sure beats the hell out of Houston," Doc agreed.

Chapter Twenty-six

It took them four days to get back to Chimayo, spending a night in San Xavier and one each at the Apache and Navajo missions that they had bypassed on their way south. They had called ahead to Ben who had rooms reserved for them but he had not mentioned the other guests that would be in residence. When they maneuvered the motor home up the drive, they were assaulted visually by the pink banner now adorning Ben and Ruthie's porte cochere and then by the crashing sounds of Hell's Fire accompanied by Ben on guitar and Ruth on electric piano.

"Welcome guests of honor," Carl screamed into the microphone as they disembarked. "In celebration of your return, Hootin' Holler Productions is proud to bring you, live from Hacienda de Chimayo, tonight only, Hell's Fire featuring the Magnificent Marones!"

They were greeted by priests, bodyguards, and janitors, bartenders, cops and a cardinal as well as a horde of people about whom they knew neither name nor occupation. Ben put out a buffet for a hundred and when that disappeared, he had another load of food brought out and watched gleefully as that vanished as well.

Carl had trucked cases and cases of beer up the mountain and had to dispatch vehicles twice more to the restaurant, leaving nothing in inventory for the bartenders there but wine coolers and hard liqueur. The band played, with one to three Marones up front, till almost two, then they retired to the porch for two hours of acoustic jams. George was the only one of the travelers who made it to sunrise.

They were all a little shaky the next morning, except George, either from too many long necks or too little sleep, but they reconvened on the veranda at eleven for brunch. After two cups of Ben's special blend Jamaican coffee, Maggie was able to initiate substantive conversation.

"Well, boys and girl," she said, "do you think that was the last official engagement for the Magnificent Marones? Personally, I don't think I can handle the lifestyle."

"Hell, Mags," George grinned at her, "you can't tell me you weren't havin' fun. You were a regular Janis Joplin up there."

"That's exactly what I mean," she answered. "Look what happened to her. And how much sleep did you get, brother dear?"

"Oh, a couple hours," he said.

"That's just unnatural, George," Doc said. "I feel like I got dragged behind a horse and you look like Buddha does New Mexico. It isn't fair."

"Life ain't always fair, laddy. I got all them sturdy Marone genes runnin' around inside me plus twenty years of judicious Elixir therapy. I am a man amongst boys!" he declared, thumping his chest.

"Are we about ready to put our act back on the road, fellers?" Maggie asked. "We could be home by midnight or so the way Junior–I mean Bartolo–drives."

"Ah, Ma? I'm goin' to stick around here for a while. Help Frank get things goin' again. Until we hash out the Estiban business anyway."

"I don't suppose that fine lookin' redhead yonder had any part in that decision," George said.

"Yeah, a course she did," Junior answered. "If I can help it, I'm never lettin' her out of my sight again. But that ain't–isn't the reason I'm staying. But it sure doesn't hurt," he added.

"Up to six, down to three," Doc said. "The vagary of the open road."

"Two," George said.

"Two what?" Maggie asked.

"Down to two. You're down to two. I'm flying back to Houston this afternoon. Ben's gonna run me down to Albuquerque. He said we ate everything in the joint so he's gotta go to the restaurant supply house anyway."

"I think I'm going to cry," Maggie said, a quiver in her voice. Doc moved closer and put his arm around her.

"Come on, Ma. You aren't losing a son," Junior said. "You're gaining a fiancée-in-law to go with your new mother and father-in-laws, your sister-in-law, you even got an uncle-in-law out a this," he grinned. "You might even get some grandkids to baby sit. When was the last time you cleaned a big pile a crap out of a stinky diaper? Christ, you gotta be missin' that."

"Artoro Marone de la Madre! Palacio. Junior! Whatever your name is. I'm thirty-seven years old. If you make me a grandmother before I turn forty, I will never speak to you again! Do I make myself clear?" she said as she pulled him to her. "Promise me you'll be careful," she said in his ear. "And don't lose Kate, ever, understand?"

"I got it, Ma," he said. "You like her. And you like me too."

After the others had unloaded their stuff and after another round of good-byes, Doc backed the motor home down the driveway. He paused as he put the transmission in drive and looked over at Maggie.

“Are you ready to go home, my love?” he said. “We could do a little sight-seeing if you’d rather.”

“Nope,” she said. “I think it’s time for me and my man to git on home. Giddy up, cowboy.”

They hit the Llano County line at midnight and were in bed and wrapped in each other’s arms by one.

Chapter Twenty-seven

Maggie and Doc were lying in the hammock beneath the live oak, their clothing piled haphazardly on the ground, Maggie's head nestled in the crook of Doc's right arm, a beer in his other hand, both of them enjoying the relative coolness of their surroundings. It was mid-September and still hot in the daytime sun. They had worked in the orchard all afternoon, the last of the pears finally boxed, the processing to begin tomorrow.

Maggie had dozed off, purring gently in his arms as he admired the view down the length of her nude form, a slight sheen still glistening on her skin, her scent both salty and sweet, the look and smell of her requiring him to shift his position slightly to get his stiffening member uncramped. As he arched his shoulders and tried to pull his right leg partially out from under her, he cocked his head, listening.

"Hey, I'm sleeping here," she murmured to him. "What kind of pillow are you anyway?"

"Someone's coming," he said.

"Let me take a little nap first, please. I swear you are the horniest man in the world."

"Maggie, darlin'," he whispered to her. "Someone else is coming. A vehicle or vehicles, it sounds like more than one." Her eyes popped open and she raised her head up off his chest.

"Oh, shit," she exclaimed, sitting up and tipping them both out of the hammock.

Maggie had time to slip on her tee shirt, the scrap of cloth barely adequate to cover her breasts but she was still wrestling with her shorts, bent over with her butt aimed at the driveway, when two motorcycles roared around the last turn and came to a gravel spewing stop.

"Nice greeting, Ma. You moon all your company or is that a special hello just for kin," Junior yelled.

Doc had not moved, too busy laughing to even try to get dressed himself. He finally climbed into a pair of ratty shorts, then stood to greet their guests, kicking the leftover clothing beneath the hammock.

"If you called more than once a month," Maggie said, "I might have known you were coming."

"And then you'd be all prepared and shit," Junior said. "That wouldn't be any fun."

"Are there more of you?" Doc asked, cocking his head again. "I still hear vehicles."

"It's Uncle George," Junior said. "And a few of his guys. We just got back from Mexico!"

They walked through the gardens and were starting up the driveway when a small avalanche of rock and gravel tumbled down toward them followed close behind by the blade, then tracks, of the biggest bulldozer Doc had ever seen. George was perched dwarf-like behind the controls, waving to them and beeping the horn. He ground down to their position and eased off the throttle.

"George!" Maggie screamed. "What the fuck are you doing?"

"Improvin' yeur driveway, Mags. You don't need her all rutted up now and I can't get my trucks down here without doin' some regradin'," he hollered back.

"Trucks for what?" she shouted but he just waved at her and continued pushing the stone out of his way. As George pulled on a lever, turning the dozer one hundred and eighty degrees in place, one of his trucks came into view backwards and dumped another load of gravel at their feet.

"Two A modified," Doc shouted in her ear, pointing at the stone as if the construction jargon made everything clear. George launched his dozer as soon as the tailgate on the truck slammed shut and went chugging back up the hill, pushing the new pile in front of him.

"Does anybody," she asked, "know what is happening here?"

"Maybe it's best if George explains it, Maggie," Kate offered. "It's pretty much his show."

They retreated to the deck and Junior served them beer and they listened to the grinding of metal on rock and the roar of thousand horsepower engines. They could see plumes of black smoke over the hills and occasionally catch a glimpse of a yellow tracked machine or a red dump truck as it turned around in front of the gardens.

Finally, after several hours, the decibels dropped off as the machines idled into the pasture by the pond and came to a stop. Maggie counted two bulldozers, a steam roller, a track hoe, four dump trucks, three with trailers attached now, a tanker truck, and one tractor rig with a much larger trailer, all followed by three crew cab pick-ups full of hard hat clad men and last of all, a cherry red box van with Marone Brothers Construction painted on the side.

George tramped up the outside path at the head of a column of red shirted men. He shouted out names and pointed to his people individually by way of introduction. After a few minutes of hand shaking and view admiring, the men marched back down the steps and were soon bivouacked in the pasture, tents pulled from the box van erected in two neat rows, camp fires crackling under iron pots, a dozen brown bodies splashing happily in the water.

"George?" Maggie asked. "Are you going to tell me why you're here, in force as it were?"

"I done told you already. I'm just doin' a good deed for my only sister. Why do you always think I got an ulterior motive?" he said. "She is one suspicious woman, Doc. I was kinda hopin' you could break her of that." Doc looked off in another direction, whistling tunelessly.

"George?" she repeated. "Look at me, brother dear. You just happened to be in the neighborhood, with..." pausing as she counted, her fingers dancing in front of her, "fifteen trucks and heavy equipment and, oh, twenty-five men. That is one hell of a coincidence. So you just dropped by to fix our driveway, right?"

"Yeah, pretty much," he answered. "Although we might as well build an air strip while we're here, don't you think, boy?" he said to Junior.

"You know, that's amazing Uncle George. I was sayin' to Kate just the other day, Ma needs an air strip." Kate looked at Doc who winked at her and then she began to whistle along with him.

"An air strip," Maggie said. "That *is* amazing. Why Doc and I have been not talking about an air strip for, oh, I guess forever. Maybe even longer. In fact I've always not said how much I don't need an air strip."

"Well good, that's settled finally," George said. "Now. What's for dinner? I'm starvin'."

"You got a lot a 'splainin' to do, Lucy," she said. "But I'll feed you first so you have the strength for the job."

"I'll help," Kate said.

"Good. I'm dying to hear what you two have been doing."

An hour later they had eaten and a half hour after that they were back to lounging, watching the campers below and the sun set above."

"Okay, George. I cooked, now you talk."

"Well, Mags," he said. "I want to borrow you and Doc for a bit. To build Sinaloa's hospital. There's a twin engine Beechcraft flying in here in three days to pick you up. The strip in Magdalena's already done. And," he added chuckling, "we built one in Chimayo while we were at it."

"That's it?" she said.

"Yep," he answered, palms up. "That's it."

"What do you think, Doc?" she said. He nodded his head, grinning at her and she turned back to her brother.

"Okay," she said. "But it's going to have to be pretty much done in about seven months, cause I want our baby to be born in Texas."

Sinaloa's facility wasn't quite done when Maggie pulled Doc aside on the site one morning in early April and said, I'd like to go home now, her hand absently sliding up and around the taut melon she'd been carrying for the last couple months, but it was close enough that Doc was not concerned about leaving his foreman in charge. Sinaloa insisted that no one was going to deliver her niece or nephew but her and Rosario said simply, I'm going too. They loaded a few things in the Beechcraft and Doc flew them back to Llano.

Francis Estiban Marone was born two days later in front of a standing room only crowd that included George and Gina, Daniel and Teresa, Maggie's parents, Rosario and Doc with Sinaloa at the controls. Junior and Kate, with Frank strapped onto the back of Kate's Harley, flew down the improved driveway a few minutes later and charged into the bedroom just in time to be handed a sloshing plastic bag and ordered by Sinaloa to 'bury it deep so the coyotes don't get it.'

After they had passed the baby around the circle, twice, Doc placed the child on his mother's breast and herded them out of the room. They adjourned to the library and he hand delivered a dram of Elixir to each of them.

"Thank you," he said, "for making me part of this family."

Epilogue

The official Grand Opening of Sinaloa's hospital was delayed until May fifth so that the celebration could be combined with Cinquo de Mayo. Estiban hosted a party for five thousand. Cardinal Garcia came with Kate, Junior, Father Frank and an entourage of thirty plus in a fleet of limos to give the benediction. The Marone clan flew in on a chartered Leer. Hell's Fire played for six hours to the delight of the crowd, George singing dozens of Spanish ballads along the way.

The three 'Margaret Marone' Centers that had been under construction had been finished the previous winter. Their completion allowed Junior and Kate to concentrate their efforts on expansion and they were planting orchards in southern California, central Texas and eastern Colorado.

Junior's plan for legalizing Elixir production required a substitute for both the cocaine and peyote additives. Doctor X was brought on board as Director of Distillation and in short order, discovered acceptable substitutes. The 'new' Elixir lacked some of the punch of the original but it retained most of the therapeutic qualities and could be generated on a much larger scale. All of the

Arturo Senior missions maintained their private stills and cooked small batches of the old recipe for 'personal use'.

Bartolo and Kate were married in the fall at Santuario de Chimayo, Father Francis presiding at the private ceremony. The reception at Casa de Chimayo was not so private. Although not as large as Sinaloa's grand opening bash, Cardinals, priests, friars and brothers from all over the southwest and northern Mexico were in attendance along with almost the entire Mountainair Clan and a couple hundred other assorted friends and relatives. They kept their promise to Maggie, however unintentionally, Kate delivering their first child on the eve of Maggie's forty-first birthday. With two of her own by then, the girl Rosario Katherine almost two, being a grandmother prematurely had lost much of its significance.

By the time of his death the following spring, Estiban's fortune had been mostly depleted but there were seven operating health care facilities in Sonora and Chihuahua provinces bearing his name and six more fully funded operations under construction. Doc and Maggie, flying thousands of miles each year with the kids in tow, helped to build most of them. Bartolo and Frank retained an investment fund of nearly forty million, the income used to offset shortfalls in donations for funding grass roots operations in the U.S.

By the birth of Kate's second son, the 'Elixir Fellowship' was the nineteenth largest international foundation in the world with a total estimated yearly clientele of over ten million and a growth rate of twenty percent annually.

Doc banked the turbo prop in a low circle over the ranch, the orchards in full bloom, the pastures a riotous quilt of wild flowers, every mesquite and oak budded in a palate of healthy green.

"We had some good rains," he said to Maggie who was bouncing Rose on her lap. "The tank's full."

"And our flowers are *all* blooming, aren't they, Sunshine?" Maggie said, tickling the giggling toddler. "Now, you need to climb in the back and strap yourself in. Daddy's going to land," she said as she scooted the girl into her flight seat and buckled her tight next to her sleeping brother.

"Have I mentioned lately how madly in love I am with you?" Doc said.

"Not in the last hour or so you slacker."

Doc brought the plane around and set it down gently, taxiing up to the hangar behind the house.

"I'll have to work on that," he said as they prepared to disembark. "I keep meaning to tell you every time it occurs to me."

"Works for me, cowboy," she said, her marvelous laughter ringing out. "And I love you too, you handsome, silver-tongued Devil!"

The End

www.ingramcontent.com/pod-product-compliance
Lightning Source LLC
Chambersburg PA
CBHW031253170626
46807CB00001B/123

* 9 7 8 0 6 9 2 2 3 0 5 2 7 *